# PEA WARRIOR

Steven L. Hawk

Peace Warrior
Copyright © 2010 by Steven L. Hawk

All rights reserved. Without limiting the rights under copyright reserved above, no part of this publication may be reproduced, stored in or introduced into a retrieval system, or transmitted, in any form, or by any means (electronic, mechanical, photocopying, recording, or otherwise) without the prior written permission of the copyright owner.

First Paperback Edition - July 2010

ISBN-13: 978-1-4528-9166-8

Cover concept and art by the author.

Background cover art by Sabrina C. Kleis

www.SteveHawk.com

*This book is dedicated to two of the driving forces in my life:*

*To my wife, Juanita, for your patience and endurance during the hundreds of hours I spent in front of my PC. You believed in me – even when I didn't.*

*And for my Sister, Deb. One of my earliest memories is of you teaching me how to read and write the alphabet. I love and miss you.*

# PEACE WARRIOR

## PROLOGUE

Death was not lonely.  He had his thoughts and memories to keep him company.

\* \* \*

"Sergeant Justice? He's one of the best I've ever seen," he heard his commander, Colonel Bishop, remarking to a huddled group of nodding generals and politicians. Grant halted less than 10 feet from the group and turned quickly away, not wanting to intrude on the private conversation. The VIPs had been observing field maneuvers for more than a week and had just reviewed the final two days of war games in an attempt to learn how Colonel Bishop's forces had overcome a much larger and better equipped opposing force. The battle scenes were recorded by numerous ground-, aircraft- and satellite-based cameras. All showed the same vivid scenes of Grant leading his men against the enemy.

"I don't know anyone else who could have pulled out a win under those circumstances," Grant heard the colonel continue. "Hell, the exercise was designed to have them lose this. . ." Slightly embarrassed by the remarks from the man he admired above all others, he marched quickly away.

\* \* \*

*Just another memory.*

He now knew that death was made up of infinite darkness, random thoughts and old memories.  There was *awareness*, but that awareness was without a body.  There was no touch, no sound.  No smell or taste.  His consciousness was a dark sea of remembrances; and, with a few exceptions, he allowed the sea to carry him as it wished. The sea was not overly large. Its boundaries were the borders of his mind. Its waves were the recollections of his thirty-two years.

Even now, after what seemed like an eternity of death, he occasionally stumbled upon a new memory. When that happened, he viewed it in his mind and studied it for every detail. Then, certain that he had recalled it to the best of his ability, he filed it away. He no longer gorged himself as he had in the beginning, replaying each new recollection over and over and over. Now, he stored them away like precious possessions – treasures to be taken out and viewed only when the dark walls of death pressed closest, seeking to finally extinguish the flickering remnant of his existence.

He understood he could not remain aware forever. At some distant point, he would relent – allow the void to crush the thin eggshell of his awareness. But understanding is not the same as conceding and, for now, he fought.

He fought with memories.

And the one he always came back to – the one he visited most often – was the memory of his death…

\* \* \*

The receiver buzzed noisily as the outpost radioed in.

"…geant Justice, this…" the transmission was garbled badly. "… your wa… can you see…"

Justice looked at Sean Taylor, the young corporal lying in the snow next to him. The soldier, a six month veteran to the team who had proved his abilities time and again over those few months, also had a receiver in his ear. A shake of the corporal's head indicated that he had not heard the transmission any better.

"Damn," Justice muttered. The sub-zero temperature was severely fucking with their reception. And this was not a good time for fuck ups. Grant cursed the supply sergeant who had issued his team the older, less reliable sets and asked the soldier on the other end, a buck sergeant and a tested veteran, to repeat his last transmission.

For the effort, he received more static.

*For a mission this important, you'd think they could find us something manufactured in this century,* he thought. Instead, the communications officer had issued them forty-year old voice activated radios that only worked half of the time under normal conditions. And the blowing snow and frigid cold surrounding the team were far from normal.

*Check that,* he corrected. *The snow and cold used to be far from normal.* Even though they were just north of the imaginary boundary that defined the Arctic Circle, Justice knew these conditions were once uncommon for mid-August. Not so much anymore. For the past ten years, the world's climate had grown quickly and progressively colder. The average annual temperature had dropped more than 5 degrees over that span of time. To a soldier like Justice, that didn't seem like a lot, but he knew that scientists were concerned. Sixty years earlier, scientists had argued relentlessly about the possibility of global warming. Now, all they argued about was the ever-present cold fronts, decreasing temperatures and the expansion of ice flows moving south. Some argued that the next ice age was upon them. Others countered that this was just a temporary meteorological blip caused by *yadda-yadda-yadda.* At this moment, Justice didn't care. All he knew was that the weather was an obstacle for him and his team.

The briefing Sergeant Justice's team received from the unit's intelligence officer, a younger-than-usual-looking first lieutenant who was rapidly becoming known throughout the brigade for his faulty analysis and missing data, informed them that a heavily armored European Front column was headed their way. If the intelligence was correct, the fission powered tanks and personnel carriers should be passing through this mountain pass any time now, and Justice had a gnawing suspicion that it was getting close. Perhaps that was the info the garbled transmission was trying to pass along. He cursed silently and peered down along the road trying to make out anything in the blowing snow.

His team, or what was left of it after two years of action on the front, had a hard-won reputation for success. They had been given this latest mission of slowing down – stopping, if possible – the armored column. They had been helo'd onto the mountain three days ago, a day before the blizzard set in, and had been waiting for the enemy ever since. Waiting is never easy for a soldier, but it takes on a hellish quality when it happens under extreme conditions that sap the strength and concentration from even the toughest men. And a blizzard is about as extreme as it gets.

In view of the missions they had been drawing lately, Justice had given considerable thought to how long they could remain effective as a fighting team. The odds were high, and had been for some time, that they would eventually bite off more than they could chew, and even money was on it happening sooner rather than later. Grant had recently heard rumors of bets being taken on when they would get their asses chewed up. Normally, it was the kind of thing that Justice would shrug off as inane gossip, started by troops who had too much time on their hands, but lately he had begun to wonder if there might actually be some truth to the rumors. He and his soldiers kept getting sent to the middle of no-fucking-where with instructions to shoot up every-fucking-body.

But his team always performed well and, so far at least, had always made it back from the abyss. They were usually down a few men, but they always returned having dished out much more pain than they had received. This assignment was different. At least it felt different to the veteran fighter. Other than the element of surprise they held, which was not a minor card, the deck was stacked heavily against them in just about every other way. At twenty-six men, they were down to half of their normal fighting strength, which had led him to insist on double rations of ammo for every man. They were also fifteen miles behind the enemy's front line, freezing their balls off in single digit temperatures, and about to face off with a heavily armored column of the enemy's latest and greatest weapons and vehicles. In other words, they were in one hell of a shitty situation, and the entire team knew it.

*Maybe those clowns back at the Division HQ do have a few bucks riding on this,* he thought. *Fuckers.*

"LP One, this is Sergeant Justice. Say again, over."

He thanked God and the Army that the radios were encrypted at least. He couldn't imagine encoding messages in this weather.

After a few more failed attempts, he spoke to the corporal next to him.

"Tay, go see what's up."

Justice could tell that Taylor did not enjoy the thought of making his way through a quarter mile of frozen terrain. The young infantryman did not hesitate, though. Like the rest of the team, he was a good soldier. An order was an order and the only way to get through with the task was by beginning it.

Again, Justice thanked the higher powers. This time he thanked them for the men that he led. Unlike the equipment and the assignments, only the best recruits were assigned to his team and he had a final say on who stayed and who didn't. If they excelled in every task, they stayed. If not, well... All prospective candidates knew the rules and it was a distinction within the Democratic Federation Army to belong to Grant's hand-picked team. The division commander, upon hearing about the team's series of successes, had once made an off handed remark in a staff meeting that the team fought like a group of hell's own warriors when up against the enemy. Word of the comment had spread and, for months after, the team's informal name was Hell's Warriors. Their commander, Colonel Bishop, liked the moniker so much, he petitioned the Army to make it an official recognition. It was eventually approved.

At first, Justice was ambivalent to the name and never used it, but those soldiers who were good enough to be on the team embraced it wholeheartedly. They quickly began tattooing the words across various parts of their bodies. Within weeks, a strict code had been established among the team that allowed only those who had been with the team longer than six months to get the words inked into their skin. Soon after that, the preferred location for its placement became the outside of the right calf, and that was made the "official" location by the veterans.

In deference to their leader, the members of Hell's Warriors incorporated a scale of justice as a key component of the tattoo. Above the scale, in an arch, the word "Hell's" was written in black. In a reversed arch beneath the scale, the word "Warriors" was placed. Those veterans who already had a tattoo on another part of their body went back under the needle and had a second, official version done. It fostered esprit de corps and gave newer recruits a goal for which to strive. In sum, it provided a positive foundation that helped the team train harder and fight better.

Sergeant Justice saw the benefits of the practice and quietly allowed it to occur. Finally, one night after a few beers, and at the insistent urgings from his team's veterans, he marched himself into the local tattoo parlor and sat down for his own "Hell's Warriors" tattoo. He wore it with pride and thought of his team every time he saw it.

Justice fought off the urge to let his mind wander and focused on the task at hand. He passed word down the line to be alert. He had a feeling that the listening post's last transmission had to do with their intended target. Corporal Taylor should be back soon and he reviewed their position and plan while he waited.

Their ambush position was classic. With the exception of the outpost, they were dug in on a ridge line less than a hundred feet above a narrow, half-mile stretch of winding mountain road. The tanks would be traveling along the road below from right to left on their way to the front. The plan was to allow the column to pass below until the lead vehicle reached the furthest man in the ambush line. When that happened, they would spring their attack and, with luck, be able to knock out most of the lead vehicles and block the road to the rest of the column before having to haul ass to the pick up zone a mile away. With more luck, the weather would allow their transport to actually be there when they needed it.

The road was a thin two-lane, and on the far side of the winding blacktop below them the mountain fell off sharply in a two-hundred foot drop. At the bottom of that cliff-like drop was a deep mountain lake that stretched for more than a mile on either side of the ambush point. A thick layer of ice, still evident despite the time of year, covered the lake. If the team succeeded in blocking the road below, there would be no way for the vehicles in the rear of the column to go around easily. They would have to halt until the road was cleared. But Justice and his men had no intention of being around for that exercise. Once their job was done, they would hightail it to the pick up point and hope their ride was waiting when they got there.

Justice was playing out this scenario in his head when one of those heavy tanks appeared on the road below. The large grey goliath seemed to rise quietly out of the snow. The gusting mountain winds muted what little noise the tank's nuclear-powered engine made. The silence of the vehicle made it seem even more deadly to Justice.

"FLASH! FLASH! Enemy tank approaching."

Sergeant Justice passed the sighting along to the other men down the line, alerting them to the approaching column. He hoped his transmissions were not garbled by the weather.

"It is passing my position now. Okay, fellas, let's do this thing just like we planned. Hold your fire until Sgt. Macon torches the number one tank, then give 'em hell."

The familiar surge of adrenalin kicked in as the instructions were passed along. Sgt. Macon was his best missile gunner and the farthest man along the ambush line to his left.  He was positioned roughly a quarter of a mile along the ridgeline, and Justice knew that, even if he had not heard the transmission, he would be ready.

The column passed below the team quietly, but quickly. The second tank in the column had a plowing device attached to its front and was easily pushing the 18 inches of snow aside. Justice knew the tanks did not need the road plowed, but the smaller, support vehicles that would follow did.  He also knew that the enemy had to be feeling somewhat exposed on the small dual-lane road.  After all, it was a great place for an ambush.

Justice wondered why there had been no further transmissions from the listening post as he counted the vehicles below and waited for Corporal Taylor to return. The vehicles were spaced closely together and he smiled at their first turn of luck on this mission. The closer they were spaced, the more his team could torch before having to bug out.  He sighted onto each vehicle as it came into view, wanting to hit the one that was the furthest back in the column as possible. He knew it could not be much longer before Sgt. Macon took out the first tank. When that happened, it was up to Grant to take out the one in the rear-most visible position.  As the team's leader, he always assigned himself an important role in the mission. It was an act that his team noticed and respected. He never asked his men to do something that he was not also prepared to do. "Lead by example" was his personal credo.

Still sighting on the tanks below, Justice heard the muffled steps and ragged breathing of Corporal Taylor as he returned from the listening post.  A glance toward the soldier showed Justice that Taylor had returned with Corporal O'Keefe and Pvt. Broussard, the soldiers manning the listening post.

"Sorry, Sergeant.  But these damn radios don't work for shit," O'Keefe explained through ragged breaths. Justice knew that their rush back through the drifting snow had been difficult. The need to keep low to the ground, staying out of sight from the vehicles below, had further slowed their progress as they made their way carefully but quickly along the steep, icy ridge of the mountain. Justice doubted that they could be seen by those below, but they were well trained and staying out of sight was a self-preserving habit that you either picked up early in wartime, or died because you didn't.

"Not your fault, Corporal," the Sergeant replied. "Taylor, take your place and get ready. The show should begin any second now. O'Keefe, take Broussard and head out to the pick up point. Your job is over."

"If it's okay with you, Sarge, we'd like to stick around for the show. You might need our help." Broussard nodded his agreement. He was a newer addition to the team but, in the four months that he had been with them, had proved to be a good trooper. He didn't say much but he went about his duties with determination and confidence. Justice thought he was a shoo-in for getting his team tattoo in another two months.

Justice's face was covered against the cold, so he did not try to hide his approving smile. Manning the outpost for three days was a lonely, tiring assignment and, by team rules, the men did not have to join in the firefight. It was not standard Army procedure, but it was Sergeant Justice's procedure. There were a lot of things that Justice practiced that were not standard Army procedure.

"Sure, O'Keefe. Head down the line a ways and hurry it up. We don't have much time."

O'Keefe and Broussard moved toward the head of the line, keeping low. They were less than ten yards away, when Macon fired on the lead tank. Within a few seconds, the rest of the soldiers in the ambush line opened fire. The severe wind and swirling snow did nothing to dampen the explosions as the laser-guided missiles found their targets.

Justice was lining up his second target when O'Keefe yelled frantically from the left. In the confusion and noise of the ambush, he couldn't make out the words. He put the corporal out of his mind. Concentrated on the target below. Exhaled. Fired.

The explosion indicated a direct hit. A volcanic spout of flame blew the target's top hatch twenty feet into the air, confirming it.

Justice smiled. Looked over to the corporal.

O'Keefe was shouting and pointing at something down the steep, snow covered slope. Justice looked in that direction and saw Private Broussard tumbling, sliding down the steep grade toward the column of enemy tanks and personnel carriers below, many of which were now on fire and smoking heavily. The chaos of war had begun.

"Shit," Justice cursed. He fired off his third and final round at one of the armored personnel carriers accompanying the tanks. His missile hit the target, but not before its cargo of armed men began pouring from the rear. *Damn, they're well trained*, he thought as the armor piercing shell found its target. In a spectacular show of force, the explosion lifted the carrier from the road and tossed into the frozen lake below. He heard the explosions and felt the heat of multiple blasts as his men found their targets.

Justice scanned his team, saw that they were okay, and searched the base of the slope below for Broussard. He spotted the private near the bottom of the incline where he had stopped tumbling and, as he watched, the soldier reversed his direction and began a frantic crawling climb back up the icy slope.

"Shall I go help him, Sarge?" he heard O'Keefe shout.

"Negative! Hold off." The last thing he wanted was for another man to get trapped below. The best thing they could hope for was that the young soldier would make it up on his own, and he appeared to be doing surprisingly well. He was unhurt and moving in the right direction. The enemy was scampering for whatever cover they could find. The initial chaos and smoke from the burning vehicles helped shield Broussard from view. Their luck was not going to last, though.

No sooner had the thought settled in his mind, than he was proved correct. Broussard was halfway up the icy slope when he caught a round in the right leg. Justice watched the blood splash the snow-covered embankment and the young man fell hard against the frozen slope. He did not lose much ground, but Justice knew the climb would be too much for the wounded soldier without help.

"Cover fire," he ordered. The men around him immediately concentrated suppressive fire on the enemy positions below. The enemy fire was minimal, a predominately uncoordinated effort by a few of the enemy soldiers. Soon enough that would change, and Justice did not want to be around when it did.

"Corporal Taylor, watch my back!" Without waiting for a reply, Justice leaped from his fighting position and vaulted over the edge of the ice-covered slope.

The move was doomed to failure almost as soon as it began. His first step hit a rock buried in the snow and immediately turned his descent into an uncontrolled, headlong slide. Instead of fighting the slide or trying to stop himself, Justice rode with it. Within a few yards he gained enough control of the slide to affect his direction. His momentum was another story, and he continued to pick up speed. Justice struggled to stop, or at least slow, his course but to no avail. Within seconds, the slide carried him quickly to where Broussard was fighting his way up the hill on one good leg.

Justice hoped the soldier recognized the situation and held out his arms.

Broussard came through. As Grant reached his position, he fell neatly on top of the sergeant and jammed his booted toes firmly into the snow and frozen turf. They lost ten yards of progress, but he managed to stop a full out tumble to the bottom.

Unfortunately, the rounds fired by the European soldiers began arriving in earnest at the same time. Bullets kicked up frozen dirt, ice and rock all around them as Justice wrestled his body out from under Broussard. He quickly freed himself and turned back to face up the frozen hill. He reached out for Broussard.

"Grab my arm," he growled to the wounded private, who promptly complied, and the two men began a slow but steady crawl toward their team and the relative safety above. Suppressive fire from the ridge above increased as the entire team recognized what was happening below. The increased support caused the enemy to seek cover once again.

The fire directed on the two soldiers waned significantly. However, the occasional bullet still ripped into the frozen ground around them and Justice noticed something unusual. The bullets were creating small craters in the frozen hillside.

"Shit, explosive rounds."

Justice knew that the bullets being fired toward them were the new explosive-tipped rounds that the European soldiers had recently begun using. This was his first encounter with the new ammunition but the realization spurred a renewed burst of energy. He stared at the frozen ground in front and above them and redoubled his efforts to reach the top of the hill. Broussard tried to increase his pace, but the injured leg wasn't cooperating. Justice refused to stop or be stopped and was now mostly dragging the young private up the slope. The fire from the enemy slowed even further and the sergeant suspected that Corporal Taylor and the others above were now honing in on individual targets.

"Broussard, when we get out of this shit remind me to make Taylor a buck sergeant."

"You got it, Sarge," the wounded private gasped through clenched teeth. The pain and loss of blood had to be sapping his strength, but he continued to fight as they struggled up the hill. "We're almost there."

Justice looked up from the frozen ground in front of them and saw that they were almost to the top. Through the blowing snow, he could even see Taylor, O'Keefe and several others firing their automatic weapons at the enemy soldiers below.

Justice groaned with effort and, with a final surge, found himself at the top of the slope. He wrestled the injured private over the lip of the ridge until the man was secure on the flat surface. Once satisfied that Broussard was not going anywhere, Justice began to pull himself over and –

– slipped.

His right leg was raised when his left foot lost purchase. One moment he was planted firmly on the ground, the next he was pitching forward toward the hillside.

His chin slammed into the hard, frozen slope. Through an explosion of stars and sudden, searing pain, he had a dim awareness of tumbling and sliding. With a sense of calm that he later recognized as shock, he only had time to think, *Okay, here we go*, before he gave himself over to the darkness.

The darkness was obviously short-lived because, when he regained his senses, he was still in a free slide down the hill. His face covering had been stripped away and the immediate splash of frigid wind and freezing snow helped bring him to complete awareness.

Unlike the first trip down the hill, this time he had no control over his direction. He tried to stop the wild descent, but it was no use. The icy slope had him in its embrace and there was no slowing down. The speed he had gained while star gazing carried him quickly to the bottom of the hill…

…and beyond.

Justice found himself sliding uncontrollably across the frozen road. Hurtling toward the 200 foot drop on the far side. As he passed through the enemy column he caught a brief, blurry glimpse of a tank burning to his left.

He crossed over the far side of the narrow lane at top speed.

His last thought before dropping off the cliff was that the heat from the smoking hulk should have melted the fucking ice on the road.

The sergeant made a desperate grab as he dropped over the edge. His right hand struck something solid. Snatched. Held on. His fall halted with a hard jolt that wanted to tear his arm from his shoulder. He cried out from the sharp tearing inside his body and looked up. A jagged outcropping of rock, a good distance below the cliff's edge was the reward of his effort. His plunge to the lake's frozen, snow-covered surface was stopped short by roughly a hundred feet.

"Aw, damn, that was close," he muttered. And in that instant, he first considered the possibility of his death and what might lie beyond.

He thanked the fates at having been spared. For the moment.

Then, reality dawned. He was hanging by a hand and an injured arm over a long drop to a frozen lake with a lot of enemy soldiers between him and his men. *And they probably think I'm hitting bottom about right now*, he thought.

"Fuck me to tears," was all he could think to say.

Justice tried, unsuccessfully, to pull himself up onto the rock outcropping above. He was able to get his left arm up so that he now had a hold with both hands, but the pain in doing so informed him that there was additional damage to his body. It felt like he had at least one broken rib, and the pain in his right shoulder was getting worse. He knew then that he was finished, one way or another. His only hope was that someone would pull him up and that was a slim hope at best. The team had less than twenty minutes to make it to their pick up point and they had been trained to put the mission, and the safety of the group ahead of the individual, unless there was proof that the individual was alive. Those were his rules and he could expect them to be followed.

His expectations were proved correct; the sound of fighting died off over the next couple of minutes and he could picture the team departing from their positions on the ridge above and heading out to the pick up point. They were his team, his family and he would miss them, but he did not fault them for doing their duty. It was what he had trained them for and he felt a familiar surge of pride in how they had performed today.

Several minutes passed without any sounds from above except for the occasional sound of a secondary explosion as the rounds in the destroyed vehicles cooked off. The only thing Justice could do was to wait for his strength to give out and he was determined to hold on as long as possible. It was not in his nature to give up, even when he knew the outcome, and he hung on to the outcropping of rock, determined to refuse death's claim as long as he had an ounce of effort left.

His thoughts had traveled once again towards death and what it would be like when he heard voices on the road above him. He spent precious energy to look upward and saw the uncovered faces of three soldiers. They did not appear happy and they were not wearing the same uniform as he was.

"Shit."

His body continued to throb and he wondered how long the men would stand there and watch him hang. Probably until I fall, he thought.

Justice looked down for the first time at the drop that awaited and noticed that the lake beneath his dangling feet was closer than he had thought, only about a hundred and twenty feet or so. He debated whether he could safely let go and knew that, although he might live through the fall, he certainly wouldn't be well enough to escape from those above him. Even with the thick covering of snow on the icy surface, he could expect several broken bones at a minimum.

He also noticed that the ice covering the lake was peppered with several large holes and he was struck by the pleasant realization that they were caused by the falling vehicles that he and his team had knocked over the side with their missiles. He briefly considered that the personnel carrier he had fired upon had even caused one of them and could not suppress a grin at how well his team had done.

He was jerked from his contemplation of the lake's surface by the sound of a metallic "clicking" from above.

A glance upwards identified the origin of the noise. One of the soldiers – there were more of them now, nearly a dozen – had chambered a round and was aiming his weapon towards the trapped man. Justice could see from the man's uniform that he was an officer, but his position did not allow him to see what rank he held or what branch he served. From the way the man smiled, an upturned snarl that did not reach the eyes, Justice was certain that he was not pleased with the events of the day. Where Justice had felt pride in his team's performance, he knew that this man felt the opposite. It was not a good sign.

The officer pointed to Justice's left and the stranded sergeant looked over at an outcropping of rock about six feet from where he hung. A large chuck of the rock dissolved into a spray of fragments, several of which stung his face and arms. The bastard fired an explosive round, Justice thought as he felt a warm trickle run from his forehead into his left eye. One of the rock fragments had opened a cut that began to bleed heavily. In a matter of seconds, Justice could not see very well from his left eye.

Justice turned his bloody face towards the officer whose smile was now beginning to include the eyes. The man was beginning to enjoy himself.

The officer smiled even broader and pointed at Justice as if to say, "It's your turn now." He then turned to those lined up next to him on the road's edge and spoke a few words that Justice could not make out but that caused the others to laugh. Like the officer, they were obviously amused with this new-found sport.

"Fuck you, assholes!" Justice spat loudly at the group above. They apparently understood the gist of the words, if not their exact meaning, and their good humor left their faces. They were no doubt remembering the damage that had just been inflicted upon them, and their dead comrades lying on the road above and at the bottom of the lake below.

The officer muttered again and all of the men around him nodded. Justice guessed that he was about to die so he gave them his best smile, held on to the outcropping as tightly as he could and waited for the bullet. The officer raised his weapon and sighted along the barrel.

The smile disappeared from Justice's face as the round struck his right leg, just above the knee. The force of the round nearly pulled him from the ledge, but he refused to let go.

"SHIIIIT!"

His cry caused a small cheer from the soldiers above him. Justice forced himself to hold onto even tighter and bit his tongue against further outcries. The pain in his leg was a hot fire that drove itself up through his body and into his brain. Stilling himself for what he knew he would see, he forced himself to look down at the wound. To his horror, he saw that his right leg was gone just above the knee. Looking past his damaged leg to the ground below, he noticed a small red patch near one of the holes in the lake's icy covering. That's my leg, he realized.

"Oh shit," he wavered into the side of the cliff so that those above would not hear. "These fuckers are going to play with me."

He took a deep breath and looked up to the animals above him. They were no longer soldiers, or even men, in his eyes.

The officer moved farther down along the edge of the cliff and Justice knew he was getting ready for his next shot. The officer pointed to his right leg and raised a finger, then pointed to his left leg and raised a second finger. Justice got the message.

The weapon was raised and the shot sounded. Pain slammed again into Justice and he killed the scream that begged to be released from his body. He could not stop the single tear that escaped his left eye and froze to his cheek and he knew that his left foot had just joined his right on the ice below.

"Fuuuck youuu!" he screamed at those above him. Through the fiery pain and anger that threatened to engulf him, he forced a smile onto his face.

"Hahh hah," he laughed, almost maniacally. "Is that all you got?!"

He received a small measure of satisfaction as a brief look of confusion crossed the countenance of the officer with the rifle. It was short lived, though, as the man snarled and raised three fingers and pointed at his right forearm.

Justice's mind raced with pain and adrenalin. His body could not take much more and he came to a sudden decision. If he was going to die, he would make sure that the barbarians above remembered his death for the rest of their lives.

With his left hand, he renewed his grip on the rock outcropping and still smiling, held out his right arm as an offering to the shot to come.

He did not have to wait long. The force of the bullet again nearly pulled him from his precarious perch but, unwilling to give up, he held on resolutely and stared in macabre fascination as his right arm disappeared in a splash of red gore. It took a second more to realize that the arm no longer belonged to him, and he stared at the stump that began to pump red just above his right elbow.

Justice realized that he was in shock from the torture and loss of blood, but he concentrated fully on becoming a nightmare to those above him. With a snarl, Sergeant First Class Grant Justice, laughed ferally up at them. To his satisfaction, he saw several of those watching his hideous show step back from the cliff's edge. One of them got sick and turned away.

"What's next?!" he yelled in defiance of the officer, who still held his weapon. Justices eyes bore into the man and dared him to finish the job. Whatever caused some of the watchers to turn away did not affect the man holding the rifle. He grinned evilly, raised four fingers and pointed to his left arm. Justice just acknowledged the other's intent with another laugh and nodded in crazed agreement, knowing he had nothing left to lose but another arm. If the fall to the lake's surface didn't kill him outright, the loss of blood would quickly finish the job.

The officer must have known what he was thinking because he shook his head no. Then he raised a fifth finger, pointed to surface of the lake and then to his head. Justice received the message. He would receive a bullet to the head while he lay on the ice.

Justice merely cemented a smile onto his face, looked the gunner in the eye and waited.

The round hit home.

Justice came to on the ice and his first thought was, I'm still alive! His second thought came immediately on the heels of the first, But not for long. That thought was followed by the sight and sound of a foot-sized chunk of ice being blown from the lake's surface not two feet from his head.

"Son of a bitch," Justice muttered as he lay unmoving. The fucker was trying to finish the job. He had no feet and no arms and the fucker was still taking shots at him, trying to take his head off also.

"He can't have it," Justice vowed and raised his head to look around. The first thing he saw was a bloody boot and he realized it held his right foot. A portion of the leg was visible above the boot and he caught a glimpse of the word "Warriors" from his team tattoo.

The second thing he saw, less than a dozen feet away, was one of the large holes in the lake's surface. It seemed a lot larger than it had from above and a plan quickly formed. The lake... he had to make it to the hole and to the lake below it.

He tried to move toward the hole and found, to his pain and surprise, that he could move using the stumps that were left of his arms and legs. He began to edge toward the hole. He edged toward the hole as another, more rational part of mind, argued against the attempt.

*I'm dead anyway, what difference does it make if I freeze to death, bleed to death or get my head blown off?*

But he knew there was a difference. It was a difference that counted. If he died from blood loss or from a bullet to the head, it would be the gunner's doing. But if he made it to the hole, it would be his choice, his decision and not the officer's. For Justice, it was enough of a difference to silence the weaker part of his soul, the part that cried out for peace and surrender, for an end to the pain and misery.

He began dragging his body toward the hole in the ice and another chunk of frozen lake exploded next to him. He ignored the agony that was his body and the ragged stumps of his arms pulled while the stumps of his legs pushed. He moved slowly at first but, as the decision to act settled more firmly into his being, he picked up the pace and clawed wildly at the ice in desperation and need. He was halfway to the hole when another round punctured the ice beside him. He thanked God that the officer was a piss poor shot and looked briefly at the place where the shot hit. He saw the blacked crater of ice and saw a bloody hand, his hand, lying next to it. That's my hand, he thought, and clawed even harder at the ice with the bone and muscle that once held it to his body. The rage drove him faster.

Only four feet to go. He felt a jolt as a round struck him somewhere beneath the waist, but he did not slow down or pause to examine the wound. The only thought that drove him was the lake, the lake, the lake. *Got to get into the lake.*

The bloody, ragged stumps that were once his arms and legs continued to pull and push his torn body toward the hole. His mind was no longer an active participant in the process of reaching the dark water beneath the ice and the victory for which it stood.

Two feet. Another round took more of his right arm; it was gone now, nearly to the shoulder but he was close enough he knew. He could see the calm water now. Already a thin film of ice and snow had begun to cover the hole and he wondered briefly whether it would be enough to keep him from his goal.

He threw himself forward, past the ragged edge and the thin crust gave easily beneath his weight. His head, his shoulders, and then the rest of his broken body entered the frigid water.

*Learn to shoot, asshole! I beat you.*

He laughed, suddenly eager for the darkness and death that waited below. His lungs filled and he sank.

## CHAPTER ONE

Earth formed its Leadership Council more than three hundred years before the arrival of the Minith.

When the human wars ended and Peace came to the world, each of the six remaining Major Cultures sent a representative forth to speak for its citizens. In so doing, the Leadership Council was formed. In the initial years, the Council floundered in a lack of cooperation and self service as it fought to right the wrongs caused by so many bloody wars and endless years of fighting between the remaining cultures. Culture Leader faced off against Culture Leader at the Council's table as each sought only to better the lot of his or her own kind. War had left them scarred and untrusting of each other and arguments broke out often as old differences renewed daily.

But as the decades passed, the struggles for dominance churned sufficiently through the lengthy process of healing and recovery until, at last, the Council's representatives began to change as the world about them changed.

As the soldiers of the old wars died off, their children and the orphans left in war's wake took their place. In time, the soldiers' grandchildren and then their great-grandchildren took their turns at leading the world and, with each successive generation, the changes became more pronounced. The Earth began a steady evolution toward a safe, gentle place where each Culture and each individual was respected. Eventually, the members of the Leadership Council stopped their internal squabbling and tendered genuine interest in each other's suffering. For the first time ever, the Earth's population was viewed by its greatest leaders as a whole, with each separate group contributing its own unique strengths, abilities and traits to the benefit of all. Their power was channeled into easing the pain and suffering of the less fortunate, regardless of their race, background or location in the world's previous command structure.

Earth became a planet where peace and understanding were cherished above all else. Scenes of violence, civil disorder and even personal outrage became acts of the rarest kind, abhorred by all but the most antediluvian humans.

At its peak, the Leadership Council cared for their world and all its people like a doting Mother on a newborn. In turn, the members of the Council were loved and praised by those they represented. There was no higher honor anywhere in the world than to be selected by one's Culture to be a representative on the Council.

But the Council's peak was now twelve years past.

The current Council, which consisted of four women and two men, were still the most powerful and influential humans on Earth, but they no longer controlled the interests or well being of their planet or its people. Earth and all of its people and Cultures were locked in the chains of bondage by a race from another world -- a race of cruel slavers.

This morning, the six members of the Leadership Council took their seats quietly, without preamble. They were alone and, as they did every third morning, they settled in to begin the business of leading the sixty billion men, women and children of Earth.

As was tradition, the Leader Elect, Primo Esteval, waited patiently for the other members to look toward him to begin. The even number of members required the Leadership Council to elect a leader from the group and they did so every five years. This responsibility was most recently bestowed less than a year before, by a five to one ballot, on Primo Esteval, representative of the S'mercan Culture. Esteval had been the lone nay vote in the election, casting his own vote for Sabatina Sabontay, the Urop'n representative.

A modest man, Esteval often jested with the other members of the Council that it had been a fixed ballot. The rest denied the claim and adamantly stated – often behind sly smiles and winks of their secondary eyelids – that it had been a fair and just ballot.

"This session of the Leadership Council of the Members of the Peaceful Earth is begun," Esteval intoned in Earth Standard language.

Like all humans for the past two hundred plus years, Esteval spoke Standard from early childhood. Unlike his own culture's language, Standard seemed stilted, pretentious and overly formal. The formality had purpose, he knew. It was meant to help overcome potential misunderstandings and thereby foster Peace. But it was not natural for him. Esteval often imagined the old kings and queens of ancient Engl'n as they conversed in similarly regal tones.

"Member Suyung, what is on the session agenda for this day?"

Suyung Trey, the As'n Culture representative, cast her dark brown eyes around the table as her small, delicate hands adjusted her prepared notes. It was a stalling tactic and all of the other members knew it; Suyung was prepared for the request as always.

"Leader Elect Esteval, yesterday we received a communication, via human courier, from the Minith Minister of Production." Suyung paused, and Esteval noted how the news registered with the others at the table. The Musl'n representative, Quasan Alla, bowed his head and Esteval knew that he was offering a prayer to the culture's God.

Unlike the earlier years of the Minith domination when the council had received almost daily directives from the aliens, this communication was the first the Council had received from the Minith for almost a year. Everyone at the table knew it could not be good news and, when Peace settled among the group, Diekela Mamun, the Afc'n Culture representative, cleared her throat and looked to her diminutive counterpart from the As'n culture. Diekela was large, dark and dressed colorfully as was her Culture's way. When she entered a room, heads turned. She exuded an exotic mixture of intelligence, pride and gentleness.

"How much?" she asked. Her normally deep voice seemed strangely hushed and Primo Esteval noted a slight waver. It mirrored his own inner voice.

Suyung lowered her eyes and hesitated, clearly not wanting to answer.

With each previous communication from the alien production minister, came an order to raise production; and with each increase more and more humans were forced into slavery for the Minith. Already, the needs of the sixty billion humans that made up the native population of the planet were barely being met in order to meet the Minith's requirements.

"Member Suyung," Esteval prompted. "Has there been a demand for increased production?"

Like all humans, Suyung had been raised to be peaceful in all respects and her voice betrayed none of her internal emotions.

"The Minith are requiring a twenty percent increase in all areas," she responded quietly. "Effective with the next cycle."

Everyone at the table drew quick breaths. Several whispered Peace mantras.

Randalyn Trevino, the N'mercan Representative, struck the top of the table with her pale white fist. Had the act been under different circumstances, the members of the Council would have been taken aback at the show of violence. As it was, they barely registered the act.

A twenty percent increase in the quotas that they delivered to the Minith meant that nearly fifty million more men, women and children would be pulled away from serving the needs of their fellows and be given over to the needs of the alien race. Teachers and their students, carpenters that built and maintained their shelters, scientists that were working on improving all of their lives – all would be needed to meet the latest demand. Even worse, the Council knew that a twenty percent increase would require them to divert workers from the sub-farms that supported hundreds of thousands of families.

The Urop'n representative, her transparent lids opened wide in the darkened chamber, looked around the circular table to Quasan Alla. The Musl'n representative acknowledged the look with a slight nod, and Quasan raised a hand to signal the Leader Elect. He received a silent bid to proceed.

"Member Sabontay and I would like to know where the resources for this twenty percent are to be found," the robed man began. "We also wish to point out that our two Cultures bore the weight of the last increase."

"Your concerns are recognized Member Quasan," Esteval replied. He turned to Sabatina and nodded to her as well. "As are yours, Member Sabontay. The resources will be obtained through a mutual agreement of the Council, as you know. The Council is aware of the contributions of your respective Cultures."

Esteval met each representative's eyes as he responded to the concerns.

"No one here wishes inequity in meeting this new burden," he intoned. The Standard language sounded overly formal when discussing such personal issues, but could not be helped. "The sacrifices of your Cultures, as well as those of all of our Cultures, will not be discounted in whatever ballot comes to vote.

"Member Suyung, was there a penalty contained in the latest communication?"

All of the members leaned forward.

In the earlier days of Minith control, the Council had argued against each quota increase and, on several occasions, the humans had failed to reach an established quota. The Minith monsters had quickly learned, though, that these shortages could be prevented by retaliating against the human food processing centers. After the second missed quota, a month after arrival of the alien race, Minith ships had targeted and destroyed a hundred of the human sub-farms. The Council, knowing that they could not afford additional losses, had met each quota since – but not without paying a terrific penalty in human life and suffering.

"For each percentage we are short in the quota," Suyung informed them in a voice barely above a whisper, "the Minith will destroy thirty of our sub-farms." Her normally unaccented Standard wavered with a hint of her native Culture-language.

"Thirty? For *each* percent?" Randalyn Trevino, the N'mercan, asked. Her quiet voice held a hint of anger and the other members drew back, surprised at the outburst. Randalyn often expressed strong emotion when their discussion turned toward the Minith, and Esteval feared this latest news might push her into violence.

As if sensing their fear, the N'mercan representative gathered a deep breath, lowered her transparent set of secondary lids, and assumed a classic tranquility pose. The act did much to dispel the other Council members' anxiety and they visibly relaxed while the Culture representative tried to calm herself.

"It is time to act," she said. The Culture Leaders knew what was coming and several of them shook their heads. "We cannot allow them to control us any longer. We must proceed with the experiment."

"Never, Member Trevino," Diekela Mamun, the Afc'n, replied. Her voice sounded calm and strong, but Esteval detected a slight undercurrent of doubt. "We do not know where this will take us."

"It is too dangerous," Quasan Alla contributed.

"What if the Minith discover what your Culture has been attempting?" Diekela asked. "How will they punish us if they learn what your scientists are doing?"

Esteval knew the N'mercan Leader was fighting to maintain Peace. After a few moments, Randalyn responded, her voice devoid of any emotion.

"Diekela, you know as well as I that the Minith care nothing for what we do as long as our quotas are met. They do not think that we are capable of resisting them."

"That does not mean that it will always be that way," the Afc'n delegate replied. "Besides, it is against Minith law for us to work against them. Do you dare risk angering them and bringing more of their violence upon us?"

The N'mercan was undeterred. The Minith's demands for increased production strengthened her position and she pressed forward.

"Fellow Members, I have never hesitated to express my views with you. You know that I struggle with Peace more than any other at this table. But I promise you that I am a firm believer in Peace and know that it is how we must live our lives under normal conditions."

The N'mercan Culture Leader pushed herself from her chair and began a slow pace around the table.

"But these are anything but normal times," she continued as she paced. "We have been turned into slaves by a race of alien barbarians who care nothing for our race, our Cultures, our beliefs. In fact, our beliefs have merely allowed them to enslave us without a struggle.

"Hundreds of years ago, we did away with war. We defeated our violent emotions and made this world one of Peace, one where no one feared for their lives or for their property. It became a world where we lock away the violent and sow goodness in those who remain. But now…"

Randalyn paused to massage her temples and Esteval wondered if his friend was feeling well. Before he could ask her if she was okay, she pressed on.

"Now we struggle as a race enslaved." Her voice rose slightly and her pace increased. "Our people struggle daily to make quotas that cannot be met! And when they are not met, our oppressors destroy our food supplies, which further hinder our ability to meet their demands."

The N'mercan's pace quickened and the Standard flowed to match her steps.

"We are dying as a race and all I've heard lately is how we cannot risk the ire of the Minith. Well I say to you that by not acting against our slavers, we welcome their violence and their power over us with open arms, led like the ancient lambs to slaughter. And for this, there is no need.

"I assert that violence, created by the hands of Peace-loving humans, has a place in our world."

Gasps circled the table and heads shook in denial.

The promotion of even the mildest form of violence by a Culture Leader was taboo and cause for immediate dismissal. The N'mercan was advocating fighting the Minith. She was crying for war. Esteval knew her words would either sway her fellow leaders, or they would be her undoing.

"I assert that violence, used against the Minith, is the only way in which we can truly free our people!" Randalyn pushed onward. "Distinguished members of the Leadership Council, let us proceed with the venture that my Culture has undertaken. The salvation of our Cultures – of our world – depends upon our liberation from these alien slavers.

"We have a chance to end the misery of our people. We cannot throw that chance away because we are frightened about what *may happen* if we act. Instead, let us embrace our only chance because we know what *will happen* if we do not."

She turned to face the stunned Council. Her blue eyes dared them to object.

"Fellow Culture Leaders, I implore you to consider these words and weigh them for their merit. Of the known and the unknown, the Minith represent the greater threat. Indeed, they are the greatest threat!"

Randalyn dropped into her seat. Her fellow leaders looked around at their peers. Randalyn's eyes were cast downward. Esteval knew she was not used to emotional appeals and the effort seemed to have left her drained. Whatever the Council's final decision, she had spoken from her heart and Esteval waited for someone else to speak.

He did not have to wait long.

"I propose we ballot the decision of the N'mercan Leader's proposal," Sabatina Sabontay stated quietly. It was apparent that she had been swayed by her friend's words. Suyung Trey nodded her assent; she too agreeing that they could no longer sit idly by while their world suffered.

Diekela shook her head, clearly not agreeing with the N'mercan's position. Quasan Alla merely stared at the table.

Randalyn lifted her eyes toward the Leader Elect. The blue iciness of her stare caused him to take a deep breath and whisper a Peace prayer before speaking.

"I concur that something must be done," he spoke quietly. He paused. Briefly closed his eyes. "But before we decide, I propose we speak with the scientist who is heading up this challenge. If we are to proceed with this experiment, we should know what it entails. He should speak before the entire Council."

Several of the others quickly agreed and a quick vote was cast to seal the proposal. By a vote of 5 to 1, it was agreed the scientist would be brought before them to describe his work, and to answer the questions of the Council.

At the conclusion of the ballot, Randalyn surprised them once more.

"If it pleases the Council, I have asked Senior Scientist Tane Rolan to accompany me on this session trip. He is waiting in my readiness chamber."

Looks were cast around the table and more than one head shook at the N'mercan's statement. Esteval did not comment on Randalyn's presumptuousness in assuming that the scientist might be called. Instead, he suggested to the rest of the council that they grant entry to the scientist and complete the business in front of them now instead of at a future date. Gaining majority approval, Esteval instructed Randalyn to request the scientist's presence.

A few moments later, the N'mercan Leader returned with a smallish man dressed in the standard, blue-gray tunic of a Senior Scientist. The tunic was ill-fitting and baggy, but clean. At just over 5 feet tall, and carrying a mere 130 pounds, the thin framed scientist did not make an intimidating entrance. He was young -- far younger than any of them might have guessed for a Senior Scientist. Most scientists never achieved the highest rank of their profession, and the few who did were typically well into their sixties before attaining the post. The man entering the room was no older than thirty standard years and that alone attested to his considerable abilities.

But it was not the scientist's age that made the Leaders sit up and reassess the man as much as it was his eyes. When he looked at the Leaders seated around the table, meeting each one's gaze directly and without apology, Esteval was touched with an undeniable sense of power, knowledge and strength.

Beneath the secondary lids, Tane Rolan's blue-gray eyes matched his tunic. And they shined brightly, with a heavy mixture of intelligence and fierce determination. The Leader Elect sensed other, more troubling emotions bubbling beneath the senior scientist's calm exterior and wondered if this servant of the people and of science was not wholly at Peace. The intelligence and determination in the scientist's gaze appeared bound by a quietly restrained anger and, for the first time since the Minith had come to Earth, the Leader Elect felt a glimmer of hope.

The scientist approached the raised platform reserved for guests to the Council and stepped onto it with quiet confidence. He turned toward the Leaders and waited. Unlike most visitors who stepped upon the platform, he did not appear nervous or anxious in the presence of Council.

"Good day, Senior Scientist Rolan," the Leader Elect greeted the young man. "Do you understand why you have been requested to speak with us today?"

"Yes, Honorable Member Esteval," the scientist replied in Earth Standard speech. There was no trace of Culture accent in the words. "You wish to hear about our recent experiments."

"Yes, Senior Scientist. We would like to know more about your research and your theories." Esteval waved a hand toward Randalyn.

"Your Culture Leader has briefly explained your work, but we would like to hear from you. Are you prepared to address the Council?"

"I am, sir."

"Very well. Please begin."

\* \* \*

Tane Rolan paced anxiously outside the Council's Chamber.

His impatience was a curse as well as a blessing and he tolerated the wait as well as he could. As a child, his inability to wait for others was well known among the adults and teachers in his life. Unfortunately for Tane, anyone who expressed emotions that conflicted with the norms of "patience" and "peace" were singled out as possibly being a Violent and he was no exception. It made for an awfully lonely childhood and one where he was constantly monitored and "re-counseled" on a regular basis.

As an adult, his inability to be patient and wait for others to take charge often helped him to reach his goals. As a junior scientist he pushed for results in his work and, where others may have held back, he charged forward.

At first, he had been labeled a scientific apostate, lucky in areas where other, older scientists had failed; but as his string of successes grew, so did his reputation as a skilled scientist. As a result of his efforts, incredible discoveries were made in the areas of human engineering, bio-genetics and cloning. Science that had been stagnant for centuries was reinvigorated and raced quickly ahead. Tane's advances were so extraordinary that he was soon recognized by those in the scientific community, reluctantly or otherwise, as a genius on par with da Vinci, Einstein, and Candleman. He was awarded the rank of Senior Scientist at the age of twenty-seven, making him the youngest, by more than two decades, to ever achieve the rank.

Now, at twenty-nine, Tane was once again waiting for others to agree with him. To grant an approval of a decision that he had already made. A decision that he planned to carry out regardless of what the Council decreed.

He was considering how he would continue his work without the Council's knowledge when the Chamber door opened and he was waved back inside.

"Senior Scientist Rolan," Leader Elect Esteval began. "You will return to your work. This Council, through your Culture Representative, will monitor your experiments and provide any assistance that you may require. We wish you Peace, and hope that your efforts deliver us from the Minith."

*It's about time*, Rolan thought.

Once again, his impatience had been rewarded.

## CHAPTER TWO

As a space-faring race, the Minith would be considered infants by many worlds in the universe. Less than three hundred Earth years had passed since their first interstellar flight had taken place.

As a race of thugs and thieves, however, the Minith were far from infants. Those particular crafts had been honed for millennia. First, they destroyed all competing life on their planet. Then they turned to fighting and robbing each other. Clans fought against clans, families against families, brothers against brothers. Aggression was a pleasure and cruelty was polished to an art.

Their way of life ended only with the arrival of another race to their world.

No Minith alive could tell you the name of the visitors that landed on their planet. That was of no importance. What was important was that they brought the gift of space travel. And with that gift came other planets to pillage. Other races to fight and to destroy.

Space travel united the Minith as a race for the first time in over a thousand years. They quickly spread into the stars.

\* \* \*

Zal, the new Master Minith and his predecessor, Brun, marched from the alien carrier vehicle and into the field. They stopped after a dozen feet and scanned the human sub-farm that surrounded them.

Zal knew the laborers had observed the carrier as it approached, and finally landed, in the field. The brighter workers moved quickly away from the descending vehicle. Others were not as quick in their thinking and were within earshot of the aliens. The workers remained as silent as possible and no one looked directly at the two giants. To Zal, it appeared as though they were trying to become invisible, to disappear into the field that they cultivated.

The two aliens were massive, both in the presence they exuded as well as in actual size. They had nothing to fear from the flock and they stood even taller, secure in their knowledge that the human-sheep posed no threat. The newly appointed Master smiled as he watched the weak animals. Had any of the flock had the backbone to look at him, he had no doubt they would shudder at his not-quite-human appearance.

At over eight feet in height, and weighing more than three hundred pounds, Zal towered over the tallest human in the flock. Brun, the Master that he was replacing, was slightly shorter, but still at least two feet taller than the average human.

Like humans, they possessed two arms and two legs. Their faces were faintly simian in appearance, and their heads were topped with large erect ears that made them resemble – from the neck up, at least – large man-like bats. Their bodies were hairless and covered by greenish skin of hardened leather. Each of their hands held an extra thumb. Many humans had begun calling them "Batmen", but never when the creatures were near.

"They are a weak flock, Zal," Brun complained. The pointed auricles of his overlarge ears, decidedly the most un-human like characteristic of their race, twitched. "They are not strong and have no courage. The only benefit of human-sheep is their docility. They do as they are told and they do not protest."

Zal looked at the flock, disgusted at what he saw.

"They cannot even consider the prospect of violence or defense."

"It seems unlikely that any creature, even one so weak as a human, would allow themselves to be enslaved without a struggle. Especially creatures as advanced as these seem to be, eh, Brun?"

Spoken in the low voice, Zal's words, like those of his predecessor, went unheard by the humans in the field. The Minith were cruel and aggressive, but they were sensitive to noise and, as a result, their respect for silence and quiet was very great. Not a few humans had learned this lesson the hardest of ways – with their lives. Not long after the Minith invasion it became common knowledge among Earth's population to be careful of making any loud noises when near the Minith. Zal knew that human mothers gathered their children when around his race. Their fear of an accidental noise that could draw the wrath of an irritable master was becoming. He saw now that the workers in the field were careful in their work and smiled. Hoes and shovels, for there were no motorized tools or equipment, were wielded quietly.

Fortunately for these sheep, the Minith presence on the planet was small. He knew that most of the humans on Earth never got within several thousand miles of his kind. No more than a hundred of the aliens were posted to Earth. Not many were needed to keep the tame humans in line and meeting their quotas. Use of destructive measures against the human farms was all it took to keep the workers in line and the quotas being met.

Other than oversee the mining production and conduct shipments to their home world, most of the Minith rarely left the monolithic Mother Ship that was the center of their domination. This was good for these humans, for on those occasions when Zal's kind left the ship, human deaths often followed.

Unknown to the humans in the field, the recent increase in quota levied upon the Leadership Council was the reason for the Minith visit to the sub-farm today and Brun raised the subject with his brother Master.

"The quota?" Zal asked, unsure of the connection between the quota and this sub-farm.

His eyes scanned the workers and instinctively planned a defense from attack. His briefing for this assignment informed him that an attack from these creatures was unlikely. Still, he was new to the planet and it was an inconceivable concept. None of the Minith understood the concept of non-violence. Instead, they typically craved an excuse to kill some of the flock.

"Certainly, Zal. The quotas. That is how you will be judged by those who appointed you as my successor. The quotas. If you fail to meet them, you will be labeled a failure."

"I would expect no less, honorable Brun," Zal replied. He did not mention that their own masters had said as much before he was sent to this planet. He also did not mention that the reason he was replacing Brun was because their superiors felt the current Earth Master was too soft on the flock. "But what does that have to do with a human sub-farm? We do not care what these animals eat or grow."

The smell of fear wafted from the workers like a drug and Zal found it difficult to listen to the other Master. Zal's heart raced wildly and he turned away from the flock to focus on his predecessor.

"That is true, Zal. We do not care. But –," Brun waved a hand at the humans in the field. "However, it would bode well for you to remember that *these humans care about little else*. If our time together leaves you with nothing else, you should remember that."

Zal noted the rise in Brun's voice and took inventory of his posture. The intoxicating smell of fear was having a similar affect on his companion and it served to feed his own urges. He held back though and listened to what he was being told.

"If you ever have trouble with the quotas, you have only to threaten one of these farms. The sheep will work themselves to death to protect their food source."

"Or if there should be trouble with a rebellion by the flock?" Zal questioned eagerly, anxious to be at battle with any human-sheep who would dare to resist.

Brun expressed what passed for a Minith sneer at the thought of rebellion and replied, "That is one thing you need not fear – or desire."

Zal swallowed the urges welling up inside him and knew that his predecessor had read his thoughts. Had probably even had similar thoughts. He rankled that the other would dare to lecture him.

"These animals are incapable of rebellion. Nay, they are incapable of violence of any kind. From birth they are trained against raising their fists or their voices and are rebuked for the mildest outbursts. At least that is what our historians and the humans tell us. As far back as they can determine, these animals have trained themselves to be sheep."

Zal had been instructed by the very same historians, but still he refused to believe. In fact, did not want to believe. Again, the Master Minith of Earth read his thoughts.

"Ah, so you deny it to yourself." Brun laughed and pointed out at the flock. "It was the same with me upon my appointment four cycles ago, but I quickly learned. I will show you as it was shown to me by Zorn, my own predecessor. Hand me your weapon and summon one of the animals."

Zal smiled, handed Brun his weapon and strode eagerly into to the field. He trampled several rows of the green shoots before choosing one of the quivering humans. He selected the largest male he saw and herded him back to the waiting Brun.

Brun nodded, pleased.

"It is good that you selected a larger animal. It will make the lesson even more effective." He switched from Minith and addressed the human male in Earth-Standard, a language all Minith learned to speak before being assigned to the planet.

"Male, what is your name?"

The man stared at the ground and rocked side to side, nervously stepping from one foot to the other. This male obviously knew it was never a good thing to be singled out by the aliens. Brun jabbed the human roughly with the end of one of the weapons.

"Speak!"

Zal looked toward the field, still alert for any sign of danger or assault. There was none. The rest of the flock continued to work the field, seemingly unaware of the two Minith and the pitiful male human.

"Ernest. My name is Ernest." He bowed his head up and down, up and down.

"How are the fields, Ernest?" Brun waved his weapon across the large expanse of green. The other workers toiled in silence but Zal could smell the fear growing like a weed among the humans. It excited him further.

"Ah, very good, sir. The field will be ready for harvest in another month. There will be much food if the other fields do as well as this one." The fidgeting continued and the fear poured off the male in waves.

"Very good, Ernest. But that is not why we demanded your presence. I require your assistance with a lesson in human behavior. My companion does not understand your views on violence. Please explain them."

"Uh, yes. Uh --" the man faltered and received a slap across his forehead from the weapon in the Minith's right hand. The second weapon remained pointed at the ground.

"Explain!" the alien shouted. The human wiped a trickle of blood from his face and nodded up and down, up and down.

"Yes, yes! Okay, uh... we, uh... violence is terrible!" The man cried out and raised a bloody hand to ward off a third attack. "Violence and... uh... aggression display character flaws or, uh, insanity."

"Do you believe this also, Ernest?" Zal questioned. Fear was the only thing he could smell and it was wonderful!

The man recoiled. "Of course! I mean, how else could we survive? Not to believe... I mean, to commit violence is... it's criminal!"

Zal and Brun exchanged looks and Zal asked in Minith, "Are they all like this? This is no act?"

"Zal watch the animal closely. No matter what I do or say to him or his people, he will direct no action against me." He switched to Earth Standard and addressed the human.

"Ernest, take this weapon." He held out Zal's weapon to the man, who shrank away from it in horror. The dangers of the weapon, and its violent capabilities were well known to nearly all humans. The alien gun fired beams of heated energy that sliced cleanly through anything organic.

"Take it!" Brun swung the gun at the human, opening another gash in the man's head that immediately gushed blood. The tone of his voice and the force of the blow convinced the man that refusal would not be tolerated. Slowly, Ernest reached out and took the object between two bloody fingers. He did not grip it like a weapon. Instead, he held it away from his body like a dead rodent.

"Very good, Ernest," Brun soothed. "Now pay close attention." When he had the man's attention, he held out his own weapon for the other's inspection. "This mechanism here -- when it is pushed, the weapon fires. Do you understand?"

"Uh, yes, but –"

"Quiet!" Brun yelled. The human flinched and bobbed his head. Up and down. Up and down.

Zal watched, fascinated. His temperature rose and his heart beat faster as the smell of fear washed over him. He wanted to strike the man, but it was not his place. Brun was in charge. For now.

"Listen to me, human. Do you have any family with you in the fields today?" Zal knew that most humans worked as a family unit and Brun was rewarded with an exaggerated nod.

"Point them out to me."

Earnest hesitated for the briefest moment before complying with the request. According to the Minith historians, hundreds of years of breeding and teaching made the human incapable of withholding anything from the creatures torturing him. Zal was beginning to believe it.

"My wife, Anit, is there," he pointed. "And my two daughters, Elly and Talla, are there."

"Yes, Ernest," the green alien hissed. "Now point the weapon in your hand at me."

The human gawked at Brun with wide eyes and mouth agape. It was apparent to Zal that the male considered pointing a weapon at Brun inconsistent with what he believed.

"Do it fool!" Brun kicked the sheepish human, striking his chest and knocking him to the ground.

"Get up! I have no time for your cowardice!" The whimpering man staggered quickly to his feet. "Now point the weapon!"

Zal watched as the man gripped the weapon with weak, trembling hands. The pale whitish skin of the human disgusted him and he struggled against the need to strike the worthless animal. He would not be able to stop at a single blow, so held back, gave in to Brun's dominance over the other.

The man lifted the weapon shakily and pointed it in the general direction of Brun. Zal saw that the human's finger was not on the firing mechanism but said nothing. He doubted the pitiful being could hit the Master Minith even if he did pull the trigger.

"Look to your wife, sheep."

Ernest looked to where his wife stood, but kept the weapon pointed at the Minith. It was obvious to Zal that he had no desire for further punishment.

As soon as the human looked toward his mate, Brun lifted his weapon and fired two blasts into the woman called Anit. The pieces of her body dropped as a bloody splash of red gore. The gore landed noisily in a pile between the rows of vegetables.

"Noooo!" The human screamed in agony as his wife's blood poured out of her torn body. He fell to his knees and lowered his head to the ground in anguish. Zal was unaffected by the woman's death or her mate's reaction.

"Point the weapon at me, human!" Brun's voice offered no compromise and the man looked up, dazed. He closed his tear-washed eyes and lifted the weapon toward the Minith obediently. A sound of grief and anguish began deep in the man's chest, but not so deep that it went unheard by either Brun or Zal. It quickly spewed forth as a strangled cry of pained torment.

Without waiting for any further action by the human, Brun lifted his weapon and took aim at the two young females who had turned toward the lumps of blood and rags that had been their mother. One of the girls screamed and the workers in the field turned in time to witness her death. The piercing dagger of her scream echoed through Zal's head as the second daughter ran to her sister. When the heat of Brun's weapon burned off the top of the second girl's head, the echo was replaced by the sound of blood and brains sizzling.

Zal was both amazed and excited. The man's family lay dead but the human had made no move to stop the attack. The gun lay lifeless and dead in his pale hand.

It would have been comical to the Minith except that the sound that had begun as a whimper deep in the human male's chest was now a screeching cry that brought pain to the Minith successor's sensitive hears. Having held back as long as his excitement would allow, Zal walked over to the kneeling human, grabbed his smallish head and lifted him from the ground. With a sudden twisting movement, he snapped the man's neck and dropped him indifferently to the ground.

Zal pulled the weapon from the human's grip and tucked it into his belt. He then looked out upon the other humans in the field. The smell of fear was still strong in them, but they appeared once again to be hard at work. Not one of them looked in his direction. Zal felt disgust at their weakness but also found delight in what that weakness meant.

"You are correct, Brun," he remarked to his predecessor. "They are not capable of fighting."

Ruling such animals for the next four cycles would be a boring exercise. He would have to use his imagination.

## CHAPTER THREE

Amazing. That was what Tane Rolan thought as their experiment opened his eyes and looked around at the nature-cage. No one knew what to expect. There had been dozens of conversations about what the man would do when he awoke – if he awoke. Everything from idiotic slobbering to manic rage had been predicted, and the assembled group held their collective breath while the object of their attention decided how he was going to react to his new surroundings.

\* \* \*

He opened his eyes and found himself in a garden of waist-high grass and green foliage. This was a new place, one he had never visited before. There were no trees but the point was a small one, meaningless in the importance of the moment.

He could see! And smell! The scent of wildflowers hit his nose and he felt as if his head would explode with sensory overload.

His eyes, nose and mind drank in the virgin scenery like a drowning man gasping for air. The bright green leaves and brown shoots were cool air blowing across the baked soil of his weary mind. Until that moment, he had not realized how starved for new input he had become.

He stared ahead, not wanting to miss a single detail. He milked the scene for all of its heavenly freshness – its newness. He committed the scene to memory as quickly as possible, fearful that he might be yanked suddenly back into the incessant replay of the memories that he had become. The fear threatened to consume him as it coursed savagely through his body. Was the garden a mirage or, worse, just another long-buried memory suddenly flung to the surface of his being?

\* \* \*

Cryogenics had evolved significantly since its inception in the twentieth century and, together with Senior Scientist Tane Rolan's recent work on cell regeneration, everyone in the room felt this was their best, if not their only, chance. So far, all was going well, but that could change in an instant. Tane had learned that very hard lesson from previous experiments. Still, he was cautiously optimistic.

Unlike their previous attempts, the man before them now was different. His body, or what was left of it when they found him, had frozen upon his death and had somehow managed to remain frozen for several hundred years. The minimal degree of cell degeneration had given them hope and he, like the others around him, clung to that hope now. They were captured by the sight of their work and they watched, alert for any sign of life or movement.

But he did nothing. Other than open his eyes, the man in the nature-cage did not move.

The man's body, or what was left of it, had been found still frozen by a group of Urop'n geologists studying the possibility of mining the bottom of remote northern lakes. Fortunately, one of the geologists knew of Tane's experiments with cryogenics and human tissue research, and he had the man's remains packed in ice and transferred to the senior scientist's custody.

Tane's initial reaction upon receiving the man's frozen cadaver was so matter of fact that it startled him to think of the incident in retrospect. He had submitted the remains to his lab for study, certain that the remnants of the body were not what they were looking for. Fortunately, he had a good team behind him. One of his more alert subordinates ran tests that indicated that the man had not been dead prior to his being frozen and suggested that the broken body might not be a waste of their efforts.

Tane validated the worker's results and, reaching the same conclusion, felt a rush of excitement. He cursed himself (mildly of course) for almost allowing the find to casually slip through his fingers. He applauded the alertness of the junior scientist and totally immersed himself in his new project.

A detailed analysis of the mutilated figure's body, teeth, eyes and clothes revealed the most amazing characteristic of the discovery. The man appeared to have been a warrior. That long-dead breed of human who fought and killed for Culture, money or sometimes – Peace forbid – because they enjoyed it. He desperately hoped that the man was not of the latter variety. He dreaded the thought of raising the broken man back into life just to have to destroy him later should he turn uncontrollably violent or aggressive.

The scientist spent every waking hour with the man as the experiment progressed. He oversaw all aspects of the project and conducted all of the more complicated procedures personally, often to the chagrin of his co-workers and subordinates. He was a man obsessed with his work and, in a world grown fat with underachievers, he found success. The control of the subject's body temperature was finely regulated and closely supervised as frozen cells tissues were sampled, replicated and grown. Growth led to new skin and bone, which were manipulated into the growth of new limbs.

These new appendages were similar to the old. They were cloned from the originals and constructed by the scientist and his team to be as good as, or better, than the originals. Three vertebrae, eight ribs and the right clavicle, all broken for centuries, were repaired. Most of the man's internal organs were re-grown and replaced. Numerous cuts and abrasions to the face and torso were easily repaired.

The man's skull was unmarred and, for that miracle, the scientist was downright jubilant. The knowledge, training and experiences contained in the man's brain were priceless, the Holy Grail for which they searched.

The rebuilding process had taken the team more than two years to complete and, when finished, Tane held his handiwork in awe. From a battered shell of a six hundred year old frozen soldier they had shaped a human, whole in structure and better than a real man in many respects. In effect, they had a human head on a man made body. And the body had several refinements over one provided by nature. The man now possessed enhanced arms and legs, a surgically implanted endoskeleton, and an ability to selectively shut down his body's pain receptors. In other words, he would be stronger and feel less pain than any natural-born human.

The only regret that Senior Scientist Tane Rolan held for his experiment was not being able to provide the man with the secondary lids with which humans were now born. When the man met his icy fate, that particular human evolutionary trait was still more than a hundred years from occurring in the first child born with the lids. As a result, the man's eyes, which were not replaced by newer versions, did not possess the necessary muscles to control the secondary lids. Therefore, he had to do without.

Upon completion of the soldier's new body, Tane and the other scientists were forced to await the Council's decision on whether to attempt the next phase of the experiment. Six more months passed before the approval was finally received.

Now, it was time to see if all of the efforts had been in vain and the scientists watched eagerly as the man was brought back to life.

It was Tane who suggested using one of the few nature-cages that still operated. He believed the sight of plants and flowers might relieve some of the confusion for the man. In what little amount of free time he had available, Tane studied up on the period from which the soldier lived and knew there were still numerous wild fields that had not been turned into cultivation sub-farms. His studies revealed that, centuries ago, many men and women felt more at Peace when surrounded by vegetation, running water and furry animals. It was a foreign idea to Tane but he felt the man would feel more at ease in a nature-cage, and if he were prone to violence, the cage would help to contain him. It was just another of many details that Tane had attended to during the course of his obsession.

They chose to re-awaken the subject in a standing position so they could better judge his initial motor abilities. But so far, other than the eyes, he had not moved a single muscle. The man's new body was seeded from his own cells and DNA but that, although a credit to their scientific expertise, meant little to the ultimate success or failure of the experiment. This was new ground for all of them. All they could do was wait and hope.

The time dragged as seconds passed into minutes. The minutes turned into two hours. Still the subject showed no change. No movement.

Several of the scientists left, upset that they had failed. Others, including Tane, held out more hope and stubbornly refused to give in to any thought of failure. The man in the nature-cage was their only chance at freedom from the Minith. If they failed, then all of humankind failed with them.

\* \* \*

It's so beautiful here, he thought. The grass... the plants. What kind of place is this? How did I get here?

He memorized the view in front of him to the finest detail before chancing to find out more about his surroundings. Slowly, amazed that he could move at all, he turned his head to the left just a fraction. He saw more of the same – weeds and flowers. But there, just beyond the flowers, he saw a wall and realized for the first time that he was inside a small garden-filled room.

One by one, he tested his body parts, the ones he knew he still possessed. He knew without thinking that his eyes and nose worked as well as ever. His view of the garden was clear and the smells of the garden were heaven.

He swirled his tongue inside his mouth – it was dry and he realized that he was thirsty, terribly thirsty. It was both the greatest feeling and the worst agony. His body needed liquids badly and rededicated his attentions to surveying the rest of his body so that he could turn his focus to finding water.

He clenched his teeth and was delighted at the sense of freedom that simple movement brought! Excited beyond measure, he quickly verified the existence of four of the five senses – only sound was still untested. Bracing himself mentally, he tried to speak.

"Unnh." The word 'hello' came out as a grunt, but it validated his ability to both make and hear sounds and he was thrilled. He had all five senses…

He was alive!

\* \* \*

The movement was so slow Tane did not notice. Or his eyes refused to acknowledge what they were seeing. However, all of the scientists heard the sudden grunt that came from the nature cage, and Tane watched in stunned silence as the man's head tilted slowly, undeniably forward.

\* \* \*

Grant blinked and looked again to be sure he had not imagined the arms and legs attached to his body. He quickly verified the truth of his initial inspection.

What's happened to me?

The sense of completeness, after being held in a shapeless void for so long, made him feel like running around in circles and laughing. Except that he could barely move. It was like waking up in a thick soup of heavy molasses. The desire to move quickly was there, but not the ability.

Still, he tried.

\*　\*　\*

The scientists cried out as a group as the man toppled headfirst onto the packed soil of the nature-cage. The sound of his face striking the unplowed ground ripped through the crowd like a slap of thunder.

Without pausing to consider his actions, Tane Rolan rushed to the door of the cage, deactivated the locking mechanism and rushed to the fallen man.

## CHAPTER FOUR

Someone gripped his arm and rolled him onto his back. Grant found himself looking into a bright light. A face swam into the light and Grant blinked it into focus. A young man, with brown hair and bluish gray eyes looked down. Suddenly, the gray eyes were shrouded by a cloudy shutter of skin as the man blinked. Startled by the apparition, Grant tried to pull away.

"What the fuck?" his tortured throat rasped. The bizarre eyes above him widened. The face and the hand holding his arm retreated.

"Quick, bring the sedative," the soldier heard the man with the eyes calmly state. So, there was more than one, he thought. He commanded his muscles to move and they obeyed, but with agonizing slowness. He fought his way to a sitting position before being pushed back to the ground by the man with the strange eyes. Grant felt like a baby. His uncooperative body was unable to resist being forced back down and that pissed him off.

"What the hell is your problem, asshole?" His voice was returning and the words held some of the force and authority he had always commanded.

"Be quiet," the man shoving him down whispered. His calm voice carried a bit more urgency and Grant thought he heard a hint of fear as well. "They will hear your violence!"

"Violence?" Grant considered the idea. A little violence sounded like just the right thing until he could sort out his surroundings, but his body was in no condition to cooperate. He allowed himself to be pushed back to the prone position. "I don't get you, buddy. Who are you? And where the hell am I?"

"I am Senior Scientist Tane Rolan," the man whispered. "And your other questions will be answered soon. But for now, you must lie still and say nothing."

The language was English, but old English, like how the uppity ups in Britain spoke – usually over tea and crumpets. *What the hell is a crumpet, anyway?* Grant wondered.

Grant watched the man steal a quick glance over his shoulder and saw worry in the clouded eyes of the senior scientist.

"Do you understand?"

"Yeah, sure... whatever you say, buddy," Grant nodded. Unable to do otherwise, Grant lay back without further resistance. He closed his eyes and reveled at the coolness of the ground as it seeped through the clothes someone had placed on his body. With as little movement as possible, he began a slow, deliberate check of his body. He started with his toes and worked up. His muscles slowly came alive. He flexed them to help quicken the process.

As he waited for his body to catch up to his brain, Grant opened his eyes to study the man sitting next to him. He seemed smallish, with close-cropped brown hair and a clean, well-proportioned face and body. Grant estimated his height at 5 feet, 2 inches and felt confident his guess of 130 pounds was within 5 pounds of the man's true weight. The most startling aspects of the young man, though, were his strange, cloud-colored eyes. They immediately became even stranger, though, when the clouds lifted and dropped in a sudden blink of motion. The man had secondary lids that covered his eyes!

"Good. They are coming inside the nature-cage. Try not to move as you will frighten them." The man – Tane -- blinked again and Grant gawked at his eyes for a few seconds before hearing the words.

"Frighten easily? Frightened of what?"

"Frightened of you, my friend. Of you."

"Me?" Grant asked. He saw other figures approaching from the periphery of his vision. "I can barely move. How can they be scared of me?"

"It is a long story, but one that you will hear soon."

"I can hardly wait," Grant choked. His throat felt like fresh sandpaper. "How about a drink in the meantime?"

Grant saw Tane take something from one of the figures just outside his vision and lean over his body. He was in the process of asking what was happening when he felt the pressure to his thigh and a slight prick. He never got the words out.

"Take him to the room that's been set aside," Tane said.

\* \* \*

Sergeant First Class Grant Justice awoke to find himself lying in a bed, his eyes opened toward the white ceiling overhead. He was no longer thirsty, but he still could not move his arms or legs.

He let his gaze travel down the wall – also white – and glanced around the room. It looked like a hospital room. The door opened and in walked the man from the garden – Tane something or other.

Grant noticed that the door seemed to lock behind the man, and he studied the smaller man closely as he approached the bed. He again noted the clouded, secondary set of eyelids. Other than the eyes, the man's face was nice and hinted of intelligence and humor. He liked the man almost immediately but not without chastising himself for the unwarranted reaction. For all he knew, this could be a doctor for the European Front Army with orders to perform a de-nutting.

"So, who the hell are you?" he asked, never one to let unanswered questions remain unanswered. "And how did I get here? The last I remember, I was headed for the bottom of a frozen lake. With no arms or legs." There were other memories -- memories of death, and memories of endless memories – but Grant didn't think he wanted to get into *that* with this guy. All he wanted to know was where he was and how he got new parts for what had been a *very* fucked up body.

The small man smiled and nodded.

"My name is Tane Rolan. I am a Senior Scientist of the N'mercan Culture." The lids covering his eyes rose and fell as he spoke and Grant got a closer look at the deformity. The lids appeared somehow opaque, but it was obvious that the man could see through them without any difficulty. He had seen the same trait in certain reptiles at zoos he had visited. The lids for those animals served to protect their eyes underwater and he wondered if Tane's lids offered the same benefit for him. The question was pushed out of his mind by more important ones, though.

"Okay. I can buy that. But what the hell does that mean, Doc? Where am I and how the fuck did I get here?"

"Please. Do not use profanity. It represents a verbal form of violence." He spoke as though reprimanding a child and Grant was slightly amused by the apparent scolding. The small man had balls. "And what do you mean by 'you can buy that?'"

"Wait a minute, wait just a damn minute, Doc." Grant was in no mood for answering questions. He wanted answers of his own. "Someone's got a lot of explaining to do and, seeing as how you're the only one here, you're elected!"

Grant tried to sit up and found that he could still not move his arms and legs easily. His body lifted a few inches, but it weighed a ton. Reluctantly, he laid back, took two deep breaths, and tried to relax.

"First question: What the fuck is wrong with my body? Forget that! How do I even have a body at all?"

"Be with Peace!" Tane whispered as he looked over his shoulder to the closed door. "If you cannot be with Peace and refrain from this violent behavior I will be required to inject you with a calming agent. The moment the others realize that you have awakened they will want to see you, and I must speak with you first."

The scientist's actions and obvious agitation got Grant's attention. "Okay, Senior Scientist Tane Rolan, I give up. I'm just going to lie here and shut the fu… I'm not going to say anything. But will you please just tell me what's going on?"

"Of course," Tane answered, relieved. "But first could you please tell me your name? I have worked on you for nearly two years now and the matter of what to call you has bothered me for some time."

"Two years?" Grant asked, then waved it off. "Never mind. This is going to be some story Doc," he said, shaking his head at the scientist's words. "But okay, I'll play it your way. My name is Grant Justice – no comments please, I've heard them all before. I will say that it's not a nice name to have, especially if you're a professional soldier like me, you dig? Now, you tell me what the heck is going on or I'm gonna show you some real violence."

"This is not going to be easy for me to explain. Or for you to understand. Accept that before I begin."

"Agreed," was all Grant said.

Slowly, almost too slowly at first, Grant listened as the scientist relayed the story of his rebirth. It took Tane over an hour to explain how the damaged body had been found and the steps that had been taken to resurrect him. In detail, answering as many questions as he could, the scientist explained how Grant's body had been discovered, still frozen, from the lake where he had died. He explained how the body had been re-grown, re-shaped and ultimately revived by Tane's scientific group, working as a team. He told how Grant's new legs and arms were grown in the experimental cell tissue incubators and how the damaged appendages had been replaced with newer, stronger versions. He described how broken bones and damaged organs were exchanged with man-made replacements and how the replacements were better than the originals. Item by item, like a child showing off his new toys, Tane Rolan pointed out the differences between Grant's old battered body and his new, "better" body.

Tane was describing the new body's ability to tune out pain when Grant finally had enough and begged the doctor to stop.

"Please, Doc. Don't say anything else. I'm not sure I like being your experiment."

"I'm sorry, I --"

"No more! Don't say anything else. I need time to think, that's all. Just time to think!" Grant's anger flashed briefly and was gone. He looked toward the ceiling, his thoughts rushing through his mind like a wind storm through a wheat field. He fought to raise his hand to his forehead and massaged his temples. The movement seemed to take hours.

"You sound so proud of the job you did, Doc, but I can barely move. Maybe you'd better send me back to the lab for a few adjustments, huh? I guess they don't make Frankensteins like they used to!"

"No, no!" Tane was quick to answer and laid his hand on Grant's arm. "You are fine. It will take a few days to get back to where your body is fully functional. In a couple of months you should be able to do everything you could do before your accident. Even more!"

"Accident!" Grant shouted, his body suddenly a flurry of waving arms and kicking legs. "Hah! It was no fucking accident that put me at the bottom of a lake with no arms and legs, Doc!"

Tane covered the two steps toward the bed quickly and slapped Grant sharply across the face.

"What the–," Grant managed to squeak out before he was grabbed by the small scientist and shaken roughly. In his weakened condition he could not resist. All he could do was take the abuse until, finally, the shaking stopped and Tane stepped away from him.

Grant glared at the smaller man and swore to himself that, when his body was able, he'd set things square between himself and the doctor. Tane, to his credit, just returned the stare.

"Listen to me, Grant! You must be with Peace! For your sake, as well as for mine and the entire world's. You cannot display violence where it could do harm to another human."

"Oh man, you keep talking about 'being with peace' and not being violent. Just what the hell does that mean anyway? I haven't hit or kicked anyone... yet" He let the last comment linger but Tane ignored it.

"Grant, listen to me," Tane began slowly. "The world... earth... is different now. You've been gone a long time and things have changed. People have changed. How we think, how we look..."

"How you speak also. Does everyone sound like you? All prim and proper?" Grant demanded.

"Well, I... yes, it is Earth Standard language. Everyone is taught to speak it clearly and carefully. It helps instill Peace and avoid misunderstandings."

"Yeah? Well it makes you sound like a pompous ass. Sorry."

Tane stared. His mouth hung open but no words came out. Grant thought he might have pushed the little guy into speechlessness, but it was short-lived. The need to educate obviously overcame the initial shock of Grant's taunt.

"Earth Standard is our formal language. In addition to Standard, each of the six Cultures has its own language, and most have more than one. At last count, the world had more than a hundred functioning languages. Culture languages are less formal and are reserved for conversations among families and friends." The small scientist ended his tutorial on languages.

"Got it. People talk funny now, unless they are at home. How else have things changed? How are people so different, Tane? What else besides the way you speak? Does everyone have eyes like you?" Grant asked cruelly, taking a childish verbal shot at the small scientist.

Grant felt terrible as soon as the words left his mouth, but he wanted to get back at the doctor for making him an experiment, for answering his questions, for shaking him like a small child. So he had picked out the man's deformity and used it as a weapon.

Grant was suddenly struck by the humor of the thought, regardless of how cruel it was. He imagined a world full of freaks with extra eyelids and he laughed for the first time since rejoining the living. It felt good to laugh and he never wanted to stop, but he did with Tane's reply.

"Why... yes. We all have two sets." Grant was stopped in mid-laugh, the sound choked from his throat. The man was serious. "But that is not the only change, we --"

"Wait!" he held up a hand, it came up easier now. "You mean everyone has eyes like you?"

"Yes. Well, there are a few who are born deformed, with only one set, but most have the protective lids as I do."

"Deformed with only one set? You're kidding, right?"

"I am sorry, but no. At first, those who were born with the secondary lids were considered deformed, but over the course of a few generations, the evolutionary change became evident in over ninety-nine percent of all humans. Now, less than one in 100,000 is born with the deformity of a single set.

"Some early scientists theorized that it was a changed precipitated by global warming or by the depletion of the ozone layer, a natural method of protecting our eyes from the sun's rays. Others thought the change came about as protection against constant exposure to vid-screens, computers and – what was it called? Oh yes, television.

"The human structure is an amazing thing, Grant. It protects us from harm, sometimes in spite of ourselves."

Grant was tired and wanted suddenly, desperately to sleep. He was dazed and wondered how many more answers he could take from the scientist. There was one more he had to know, though, and he refused to give in to his exhaustion until he found out.

"How long, Tane?" he asked in a hoarse whisper.

"I'm sorry... how long what, Grant?"

"How long have I been gone?"

The question seemed to catch the scientist by surprise and he tried to change the subject. "But our eyes are not the only change we have undergone –"

"How long, Tane?"

"Peace. All living humans are encouraged to live a life of Peace and to forsake all forms of violence. From the time they are born, while they live and marry, until the day they die, all humans are encouraged and trained to be at Peace with each other and all other things." Tane stepped toward the bed as he explained and Grant watched the scientist intently.

"There are no more wars, no more battles, and no crimes of violence, except for those committed by the insane. And even the insane are treated well."

"How long?"

"The earth is at Peace, except for – well, except for the... the..."

"My God, Tane," Grant whispered once more. "How long have I been dead?" The small scientist stared at Grant, obviously frightened and not wanting to answer the question. But he finally did.

"As near as I can determine from the documents we found with you, you were at the bottom of that lake for more than six hundred years."

"Six... hundred...years? Damn." Grant sank back into the bed, finally ready to embrace sleep.

Tane watched as tears slid down Grant's cheek. Then he unlocked the door and quietly let himself out of the room.

## CHAPTER FIVE

Grant awoke with a start, keenly aware of his surroundings. As a soldier he had learned the art of immediate wakefulness. The ability to change from a sleeping state to complete awareness had saved his life on more than one occasion. He did not question that the trait had not disappeared in the six hundred years since his "death". It was as much a part of him as his head was. And his head, he recalled with some distaste, was one of the few original body parts that he still retained.

The memory of how he lost his limbs came back to him as it had thousands of times. Only this time, he had a body to help him remember and his thoughts went immediately to his new arms and legs. He forced his right arm into movement and managed to push off the thin white blanket covering his body. He saw that he was naked except for a pair of loose briefs.

He struggled with his new limbs and fought his body to a seated position. Once seated, he slowly forced his legs over the side of the bed. His muscles strained, almost to the point of concession, but his feet hit the strange marble-like tile of the floor with a loud thump. He felt nothing. He looked at the feet where they rested on the off-white tile and the realization hit him like a blow. His own feet were forever gone, blown away by a bullet. The memory of that moment caused him to moan with the loss.

His new feet looked to be normal except that they were pale and appeared extremely soft. *They aren't soldier's feet,* Grant thought. There was no sign of the calluses and toughness that he had spent a lifetime building and he wondered how they would hold up over a 20-kilometer march with a 60-pound pack and a full load of ammunition. Not very well, he concluded, and his eyes traveled up to his legs.

He slowly traced the curve of his legs from the ankle, up the calf, past the knees. There were no scars on either leg and they were pale and nearly hairless, like the legs of a pre-pubescent teen. Just above the thighs, the paleness gave way to pinkish skin where (he assumed) the doctors had had to begin the re-growth process. Other than the lack of color, scars, tattoos and hair, they were a lot like his previous legs – long and muscular, built for both endurance and power. He tried to flex, first the right and then the left, but neither cooperated fully. There was movement, though, and Grant was sure he was making progress.

He continued his visual inspection and moved up to the groin. Visually, everything looked to be in place and Grant forced his right arm into movement. He tugged the waist band away from his body and completed the inspection.

The sight of his own member was a welcome sight and he felt a rush of relief.

"Fuckin' eh!" he exclaimed. There was no way the small scientist could have duplicated his dick and balls in such precise detail and Grant nodded as if greeting a lost friend. "Fucking eh."

He took stock of the rest of his body, his eyes lingering overlong on his hands and arms. The appendages were unfamiliar, the old scars and calluses gone, replaced by unmarked skin desperately in need of some sun. He recalled the missing scars with affection and mourned their loss. Each defect had represented a small part of his life. The burn scar, now missing from his right elbow, had been the result of a close escape from a burning helicopter. The aircraft had been a victim of a well-aimed burst of automatic rifle fire that had reached out to them from below. Grant, and most of his team, had managed to escape from the downed craft before it exploded with the pilot and co-pilot still inside.

The three puckered holes that had lined his left arm from the wrist to the elbow were also gone, but not the memory of the ambush that had caused the injury. He had been a cherry, a new guy on his first patrol, when the inexperienced lieutenant in charge of the mission walked them into an enemy kill zone. The platoon sergeant had warned the officer of the potential danger, but the man had ignored his NCO's advice and ordered the group on. The lieutenant died because of his stupidity and Grant, a private at the time, escaped with a damaged arm and a growing respect for the sergeant. Grant had learned an important lesson on that mission: when your life is on the line, rank is of no value. Experience is what counts. Those three bullet wounds helped him remember that lesson countless times through his years as a soldier. Now they were gone and he grieved their loss.

His sudden despondency irritated Grant, and he pushed the growing depression out of his mind as he completed the physical inventory. His entire body, which had been numb, now began to tingle. He likened it to the feeling of waking up to find your arm in pain, but useless for several minutes, while the blood flow returned. It was intensely uncomfortable and he did not chance trying to stand up right away. Instead, he sat where he was and considered his surroundings as he waited for the pin pricks to go away.

He appeared to be in some type of hospital if the white room and bedding were any indication. The room he occupied was small, the bed and one chair the only furnishings. There were two doors leading from the room, one he guessed was a bathroom. The other one, the one the scientist had used earlier, obviously led to the rest of the building. There was a sign on the wall written in a language that vaguely resembled English. He gave up on trying to decipher it and decided to risk standing up after all. His bladder, real or manufactured – he didn't know for sure nor did he care – was crying for release. And when Mother Nature called, you did not put her on hold.

He took a deep breath and planned his assault on the

door he took to be the bathroom. The wall was only a few short steps from the bed and he carefully raised himself on his numbed feet. The first step was wobbly but without incident. The second pitched him forward and he tried in vain to catch the side of the bed as he fell. His arms failed to do their part, however, and he banged his head roughly on the hard tiled floor.

"Shit!" he exclaimed. As quickly as his right arm would allow, he lifted his hand to check the lump that was no doubt rising on his forehead. But the numbed fingers could detect no sign of the injury. They came away without any blood, however, and he took that as a good sign.

He continued toward the bathroom, dragging himself with his arms as he pushed with his legs. He reached the door after some effort, and looked up to the handle. It was not a handle at all but a strange type of clasp that he quickly figured out with his eyes but not so quickly with his hands. The nearly useless slabs of meat that the scientists had given him looked normal but were nearly useless at the moment. The scientist had said they would eventually be better than normal but Grant had his doubts.

He finally managed the device and the door opened inward to reveal another strange looking device. The strangeness of the device did not hide its purpose, however, and he thankfully noted the hand rails that lined the side walls of the tiny bathroom. He fought his way onto the strange toilet and did his business sitting down, grateful for the relief it provided. His arms and legs might be numb, but the lack of feeling did not extend to his bladder. If each trip to the john turned out this badly Grant decided he might just ask for a catheter instead. It might damage his pride but at least his head would remain unhurt.

He made it back to the bed without further injury and dragged himself into it, exhausted. The scientist said that this helplessness would last only a few days and Grant prayed it was true. He had been a strong man all of his adult life and his current weakness bothered him more than he cared to admit.

Minutes later, the door to the room swung open and Tane walked in, accompanied by an individual Grant did not know. The man was portly with a waxy face and a tremendous belly. He carried himself with a self-important air that Grant recognized immediately as arrogance. The man looked down on Grant as he was introduced by the scientist.

"Grant, this is Mr. Blue," Tane declared. His voice expressed reservations about introducing the two and Grant guessed the man to be superior to Tane in rank. "Mr. Blue is the Administrator of this facility, and is charged with overseeing this, uh...uh....."

"Experiment?" Grant offered sarcastically, seeing Tane's unease in describing the present situation.

"Well, uh, yes, I guess," he stammered, still at a loss. "But, this is more than an experiment, Mr. Justice--"

"Call me Grant, Tane."

"Why, yes, certainly, Grant," Tane complied. "You see this is much more than an experiment. So much more. There is more at stake here than your new body or our regeneration of your new limbs, Grant."

"Really? It seems like a pretty big thing you've done here. I mean, how often can you bring a guy out of a six hundred year old sleep, give him a new body and a second chance at life, huh?" Grant looked at the two men and wondered if they could ever understand how he felt. "But the thing is, Tane, this is not my body. It's more yours than mine. Hell, this one doesn't work for shit!"

Mr. Blue gasped and retreated to the door. He glared accusingly at Tane who glared right back at him.

"Senior Scientist Rolan, you said he was at Peace! I cannot allow this behavior to exist in my facility. I will speak to Culture Leader Trevino about this, I can assure you!" The administrator turned to leave the room, but Tane stepped in front of the door, blocking the man's departure.

"Hold it, Blue! What did you expect? He is not like

us."

Grant watched and listened in confused silence at the two men. He had no idea what had upset the man called Mr. Blue but suddenly felt compelled to stay silent, not wanting to add any fuel to the fire.

"That does not concern me, Rolan!" Blue retorted. He stopped and looked down his nose at the senior scientist. It was apparent he wanted to leave the room as quickly as possible, but he seemed unwilling to force his way past the small scientist.

"I will not permit violence here." He looked over to Grant who diplomatically kept his mouth shut. "By anyone."

"You have a choice, Mr. Blue. You can put up with Mr. Justice and his tendencies toward violence – and they have been minor tendencies at best – or you can put up with the Minith and what they represent for the rest of your life, and the rest of your children's' lives, and their children. Do not forget what it is we are doing here. In this case, the end will justify the measures we take to accomplish our goal."

Mr. Blue looked over to where Grant lay and pondered what the scientist said. Finally, he turned back to Tane and said, "I will take what you have said into account, but do not mistake my position. Violence, in any form, will not be tolerated in this facility. Is that understood?"

"Yes," Tane answered.

"Good. You are responsible for his behavior. Make sure that he understands what is expected of him. Also inform him what behaviors will not be tolerated." The man called Blue discussed Grant as if he were not present and he had to force himself not to respond to the overweight buffoon's comments without first talking to Tane about what was being said.

"Very well," Tane answered and he moved away from the door. Mr. Blue paused to look briefly at Grant before he turned toward the door and left the room.

Tane appeared upset as the door closed, but quickly had himself under control. He turned toward Grant. "You have made an enemy, Grant. A powerful enemy."

"Who? That guy?" Grant asked, humored by the idea that the man could be of any danger to him. He had met plenty of those kinds of men before, bureaucrats who were full of their own importance and who used their positions to bully those around them into bending to their will.

"Yes. Mr. Blue is a very important man. He has been placed in charge of this effort by our Leadership Council and he has their ear. I do not believe he could stop what we are attempting to accomplish but he could slow us down if he wished, and that could be just as dangerous."

"You keep inferring that there is something going on around here that I'm involved with. Something other than just being your human guinea pig. Is there anything I should know, Senior Scientist Tane Rolan?"

"I was wondering when you would get to that, Grant," Tane said. "Yes, there is something. Something that requires your experience and background. It is the reason so much time and energy were put into your...uh, rehabilitation, shall we say?"

"Sure, rehabilitation. That's as good a term as any, I suppose. So what is this thing that I can help you with, Tane?"

The small scientist thought for a moment before telling Grant the story of how the Minith had arrived on the earth thirteen years before. He explained the hold they had placed on the world and its population. He described the quotas imposed by the aliens, their violence toward the humans of earth, he even described what he knew of their weapons. Tane relayed everything he knew, and even a great deal of what he only suspected, about the Minith to the man sitting on the hospital bed.

Grant was speechless through the scientist's tale, marveling at the turn the world had taken since his fateful dip in that ice-covered lake six hundred years ago. Tane finished telling what he knew of the Minith and Grant spoke the question he had been dying to ask since the scientist began his tale.

"So where do I fit in? I mean surely with – how many billion did you say?"

"Sixty."

"Yeah, with sixty billion people on the planet, there must be someone else who can do what you need done. I mean, how can one person have any impact on this situation if sixty billion others can't?"

"Ah, Grant, but you can! You see, it all has to do with the world's population and how it has evolved since your time. These eye lids," Tane said pointing to the transparent second lids, "are not the only changes we humans have undergone. I told you yesterday that there is no violence. That means that there are no wars, and therefore there are no soldiers. We have no way to fight the Minith and drive them from our planet."

Tane stepped forward and reached out to take Grant's hand. "That is where you can help us. We need your ability, your knowledge of battle, to help us get rid of these aliens."

Grant released an exasperated sigh. "If what you've told me about the Minith is true, there's no way I can do anything. Even if I were able to get out of this bed. With a few hundred trained soldiers perhaps, but alone? Never."

"Then you must train us to be soldiers, Sergeant Grant Justice."

"Soldiers? You get offended when I say 'shit' or 'hell.' How am I supposed to train you to be a fighting force when I can't even say what's on my mind? Damn, Tane, profanity is the fucking language of soldiers!" Tane winced at each of Grant's profanities, involuntarily driving the man's point home.

"I know, Grant, but there must be a way."

The scientist dropped wearily into the room's only chair and put his head in his hands. "We have to think of a way."

"Look, Tane, you let me know if you think of anything, alright?" Grant was finished with the discussion, unable to consider the possibility of fighting off an alien invasion when he could not even make it to the bathroom without crawling. Hell, when he was alive, aliens were just a concept carried forward by crazies, or cinematic fodder for cheap movies.

"Right now, I want to work on getting my body back in shape. Maybe if I can learn to walk again I'll be able to think about the Minith. But not now, Tane. Not now."

Tane nodded and walked quietly to the door, his shoulders heavy with the possibility that Grant could not help them. "You know, Grant," he said, turning to look at the warrior. "I may be able to help you get on your feet sooner. If you do not mind some pain."

"Doc, right now, pain would be a welcome relief. I'm so numb I can't even feel my cock. And that's not a good feeling, I assure you."

"Very well, then. I will return shortly with some medication to eliminate the numbness. Eventually, you may be able to control the nerve endings in your arms and legs at will, so that you can feel or not feel your limbs as you wish."

"What do you mean?"

"If our work went as planned, you should be able to feel pain or turn it off, as you wish."

"Okay…" Grant could not foresee a use for the ability. He had always been keenly aware of his body and could not anticipate the desire not to feel any part of it. He suspected the ability was just another feather in the scientist's cap and thought nothing more about it. He did have a question for the man concerning his 'rehabilitation' and asked, "Tane, why didn't you give me a second set of eye lids? It seems like something you would have done while I was being 'rebuilt."

"Oh, I considered it, but your face does not have the necessary muscles to control the second set and they would not have worked. Also, your brain would not have recognized them, much the same as it does not recognize your new arms and legs yet. That is why you cannot use them as you would like just now."

"So, I have to learn how to do everything all over again,

huh? Walk, fight, run?"

"Not exactly, Grant. Your brain already knows how to do those things, it just needs time to adjust to your new limbs. The signals are being forwarded to your old limbs that were slightly different in size and shape. Your brain simply needs time to recognize the limbs you now possess. It is not a re-learning process, but a readjustment to a process already learned. It should go quickly."

"That's easy for you to say, Doc. I'm the one who can't go to the bathroom."

Tane smiled. "I'll send someone in with food soon."

"Great! I haven't eaten in...what? Over six hundred years!"

## CHAPTER SIX

A week after Grant's revival, Tane was summoned to Mr. Blue's quarters to provide an update on the ancient soldier's status. He entered the over-large suite of three rooms with some trepidation. He disliked the large man intensely, yet he needed his assistance and cooperation in relaying the progress of his mission to the Leadership Council. What the Council saw in Blue, Tane had no idea, and he was unsure of how to act toward the other man whom he found resting on one of the couches that filled the primary room of the suite. The posturing of the obese administrator was apparent and Tane had to repeat one of his personal Peace mantras to maintain his diplomacy and tact.

Although Mr. Blue's position as Administrator of the facility accorded him the uncommon luxury of three rooms of living space, Tane Rolan blanched at the waste. Living space was in extremely short supply, especially larger spaces, and Mr. Blue was not even married. Tane knew there were thousands of families living within a mile's radius from the hospital who were existing in tiny, one-room shelters. The waiting list for larger housing was interminable. Tane, although permitted similar quarters as Mr. Blue by virtue of his scientific standing, held only a small one room apartment. His desire for a larger apartment was inconsequential compared to the needs of others.

Tane ignored the familiar sense of disquiet he felt at Mr. Blue's wastefulness. It was the man's legal right and he had other matters that required his immediate attention. Not the least of those was in convincing Mr. Blue that significant headway was being made by the project.

"Good day, Blue," Tane greeted the other man. He

often ignored the man's title of 'Mr.' on purpose, a soft form of rebuke and one not overlooked by the other man, he knew. It was silly to do so now that he needed the man's backing and support, but the premium apartment and all of its wasted space made him angry. Besides, as Senior Scientist, he was not formally bound by culture-tradition to address the man by his title. They were equals.

"How goes the work, Rolan?" Blue asked, countering with a similar omission of title. Blue knew the other man's own quarters were a third the size of his own. He did not know it was at Tane's choosing.

"It goes well. Better even than I had hoped. The man has extreme intelligence and an incredible amount of determination. I have never seen a man so driven to learn so much."

"Oh? And what has this man learned thus far?" Blue stressed the word 'man' as though to express his doubts about Grant's claim to the description. "It is only a week after all, Tane."

"Yes, only a week. But in that week he has learned to use his new body, almost to the level of his former ability, or so he says."

"So. He has learned to walk again, eh? That does not seem like so large an accomplishment."

"Not only to walk, Blue. He has learned much more. I would have estimated his recovery to take months whereas he has improved to a remarkable level in only a week. And what is even more significant, he elected to do so through great pain." Tane waited for Blue to comprehend the words, but the man only looked at him with a blank stare. He explained. "He was given the ability to block out pain, all pain if he so desired. He chose not to do so, and I tell you this – there was an incredible amount of pain for Grant Justice over the past week."

"So? He has a high tolerance to pain. I have heard of this phenomenon before. It happens quite often, I am told, in Violent's Prison. The fights, you know."

Tane became exasperated. "In Violent's Prison they do not have the ability to block the pain! Grant Justice has the ability but chooses not to use it. That says a great deal for the man, Blue. I am not so sure you or I could do what he has done."

"Perhaps, Rolan, perhaps. Do not get out of Peace over this, my senior scientist. A high tolerance for pain is remarkable, I grant you, but not without precedence."

The scientist shook his head, unable to express his feelings of respect for the man he had helped rebuild. This pompous bureaucrat would never understand the soldier's mentality. He tried a different tack. One that he believed would impress even Blue.

"That is not all, Blue. He has learned more."

"What else?" Blue asked, yawning with feigned boredom. He inspected his nails in the quiet light of the room.

"He has been subjected to the information-transference educator, Blue." Tane referred to the rarely used education device that was still in the experimental stages. The device used subconscious transmissions and prompts to implant large volumes of detailed information directly to an individual's consciousness in a short amount of time. Due to the short supply of the devices, they were normally reserved for individuals who displayed an above average intelligence. It was decided that the device would be tried on Grant to test his ability to learn and retain data.

"Yes, so? We have agreed that they should be tried on him, even though I do not believe he will be capable of understanding anything through the process. What is there to report?"

Tane Rolan smiled. "He has shown a remarkable...uh, aptitude, Blue."

"You mean the heathen has benefited from the lessons?" Blue raised his eyebrows at this. Tane knew the administrator considered Justice an uneducated gladiator, revived for the single purpose of fighting the Minith. He had probably never considered the man might possess any significant degree of intelligence.

"When I last visited him this morning, he had worked his way through six different languages." He watched the other man carefully for his reaction and was rewarded with the sight of Blue, all four hundred pounds of him, nearly falling from his perch on the couch.

"Six? You must be mistaken!" Blue managed to right himself, but his mouth hung ajar as he studied the scientist's face for any sign of mistruth.

"Yes, Blue. Six." Tane felt a sense of pride that his 'experiment' now knew more languages than most humans alive. "I started him out with Standard, of course, and he picked it up like a native Urop'n. So naturally, I began with other Lat'n-based languages."

"But how is this possible? The man is only a warrior. He is no linguist!"

"I have discussed the subject with Grant, himself, and I believe he is correct in his theory about this. He was frozen for six hundred years, Blue. Six hundred years!"

"I am aware of that! What is the explanation?"

"It seems that for those six hundred years our soldier was able to recall, in exquisite detail from what I can determine, the memories of his life. In fact, those memories were his only exercise. He could do nothing else but think and remember, Blue. Imagine! Six hundred years with nothing but your past to keep you occupied! It's a wonder the man is not insane."

Tane's voice raced with excitement. The experiment was a much greater success than he ever could have hoped. He took a deep breath to retain Peace and continued.

"I believe that Grant Justice has expanded his abilities of retention far beyond those of a normal human. In effect, he has exercised his mind for over six hundred years and is using that mind to learn more than we could have believed possible. Even Grant, himself, is surprised at his ability to recall the information contained on the transference tapes."

"But six languages?"

"And still counting, Blue."

"Remarkable, remarkable. I must inform the Council of this right away. When can you bring Justice here, Rolan? I would like to see this man again." Blue hesitated, clearly remembering his first meeting with Grant Justice only a week before. "He can be trusted to be at Peace, can he not, Rolan?"

"Yes, Blue. Certainly," Tane said, not quite certain of the fact at all.

\* \* \*

Grant lifted the two hundred and ten pounds over his head, completing the tenth repetition of his final set of bench presses. He felt good about his workout, he was almost to his 'pre-revival' abilities with the weights. He suddenly considered that this new body might not be as bad as he first thought.

His workout was halted by the sight of Tane Rolan entering the room. The scientist entered Grant's 'gym' with some unease, his unfamiliarity with the steel bars and plates showed clearly on his face.

Grant had requested that the room be furnished with the free weights and, after several attempts at describing exactly what he wanted, Tane had the equipment fabricated. His initial reaction to Grant's desire to increase the strength in his body was to give him a muscle enhancement drug, but Grant emphatically discounted the suggestion. He had seen enough steroid use as a soldier to put him off the idea of chemically induced muscles forever. The use of steroids in the Democratic Federation Army was completely legal, and often encouraged by those in charge. The army wanted its soldiers to be as fully developed as possible and the risks involved, although great, were generally accepted by the brass. What were a few tragedies when the army as a whole benefited from the successes? Grant personally knew of several soldiers who ended up crippled because of their massive use of chemicals and, upon taking over his own team, immediately denied the use of steroids to any of his men. Instead, he encouraged natural body development and had implemented an intense regimen of lifting weights, aerobics, and running for his team. He attributed much of his team's success to the physical training they had undertaken.

"Tane, how are you?" Grant asked in an obscure As'n dialect, the latest addition to the growing library of languages he held in his head. He still found the ability to switch languages at will – he now knew nine – exhilarating. He found the ability to switch from one language to the next about as difficult as changing his shoes. When he wanted a different language, he merely stepped into the closet of his mind and tried one on. It was that easy. And so far he had not run out of closet space.

The actual transfer of the languages lasted only sixty to ninety minutes depending on each one's complexity. The information-transference educator was placed over his head and the patterns, words and structures of each language were electro-aurically implanted onto his brain. At least that's how Tane had described it to him.

A quick and painless process, Grant had also undergone historical and socio-economic educational sessions with the machine. He now had a unique grasp of the current state of the earth and everything of note that had occurred since his previous life. He now held a better understanding of what was expected of him and why he had been revived by the Leadership Council and Tane Rolan. The reason was simple: the Minith would suck the world dry of all its natural resources within a few generations if they were not stopped.

"Very well, Grant," Tane answered. The dialect Grant spoke was one of the seven that he himself possessed. "How are you?" he asked in an even more obscure Afc'n tongue.

Grant looked at him quizzically, then answered in Standard with a laugh. "You got me on that one, Tane, but from the inflection and the similarities to the major Afc'n culture Language, I'd say you were asking how I was. If so, then I'm fine. The workout's going just great."

"Very good," Tane switched to Standard, also. "How do you feel?"

Grant was dressed in shorts and a shirt he had ripped into a passable counterfeit of a tank top. His body was covered in sweat. "I feel great, Tane. Haven't felt this good in six centuries or so, you know?"

"It's good to see you still possess a sense of humor, Grant."

"I'd be going bat shit without it, my good scientist. Absolute bat shit!"

Tane nodded, but it was clear to Grant that he had no idea what he was talking about. Grant did not feel like explaining the term "bat shit" and, instead of asking, the scientist changed the subject.

"Have you thought any more about the Minith, Grant?"

Grant smiled. The scientist's ability to change the course of a conversation to a serious topic never took more than two or three exchanges. It was easy to see how the man had reached the level of Senior Scientist at such a young age. Grant realized from his sessions with the transference machine that Tane was an exception to the rule in this world he had found himself in. He found his respect for the small man growing by leaps and bounds with each passing day.

"Yes, I have, Tane."

"And what have you been thinking?"

Grant was not prepared to discuss his thoughts in detail until he worked out all the kinks, a habit he had acquired while in the Army. He liked to study all aspects of a plan before deciding on the final details. Too many times he had witnessed the outlines of a plan become the plan itself when divulged to those in a decision making capacity.

"Not just yet, Tane. Let me give it some more thought,

and I'll let you know as soon as I can. I promise."

"Hmm. I have no choice but to trust your judgment, I suppose. Is there anything I can do to assist you with your work, Grant?"

Grant gave the matter some thought before answering. Finally, he nodded and said, "I'll need two things, Tane. First, I want everything you can get me on Violent's Prison. And I mean everything; blueprints, lists of prisoners, the crimes they committed, everything."

"What? How could anything to do with Violent's Prison be of benefit? Only criminals are sent there, persons not fit for society. I don't see how--"

"Tane!" Grant interrupted. "Can you get me anything, or not?"

"Well, certainly, but I don't--"

"Tane, don't ask me to explain. You probably wouldn't like what I'd say anyway."

"Okay, Grant. As you wish. But if Mr. Blue hears of this, he may not permit it. He dislikes even the thought of violence. If he had his way, we'd all stay slaves forever. I believe he would prefer that over any form of violence – even violence that is directed toward the Minith."

"So, don't let him find out."

"Fine. And what is the second thing I can help you with?" Tane was almost afraid to ask, considering Grant's first request.

"I need a lesson on the Minith Language."

A look of horror crossed Tane's face. "Grant! It is forbidden! I can't... I mean... there isn't a lesson on the Minith! They would never allow it!"

"Oh, and I suppose they don't mind our plotting to get rid of them, huh? Think, Tane! You're better at that than anyone else I know. What could it hurt?"

"But there isn't a Minith lesson for the transference machine, Grant. No one has ever developed one. There are only a few humans who are even allowed to learn the language and they are all imprisoned within the Minith Mother Ship. They are never permitted to leave it."

"Tane, I did a little research in the transference library. There wasn't a lot about the Minith, but I learned what there was. It's apparent that the prisoners there are kept obedient more out of their own fear than anything the aliens do to them. For Christ's sake, there aren't even any locks on the doors from what I can determine!"

"Perhaps, but there is no one willing to enter the ship and no one inside is aware of our needs. There is no way!"

Former Sergeant First Class Grant Justice smiled at the small scientist. "Wrong, again, Tane. I'm willing to go there. Better yet, I will go there. I need to learn as much about them as I can." Grant wasn't ready to discuss his entire plan yet, but he needed Tane's help to complete the first phase. He needed an accurate description of the inside of the Mother Ship if they were to succeed in ridding the earth of the Minith.

"You brought me back to help the world, Tane. Did you think it would be easy? Or without risk?"

"No, of course not, but I thought there would be more time. I did not expect things to happen so soon."

"There is still plenty to do before we are finished with the aliens, Tane, but we have to start somewhere. This is just a part of the game, my friend." Grant sat down at the bench and began another set of reps with his new weights.

"Okay, Grant. I will get you what I can on Violent's Prison...and on the Mother Ship of the Minith. Not everything has been placed into the transference library. Give me two days."

"Two days," Grant agreed in a major Musl'n dialect, another of Tane Rolan's languages. He grunted with the effort of the repetitions, but it felt wonderful. "Then we begin our war against the slave masters of Earth."

## CHAPTER SEVEN


Grant waded awkwardly through the crowded streets of Bst'n. Like the same city from his time, it was one of N'merca's largest and most populated. As he fought his way along the street, however, he realized the Boston he once knew was gone. Here, in its place, was a sprawling mass of bland gray concrete. The buildings had little character, and the teeming throngs of people that navigated the streets possessed even less. Most were dressed in jumpsuits of one muted shade or another. There were no bright colors or eccentric displays of individuality. Like the city itself, the clothes seemed lackluster, bleached of brightness and energy.

The people wearing the featureless jumpsuits seemed much the same. They moved slowly and quietly, as though dazed, and Grant wondered if their lethargy was a result of the Minith presence on their world, or just a symptom of living a Peace-filled existence. He hoped it was the former.

Few landmarks of the old city remained and he rued the loss of so much history. It was probable, he decided, that many of the historical sites had been torn down because they were monuments to the wars that had forged the old United States. For all of the city's newfound dullness, the streets were surprisingly clean, and smelled of antiseptic. Grant surmised that cleanliness came with the Peace, love and brotherhood that made up the new world. Except for the Minith, of course. They were the wild card.

Grant came from a world where war was a common occurrence – too common really. He had regularly questioned the need for war, especially those wars in which he fought. But, unlike the people surrounding him now, Grant knew war was an unpleasant necessity. These people and their ancestors had worked hard to eliminate war, to erase even the thought of violence. Those were not bad goals in Grant's view. Just unrealistic. Grant was an historian of war. He understood that fighting was sometimes needed to eliminate evils that were greater than war. Genocide, slavery, oppression, injustices in multiple forms. All were valid reasons for picking up arms and sacrificing lives. The American Civil War of the 1800's erased the practice of slavery in the United States. Grant wondered how many of the people he passed would not be alive if that war had not happened. Or how many of these people knew their ancestors were responsible for stopping that ungodly practice? And, if they did know, how many of them would be proud of their dead kinsmen and what they accomplished through war? How many would be ashamed? Grant pondered these questions as he fought his way through the crowds. He did not know the answers. But he did know that peace would not be possible as long as the Minith noose coiled tightly around the world's throat.

He felt awkward among the hundreds of thousands of pedestrians. He was surrounded by people, yet felt alone. He could not get used to the numbers of people that surrounded him, people so much like him, but yet so different. They were at home among the crowds, whereas he felt crushed by the mass of warm bodies pressing close as they made their way along the streets. Grant estimated that the crowded avenues he walked along held at least a million people. And that was a conservative estimate, he soon decided.

He looked into the faces he passed and saw men, women and children who, upon first glance, did not seem so different from the people he had once known. But there, just beneath the surface of those calm exteriors, ran a powerful current of fear and subjugation. If you looked closely, it was not difficult to see the signature of the Minith stamped boldly across the lives of these humans.

He had left the hospital hoping to better understand the world around him. He longed to see new people and new sights and had looked forward to rubbing elbows with the people who lived in the city. Six hundred years with nothing but memories to keep you company made a person lonely. But this was too much; he not only rubbed elbows, he practically held hands with them, they were pressed so closely together.

He tried to escape the mobs traveling to who-cared-where by entering various buildings, cutting down side streets, and dodging down alleyways, but it was useless. The people were everywhere. Grant quickly grew dizzy and lost his way. He looked up to find the sky spinning rapidly and went down to one knee. He was helped to his feet by a young man and his daughter, and he asked for directions. The pair pointed him in the right direction and Grant trudged his way back to the hospital. Defeated. A twenty-first century man among billions of humans who were six hundred years younger than he.

The hospital was so indifferent from the other edifices that surrounded it, Grant took most of an hour to find the large, gray building. His brow was clammy with sweat, and the relief he felt as he trudged the hallway to his room shamed him. He dropped into bed, tired, alone and lost. He was not sure that he liked the world he had awakened to, and his small room provided scant relief. He imagined crowds of men, women and children pushing against the outside of the building.

"Enough! Stop feeling sorry for yourself," he chided himself. The comfort he desired was not to be found inside the four white walls of the room.

Unwilling to hide like a hermit afraid of the world around him, he pushed his feelings aside and left the room in search of Tane. The man might know of a place where he could go to relieve his claustrophobic feelings. For the first time since his rebirth, the halls of the hospital seemed crowded, more crowded than any hospital or laboratory he had ever been in, and he wondered why he had not realized before now how many scientists were in the building. His brush with the world outside the hospital had heightened his awareness to the numbers of people around him. When he first learned the population totaled sixty billion, he had not stopped to consider the importance of such a number and what it would mean to be one person among such a population. The sense of being closed in was both unnerving and frustrating.

He spotted Tane in the corridor ahead, talking to a mob of junior scientists. He casually joined the group, and immediately noticed a shift in the group dynamic as several of the scientists moved away from him. Grant was shocked by the reaction but he understood. He was an outcast -- a violent person thrust by fate among the Peaceful. He swallowed the desire to confront them, knowing what response the action would earn. Besides, they had a right to their fears, he decided, regardless of whether they were justified.

"Ah, Grant, how are you?" Tane asked, using the most obscure of his languages. The game was becoming a habit between the two men and Grant smiled. He now knew seventeen different languages, including all of those spoken by Tane.

"I am not well, friend. I am lonely but need some space where I can be by myself," Grant said in one of the languages he knew Tane did not speak.

"I'll take that to mean you are fine, Grant," Tane said with a laugh, not realizing that Grant's words meant nothing of the kind.

"Do you know all of those here?" he asked in Standard, indicating the scientists around him.

Grant shook his head. "No, I do not think so, Senior Scientist Rolan." Grant always used the other man's title when they were among Tane's co-workers. It was one way of expressing the respect he held for the small scientist.

"Then allow me to make introductions, Grant. These scientists have volunteered to be trained as soldiers. They are your first recruits!" Tane was obviously pleased with the revelation, his face beamed with pride at the junior scientists who maintained their distance from Grant.

Grant looked over the eight men and three women he faced. Just moments before, several of them had moved away from him, scared to be any closer than they had to be. Now, he was being informed that they were to be his recruits, trainees, soldiers. It took some effort not to laugh as Tane introduced the junior scientists, several of whom were older than the senior scientist. Instead, he nodded politely to each before requesting to speak with Tane alone.

When they were well away from the 'recruits' Grant spoke. "They will never be soldiers, Tane. Impossible."

"What do you mean, Grant? They volunteered!"

"Look, Tane, I don't question their loyalty. I'm sure they want to defeat the Minith as much as you or I. It's just that they do not, uh... possess the necessary traits to be soldiers," Grant finally said, unsure of how else to describe the recruits.

"Hell, man, they can't even stand to be near me. How do you expect me to teach them anything about killing?"

Tane Rolan's face paled and he stepped quickly away from Grant. Grant used the man's fear to drive his point home. "See there, Tane! Even you. You know what needs to be done, but can't stomach the thought of hurting anyone. Even the Minith! I need recruits who are not afraid of violence. Men and women who can be taught to kill when killing is needed, Tane."

"But where will we ever find such persons, Grant? Where?"

Grant Justice looked evenly at his friend and shared his thoughts regarding the matter for the first time. "In Violent's Prison, Tane. We must recruit our army from Violent's Prison."

Grant caught the senior scientist before he hit the ground. "I'll be damned," he muttered as he picked up his friend and carried him to his room. "The little fucker fainted."

Tane came to in Grant's bed, and sat up. Grant, who was sitting patiently in the room's chair, wasted no time with small talk.

"How you feeling, pal?"

"I feel fine. What hap—"

"Nothing happened. You just fainted. But you're fine now." Not waiting for further conversations, he cut straight to the heart of his intentions. "I'm leaving for the Minith Ship, Tane. I can't wait any longer."

The scientist swung his legs off the bed and looked closely at Grant. Grant thought he might be searching for signs of insanity. He apparently saw none.

"How are you going to get there? The Minith ship is in the middle of the continent, over twelve hundred miles away."

"I can fly a carrier vehicle. The knowledge was implanted just this morning. I need your help, though, to get one."

"The knowledge was implanted? Grant, you could kill yourself if you are not careful. Carriers are very dangerous to the untrained."

"Don't worry about that, Tane. Just get me to one. I'll take care of getting it to the ship."

"And back, also?"

"Of course, I'll get it back, Tane." Grant possessed a confidence earned through numerous battles, fights and campaigns. There was nothing false about his self possession. He had driven trucks, tanks, and personnel carriers; he had even flown helicopters on several occasions in his past life. Compared to those, the carrier seemed like a toy. Prior to flight, you programmed it with where to take you and how fast you wanted it to travel. Otherwise, it did most of the work. Taking off and landing were the only two aspects of the trip that took human action and those operations seemed simple enough to Grant.

"Yes, Grant, you are probably correct. I think you are probably capable of doing almost anything you set your mind to do. I have a carrier vehicle assigned to my position. You may use it if you desire."

Grant stood up, no longer in need of a place to be alone. He was excited for what lay ahead.

"Let's go, Tane. Time's wasting and there's work to do."

Ten minutes later, with Tane's assistance, Grant was headed to the Bst'n museum.

Two hours later, he was cruising a thousand feet above the ground. The crowded city of Bst'n was quickly left behind. Twelve hundred miles ahead, the Minith Mother Ship waited.

## CHAPTER EIGHT

Grant brought the carrier down hard. His first landing in the simple, but futuristic, craft plowed a long furrow of soil and rock before jerking to a halt with a loud thump.

"Oops."

He unbuckled the safety harness and made his way back to the doorway, which sat mid-way along the left side of the craft. Although they came in different sizes, Tane's carrier was built for carrying a pilot and up to ten other riders. Although he did not comprehend all of the engineering science he had absorbed on the vehicle, he understood it utilized electronic interactions with the earth's magnetic fields to stay aloft, and simple thrust maneuvers to move side to side, up and down. It was not sleek, nor overly fast. The 1200-mile trip took just over six hours. More than anything else, the carrier reminded Grant of a large mini-van from the early 21$^{st}$ century. It was basically a large box designed to carry passengers and cargo through the air.

He inspected the outer body for damage, and found the body of the carrier in excellent condition except for a minor ding or two. He cursed his own stupidity for not taking more care in putting the unfamiliar craft on the ground.

He was six miles from the Minith Mother-ship, a mile beyond the alien imposed limit for human travel. He knew from his airborne approach, that humans obeyed this limit without question. In fact, they exceeded it greatly.

During his trip from Bst'n, he had scanned the ground closely. The entire distance had been carpeted with either cities or farms. Like Bst'n, the cities he passed teemed with humans. The borders of each city gave way to neatly planned farms that went for miles. From 1000 feet up, he could easily see thousands of workers in the farms, toiling away like ants to grow corn, wheat and other assorted crops – most of which he could not recognize. It was if every inch of ground that was not used for human industrial or residential use had been turned to food production. There were only two exceptions along the entire 1200-mile stretch.

The first was a massive dark ribbon that first appeared on the horizon in what was once southern Ohio. What Grant first thought was a river soon revealed itself to be a mile-wide chasm of mining activity that ran as far as he could see from north to south. The mine's intrusion upon the carefully cultivated fields that surrounded it was staggering and Grant slowed the carrier to investigate.

As the carrier crossed the open pit mine, Grant stared down into the darkened bowels of the planet. He was stunned by what he could and could not see.

What he saw was a beehive of activity on a massive scale. Countless men and women worked along the deep chasm. Numerous roads were dug into the sides of the steep cliffs surrounding the enormous gash and long lines of giant, empty trucks were descending into the pit. They passed similar lines of trucks that slowly made their way out the pit. Those ascending from the mine were filled with some type of ore that Grant could not define.

What Grant could not see was the bottom of the canyon. The sun did not penetrate to the pit's farthest depth. Grant turned the carrier northward to see how long the mile-wide gorge ran. He flew more than 30 miles north along the western edge of the mine before finally turning away. The northern end of the mine was still not in sight.

The second exception to the humans' careful use of land for farm or city use began fifty miles from the Minith Mother Ship. As Grant had learned from studying the human library on the Minith, this was a human-imposed border between themselves and the aliens. With the Leadership Council's blessing, this land was abandoned by the farmers when the Mother Ship landed. It kept the population a "safe" distance from the aliens.

Grant considered the safe zone as he viewed the terrain around him. His scan of the area from the sky had showed no ground or airborne activity of any type for miles. There was certainly nothing happening between his current position and the Mother Ship. He was alone and had no reason to expect that would change. His fellow humans had proven to the Minith that they were unwilling to enter this area and he counted on that fact to get him close to the ship. And perhaps inside it.

Still, he covered the vehicle with the stunted shrubs and trees that grew nearby and erased the creases caused by his landing. It could be unhealthy to have an alien patrol spot the craft and investigate the whereabouts of its driver. That task completed, Grant looked across the flat, almost desolate land, toward the object of his journey. Although still a few miles away, he could see the Minith ship clearly. It dominated the otherwise featureless horizon, a towering monument to the slave masters of earth, an expression of stature even from this distance.

Grant began the march toward his goal. As he moved away from the carrier, he noticed a scorched darkness beneath the shrubs and grass. From the appearance of the ground and the sparse plant growth that had developed, the fire had occurred several years past. Grant wondered if the landing of the Minith ship caused this damage, or if the aliens had burned the ground intentionally as a means of clearing a barrier around the Mother Ship. The blackened earth was visible as far as he could see in every direction.

The aliens had selected a location with good surrounding visibility as the site for their main headquarters. Grant knew this area had once been called Iowa, and was probably selected before the aliens knew there would be no trouble with the humans of earth. He doubted they would have bothered with site selection had they known in advance what type of population this world possessed.

He traveled quickly, covering the flat unspectacular ground in good time. His feet kept pace with his heartbeat. Two steps for every beat, it was a pace most men could not match for long but he felt good in the moment. Alive.

Grant wore a camouflaged ghillie suit with the hood thrown off. The homemade sniper's outfit was fashioned from a fishing net Grant had liberated from an unattended fishing boat moored in the Bst'n harbor. The net was covered with hundreds of narrow strips of ragged, green cloth that Grant had ripped and tied by hand during the flight. With the suit's hood pulled on, Grant could disappear into the ground, invisible to the naked eye. Just another bush. Under the bulky getup he wore a standard gray jump suit, work boots, and a leather belt. He had a six inch knife strapped to his right calf and half a dozen shuriken throwing stars tucked inside a pocket on the left side of the belt. Although lethal with the knife or the throwing stars, Grant's real defense – he hoped – was a late twenty-first century hand weapon stashed in one of the pockets of the jump suit.

While not his first choice of weapons to take on this little adventure, all were compliments of the museum in Bst'n.

What he couldn't understand was how a culture so opposed to war would leave military weapons – fully working weapons – lying unprotected by any form of security. He wasn't one to question good fortune, though. The museum placard that rested below the hand weapon had described it as a self-loading electro-pulse weapon. It supposedly killed silently and required a full charge of electricity in place of ammunition. That had been good enough for Grant. Over Tane's objections, he removed the weapon from the display and tucked it into his pocket. The knife and shurikens were just as easily squirreled away. Other than a slight stomach ache for Tane, Grant and the scientist had walked out of the museum with no problems. Security was non-existent and there were no other visitors to the section of the museum devoted to that ancient vulgarity called 'war.' If the need for solitude struck again, he now knew where to go.

Grant reached under the ghillie suit and took out the pulse weapon. Shaped like any other handgun, it consisted of a barrel, a hand grip, a trigger and a fire select switch. The switch could be moved to safe, single or burst fire mode. A tweak of the switch from safe to single and the weapon came alive in Grant's hand. He aimed for a meter-high shrub ten feet away and pulled the trigger. A thin beam of blue light, perhaps an inch in diameter, erupted from the weapon and the plant disintegrated with a muffled plopping sound. Grant flinched as bits of plant splattered his face and jump suit.

"Damn." He flicked the setting to 'burst' and took aim on another plant, this one thirty meters away. The gun pulsed in his hand again as the beam left the barrel. The beam fired continuously for three seconds before shutting off. The plant and much of the surrounding area were mush. Grant pulled the trigger again, moving the weapon in an arc. The weapon chewed up a swath of plants and grass. Again, the weapon ceased to fire after three seconds.

"Very nice."

A quick check of the charge indicator showed 98% charge remaining. He returned the setting to 'safe' and continued toward the alien vessel.

Two miles from the Minith ship Grant tugged on the suit's hood and went to ground. Information on Minith defenses was non-existent. He had no idea what detection methods the Minith used so he kept to his standard practices of silence, stealth and caution.

Slowly, steadily, he drew closer to the ship. The ground grew darker and he suddenly knew. The extreme heat of the ship's landing had scorched this ground. Grant shuddered at the deaths that the ship's landing would have caused. He cursed. He slowed his pace, trading speed for concealment. Determined to stay hidden, his purpose was now solidified in his mind.

A mile from the ship, a carrier rose from the far side of the ship and dashed away, heading in the opposite direction. Grant breathed a little easier. He knew from his lessons that the aliens traveled via human carrier vehicles whenever they left the Mother Ship. That meant there had to be a carrier fleet operation that supported the Minith – and he now knew it was located on the far side of the ship. That was one question answered and one potential problem resolved.

Hours passed as Grant crept slowly closer to the ship. The sun had left the sky hours before but he kept moving forward. There was a sliver of moon throwing some light on the ground, but it was a lack of ground cover that Grant cursed. Over the final quarter-mile, the small shrubs had given way to sparse patches of gray-green grass. Grant had spotted a potential entry port on the side of the ship hours before and headed toward it. He slowed his approach even further as he traded concealment for complete silence and maximum stealth. More than a decade of being a professional soldier, coupled with more than six hundred years of death, had given him the patience he needed. He was invisible – a mere whisper of wind through the grass as he moved a foot closer. Then another foot. Then another. Each movement was punctuated by 30 seconds of motionless surveillance.

Finally, just before dawn, he reached the ship. If there were Minith on duty his slow approach had worked or they were sloppy in their guard. Or perhaps the aliens believed the humans posed no threat, and posted no guards. Not that it mattered to Grant. For hours, his actions had been directed toward getting him to the entryway undetected. And here he was.

He stood up quietly, stretched, then grabbed the large handle inset into the ship. One turn and Grant found himself peering inside the alien ship.

As easy as that.

He stepped inside, closed the portal, and shrugged off the ghillie suit. It was covered with the blackened soil through which he had crawled.

Grant stared down the length of corridor and paused briefly. His body readjusted itself from hours of crawling to a standing position. He scoped out the interior of the alien ship as he waited.

The gray metal walls extended for a hundred meters. Doors were spaced every twenty meters or so on both sides. He covered the hundred meters quickly and stopped short, taking a quick peek around the corner of the adjoining corridor. No aliens, so he wagered another look. The scan revealed a longer, larger hallway than the one he had entered. Along its length, he saw several off-shooting paths and more evenly spaced doorways. Because of the ship's circular design, the hallway curved out of sight after a few hundred meters. Unsure of direction, he turned left and headed down the larger corridor.

He placed his hand under his belt and felt the reassurance of the shurikens. He next checked the security of his knife and removed the electro-pulse weapon. He gripped the weapon tightly and switched the fire selector button to 'single.'

He counted each door and branching corridor as he passed. Getting lost was not an option. Thirteen doors and three corridors was enough. It all looked the same. Gray metal walls, doors spaced at even distance and no sign of life – Minith or human. Grant turned around and retraced his steps. If he was going to search room by room, he might as well begin at the point closest to his exit. Grant turned the final corner and noted the ghillie suit, untouched where he had left it.

He approached the doorway on the left closest to where he entered the ship. He took a breath, readied his weapon, and turned the handle on the door as slowly as possible.

The door was not locked and he stepped quickly into a small, brightly lit room. Purple. The metal walls and all of the furniture in the room were a garish shade of purple. A well cushioned couch sat along the back wall. Purple. A low table and two cushioned chairs, colored in a slightly darker – but just as horrid – purple, rested in the center of the room. Some type of alien device sat on the table and immediately piqued Grant's interest. Two doors, one on each side of the room, were closed.

*Not bad, except for the color,* Grant decided.

He listened at each door. At the first door, nothing. At the second he heard running water and his mind immediately flashed onto the six hundred year old memory of a shower. The shower stopped.

Grant tucked the weapon into his belt and stepped to the side of the door. He waited. The Minith were larger and stronger but, with surprise on his side, he had no doubt he could take one of the creatures down without using deadly force. They were like men in a lot of ways, or so the mind transference machine had indicated.

He waited only a few minutes. The door opened inward and Grant made his move.

He reached, he grabbed, he threw.

Hard.

Human.

Woman.

"Oh, damn," Grant cursed and lifted his two hundred or so pounds from the inert body. He had been expecting an oversized alien and had gotten a human female. What would have been bad for an oversized alien was slightly worse for her.

Seconds passed. She moaned, slightly stirred.

Grant silently thanked whoever might be up in heaven that she was still alive and carefully carried her to the nearby sofa.

He laid the woman down and noted that she was somewhat attractive. He turned her face toward him and changed his assessment. She was very attractive. The oval face possessed a perfectly shaped nose and full lips. Apart from the large purple welt rising quickly over her right eye, it was an unblemished face – framed by short brown hair, still wet from the shower. Her widely spaced eyes had long lashes and Grant wondered what she might look like with those secondary lids – and just as suddenly found himself not caring. A quick check of her body showed pleasant curves clad in a thin robe of silky, purple (what else?) material. The robe did not cover much and he scanned the room for something to cover her with. Nothing. He went to the second door and found a bedroom on the other side.

Grant drew the purple blanket from the small bed. He placed the blanket over her body, covering her with some regret. After all, it had been over six hundred years since his last experience with a female. He had also spent six hundred years recalling each and every one of his previous experiences and that tended to dull those prior recollections.

Grant sat next to the sleeping beauty and felt her forehead. She felt slightly warm and he picked up her wrist gently, found the strong beat within. He looked back to her face and found himself staring into the most beautifully unclouded brown eyes he had ever seen. It took a moment for the fact to register, but it did. Her eyes were unclouded by the secondary eyelids she should have possessed. Then, he noticed her blank stare and he knew.

She was blind.

Her lips moved and she spoke slightly, almost beyond his hearing. As it was, he heard the foreign sounds and recognized the patterns of speech. The language was unknown, but his pulse quickened with the thought that this woman could possibly be speaking Minith. He answered in Standard.

"I'm sorry if I hurt you." The woman recoiled in surprise.

"You... you are human?" Her voice trembled as she spoke, and Grant guessed that his act of violence was the cause.

"Yes. Most of me anyway," he said.

"You are human!" The woman smiled and felt out for Grant. He immediately grabbed her hand in his and squeezed reassuringly, somehow knowing that the woman needed his presence.

"But how did you get here? They do not allow humans here unless they are in the interpreter's group, and I've never heard your voice before."

The words 'interpreter's group' made Grant realize his earlier assumption was correct. This woman spoke Minith. His task here was almost finished. He had only to get them back to Bst'n.

"It's a long story. About six hundred years long to be exact, but that can wait until later. Right now, we have to get out of here. Do you feel up to a little walk? The carrier is a distance away."

"What? You mean leave the ship? We cannot!"

"Oh yes, we can. And it's time we got started. Are you coming or do I have to carry you?"

The woman drew back, suddenly frightened, and began lashing out with her hands and feet. She was nearly hysterical and a lucky shot of her right hand caught Grant in the chin.

"We cannot leave the ship! They will hunt us down and kill us!" she shouted, her voice rising dangerously. "We can't leave! We can't!"

Grant offered a silent apology. Then hit her with a calm right jab.

He caught her before she hit the floor.

"I'm so glad you saw it my way," he offered as he looked about the apartment for her clothes. As before, he noticed the ugly purple tint of the furniture. Now he realized that no human had chosen the stain and wondered what the woman would think of such a loud shade if she could have seen it.

While putting her into her clothes he tried not to stare at the flawless skin and well formed body, but soon gave up the attempt. She wore a bra and panties under the robe, so he maintained her modesty, but it was impossible not to appreciate her body as he worked. He kept his ears alert for any sound of approach, but all was quiet. He quickly had her dressed and tossed over his left shoulder.

He opened the door to the corridor and looked out. No sign of any aliens. He turned right, stepped over his ghillie suit, and grabbed the handle. Then he heard the footsteps echoing down the corridor. Getting closer to this corridor.

Grant quickly stepped back to the woman's room. He closed the door and listened. He heard two pairs of footsteps nearing his position at a trot, then slowing to a walk, then finally, stopping. They had seen the ghillie suit. He recognized the faint whisperings of the language the woman had first spoken when she thought he was one of the Minith and that cemented his position. There were two Minith in the hallway. They were probably alerted by the woman's outburst and now were confronted with a dirty bundle of rags that had no reason for being where they were.

Grant lowered the woman to the sofa. He hoped she would stay quiet. Any noise she made would pinpoint their location for the two outside. Grant pulled the knife from his boot, hoping to take out the first Minith quietly if he decided to search this room.

He made out the whisperings of the Minith again and one of the aliens ran off down the corridor. The other was still outside and Grant positioned himself behind the door and waited, thinking of his earlier attempt at this very action just minutes earlier. This time he would make sure that whoever or whatever came through the door was not human before he acted. He did not want the blood of an innocent human on his hands if he was wrong.

That decision almost got him killed.

The door swung quickly inward, catching Grant by surprise. He had not heard the alien approach the door and his initial hesitation gave the Minith guard a chance to spot him. The guard was huge and well trained. As Grant lunged at the alien's neck, the Minith turned away from the blow, catching it on the shoulder instead. Grant cursed his error and was stung by a crushing backhand from the eight foot tall alien. Grant bounced off the wall and back into the waiting arms of the heavy beast.

The Minith gripped Grant with crushing force and he struggled to bring the knife into play. It was no use. Grant's arms were pinned to his side and he was forced to stare into the hideous face of the Minith. It was Grant's first experience with one of the aliens and it was not a good one. The guard's eyes were fierce with rage and the snout of the beast was set in a vicious snarl. The alien squeezed. Grant saw stars and brought his knee up into the alien's groin with the force of a sledgehammer. Grant dropped like a stone.

So the fucker had balls.

Grant sucked for breath and grabbed the knife. The knee had the same effect on the Minith as it would have had on a man. The Minith was doubled over and Grant wasted no time. A quick stroke of the knife. Dark purple blood spouted from the alien's neck and splashed wetly across Grant's jump suit. The alien fell, dead or dying.

Grant had little time to savor his victory. He heard the other Minith racing his way and jumped into the corridor to face the threat. The other guard came on at a run and his huge bulk nearly took up the passageway. He slowed when he spied Grant and the dark blood of his fellow. The sight of a human covered in Minith blood was obviously an unexpected one.

Grant did not pause in his actions, however, and drew two of the shurikens from his belt. The sharpened metal stars traced a path toward the alien. The Minith stared at the thrown pieces of metal as they whirled toward him. The first buried itself in his chest. The second took him in the throat. He dropped to his knees and gasped. The plum-colored blood from his torn throat cascaded onto the polished steel floor of the ship.

Grant sprinted to the alien and jerked his throwing

stars from the alien's body. He wiped them on the Minith, tucked them into his belt and dragged the alien's body into the woman's room. He picked up the interpreter, stepped across the two dead aliens and closed the door on the bloody carnage.

Sixty seconds later he was outside the ship and stealing quietly back toward the carrier vehicle. He wasted little time with concealment. Silence and speed were needed now. His first experience with the Minith had shown him that hearing was indeed one of their strengths. He made good time across the even ground and hoped for luck. If the bodies of the two aliens were not found within the next hour, they had a chance.

They were in the air, still hours from their destination, when the woman stirred and sat up. Grant knew he had some explaining to do.

"My name is Grant. Who are you?"

"Uh... Avery... my name is Avery." Her voice was soft and cool. She stared ahead, seeing nothing of the sky and earth outside the carrier vehicle.

"Nice name. It suits you."

"Why... thank you." Avery explored the bump above her right eye and winced. "Why did you commit violence upon me?"

Grant felt like an ass. He wasn't one for hitting women and detested men who did. She rubbed her jaw and he tried to explain.

"Sorry. I had to get you out of the Minith ship. You didn't want to come." It sounded lame, even to him. He felt like more of an ass.

"And the first time you struck me?"

Grant had hoped she wouldn't bring it up, but there it was. "An accident. I thought you... Well, I didn't know you were human. I thought--"

"You thought I was one of the Minith?" she asked. Her eyebrows lifted. "Well, that is unusual. Not many people would consider committing violence upon a Minith."

"Does it surprise you that I considered it? That I

might even enjoy it?" He considered telling her about the aliens in the corridor and immediately dismissed the idea.

"It would concern me none to see them come to harm. The excuse that violence is always wrong is weak where the Minith are concerned." Her voice was strong with conviction and the words rang true to Grant's ears. This woman was not afraid of violence if it was to be used against the Minith.

"You mean you're not morally opposed to violence?"

Her voice lowered to a whisper and she spoke in an obscure S'mercan language that Grant recognized. "I am against violence that is committed for the sake of committing violence. But violence that is directed toward freedom from the Minith should not be readily forsaken. That is cowardice."

Grant was surprised. Avery was the first person he had met since his 'revival' that shared his view. It was downright refreshing to see that not all humanity had become sheep for the Minith herd.

"Avery, do you speak Minith?"

"Yes. I am in the interpreter's group."

"Correction, Avery. You were in the interpreter's group." Grant watched as she mulled the words. Her understanding was quickly followed by a flood of tears, and Grant reached out for her hand.

## CHAPTER NINE

Zal growled at his Earth's Guard Captain. The male was obviously too soft from having served on this world for so many years.

"How can you tell me that this was no human? Who else would have killed two of our brothers, you fool? A rogue Minith? How do you explain the disappearance of the female, our primary interpreter? Did she vanish into the atmosphere?"

"But sir, the humans cannot commit violence. They--"

"Enough!" Zal pointed at the captain accusingly. "Do not deign to tell me what these humans are capable of doing and not doing! Just because they have been obedient in the past does not mean they will always be so. They are a race which is enslaved! Even the most peaceful of beings resist being ruled by a superior race."

"But sir, the humans have never lashed out against us. Why would they enter the Mother Ship and kill two of my guards? It makes no sense."

"You idiot! It makes every sense! They are our slaves and they dislike the position. I have been on-world for only two weeks but I know what subjugation can do to a race! Hear me speak: This is only the beginning. We must retaliate for this affront to our dominance. I do not care if the killing was the act of a single human or a group of them. The entire race will be punished for it. Notify the human leadership of my decision!"

"Yes, sir."

"And Captain?"

"Sir?"

"Find the female. That is of extreme importance!"

"It will be done, Minister." The captain bowed and left

Zal's chamber, intent on accomplishing his orders.

* * *

"How can they do this? We had nothing to do with it!"

Quasan Alla, the Musl'n Culture leader asked at the news that three of their farms were being destroyed in response to the killing of the two Minith guards.

"This had to be the result of a lone Violent! An insane N'mercan," the Urop'n Culture Leader exclaimed. "Probably this woman for whom the Minith are searching." Sabatina Sabontay glanced accusingly at Randalyn Trevino as if she were personally responsible for what had happened within her Culture's boundary.

Randalyn did not deny the silent accusation though she knew the woman Sabatina referenced was not of her Culture but Esteval's. She accepted the reproach because she felt acutely responsible for this situation. She alone among those in the room knew what transpired in the Minith Mother Ship. She had been briefed by Senior Scientist Rolan only an hour after the warrior's return from that place. As much as she wanted to keep the information from the rest of the Council, she could not. They were responsible for leading the earth as a group.

Randalyn nodded her acceptance of Sabatina's indictment. "I am knowledgeable of the circumstances surrounding this incident, Sabatina." The Urop'n gasped in surprise as did the other members of the Council.

Randalyn briefly explained how the deaths of the two Minith occurred.

There were a few moments of stunned silence, before Primo Esteval spoke. The Leader Elect's voice betrayed none of the emotion that Randalyn knew he felt. "This is our doing, fellow Council Members. We balloted the question of Senior Scientist Rolan's experiment. We, the members of this Council, are equally responsible for what has occurred."

"He must be stopped!" Quasan pleaded. "Tane must cease his experiment now! Before more harm is caused, he must cease!" The voices of the Urop'n and Afc'n Culture Leaders rose in agreement but were cut short by an impatient wave of the leader Elect's hand.

"Perhaps, Quasan. But let us not be hasty. We knew this to be a dangerous undertaking and not without a great degree of risk." Esteval's voice was rational and calming and the members were reminded of why they had elected this man to be the Leader Elect. "It would be foolish to expect the Minith to leave Earth willingly. Success will not arrive without sacrifice. What we must decide now is this: what sacrifices are we willing to make? Until we decide this, we will be unable to proceed on any course.

"If we sacrifice our freedom to the Minith, we know what price we will pay. It is the price of slavery and, eventually, the loss of our planet's life.

"If, however, we desire freedom from the Minith, there is also a price to be paid. My question to you, fellow Culture Leaders is this: What price are we willing to pay should we decide upon freedom?"

Randalyn looked carefully around the table. Her mind was made up, had been for some time. "I vote freedom. At any cost."

The silence lay heavy upon the other Council Chambers as they pondered the decisions and choices before them. Each Culture was represented here and each Culture would be required to live or die with their decision. Ante up their share of whatever price they agreed upon.

"Aye," the As'n representative, Suyung agreed.

"Aye," sighed the Afc'n representative, Diekela.

All eyes turned toward Quasan and Sabontay. Almost a minute passed while the Urop'n and Musl'n Leaders pondered their decision. Finally, Quasan spoke.

"Aye."

Sabatina Sabontay sighed heavily. The ballot was

already decided regardless of her vote and she knew this. It did not matter if she agreed with them or not. They would sacrifice Peace to rid their world of the Minith.

"Aye. We fight."

"Aye," the S'mercan Culture Leader and Leader Elect, Primo Esteval said, making the ballot unanimous.

## CHAPTER TEN

"Who?" Mr. Blue asked. Grant stood silently off to one side of the room watching the exchange.

"For the last time, my name is Avery. For the last four years, I have been held inside the Minith Mother Ship as Primary Interpreter for the Minith Minister of Earth."

"Yes, yes. I heard all that, girl, but what does that mean? How did you get here?" The administrator shifted his substantial weight upon the overstuffed sofa. Grant heard the unmistakable sound of the man passing gas. "Excuse me."

Grant smiled. Blue was an idiot in charge of something that mattered. He had seen it time and time again and the fact that it still happened six hundred years after his time showed him things had not changed all that much. Avery, bless her soul, ignored the man's boorishness and answered his question.

"It means that I was responsible directly to the Minith's Earth Minister, the head alien, for any interpreting that was required. And as for how I came to be here, you can ask your friend over there." Although she could not see Grant she pointed directly at him. Mr. Blue turned and found Grant staring harshly back. Blue flinched.

Grant knew it could not be a comfortable position that Blue found himself occupying. He was probably used to intimidating others by virtue of his rank and demeanor. It was unlikely that the administrator found himself on the receiving end of such a disdainful attitude very often. At least not to his face.

"Ah, um, well. Can you explain her presence then, Mr. Justice?" The overweight man flushed and wiped at the moisture beading his forehead.

"Yes," Grant replied.

Blue waited for him to continue but Grant did not intend to offer any information freely. Grant's response had the desired effect on the politician, for that was how he viewed Mr. Blue – as a politician of the worst type. Blue swallowed the lump beneath his chins and made another attempt.

"Will you explain her presence?" Grant watched the man's fear turn to anger.

He had pushed the man as far as he dared. The man might be a buffoon, but he was not without some degree of power and they were going to need his support, if not his help.

"Of course, Mr. Blue. I went to the Minith ship and I took her. I needed someone who spoke their language and she fit the bill."

"That's it? You just went to their ship and you took her!" Blue's face paled. He was no doubt imagining the repercussions of Grant's actions.

"Are you insane?! Do you know what they will do when they find out she is missing?"

"No. I don't. Do you?"

"Well, uh...no. But you can bet it won't be Peaceful!"

"Blue," Tane interrupted. "I have already informed Culture Leader Trevino of this. She is taking it before Council. She has probably already done so."

"HOW dare you, Rolan!" Blue turned on Tane. It was apparent to Grant that the administrator needed to show his power and Tane appeared to be a good target. "You know that she is not to be contacted without my knowledge! I could have you relieved of duty for this!"

Grant had seen enough of this man's theatrics, and stepped forward.

"Listen to me, you overweight sofa maggot, with your formal Standard bullshit," he said through clenched teeth. Everyone else in the room blanched at Grant's words. "We have a job to do, and we're going to do it. Now, you can be a part of the solution if you want, but if you even think about being any part of the problem, you'll answer to me.

"I did not get revived from six hundred years of blissful sleep to put up with your bureaucratic bullshit," Grant felt the lie about his sleep being 'blissful' well justified.

Avery stepped toward Grant and put out a restraining hand. "Be with Peace, Grant. This man is not your enemy. Save your violence for the Minith." The soothing tone of her voice and the softness of her hand calmed him.

"I have no intention of being violent to this man, Avery. Unless he tries to get in our way."

"Then say you are sorry, Grant. You have offended him with your behavior."

"No freakin' way," Grant growled.

Avery's hand clamped tighter around his forearm as she stepped closer. The look on her face was calm but there was no mistaking the order in her voice.

"Apologize."

At the mild rebuke, Grant took a deep breath, bit his tongue, and gathered his thoughts. He was blaming this man for more than he deserved. Sure, he was an overweight do-nothing who thrived on power, but that was no cause to threaten him. Especially when a threat was cause for a prison sentence.

Once again, he felt the harsh bite of his situation as his mind struggled to grasp reality. This was not his time. These were not his people. They were human, but their values and mores were very different. He had acted as if Blue was the cause of his being here, and knew that was wrong. He was here because another bureaucrat, six hundred years ago, had decided to send him and his team on a suicide mission. He had been unfortunate in that, but it was time to move on. Get with the program. He was alive now and he had something to live for, a goal, and he reached out for that now. He had to defeat the Minith and liberate their planet – his planet – from the bonds of slavery.

"Please accept my apologies, Mr. Blue. I intended no violence."

"It is nothing," the other man answered with a slight wave. He pulled his collar away from his neck and dabbed his forehead and neck with a square of silk from his pocket. "Be at Peace, Mr. Justice."

"I will." He was also ready to put the next part of his plan in motion. "Tane, did you get the material on Violent's Prison?"

"Violent's Prison? Why in the world would you care about that unholy place?"

Blue's intrusion annoyed Grant but he did not let the irritation show. He had gone through the same thing with Tane, and realized that the mention of the place struck a chord of terror in these 'modern' men and women. He looked at Avery and was surprised by the lack of fear on her face at the name of Violent's Prison. He briefly wondered why she did not flinch from the sound of that name.

"Because I need soldiers, Blue. Men who are not afraid to kill if killing is needed."

"You cannot be serious! I will not permit it!"

"Blue, I apologized for my earlier behavior but I meant what I said. If you stand in my way on this, I will see that you are relocated to a safe place until our work is finished. Do you understand?"

"Yes, yes, of course! I only meant--"

"I know what you meant, Blue. But that place… that prison… it doesn't frighten me like it does you. You don't have to go there. I do."

"Not alone," three heads turned toward Avery as she spoke. "I am going with you, Grant."

"I don't think so, Avery. It will be dangerous. I can't risk it." Avery laughed boldly, and he stared at the beautiful woman, unsure of what he was witnessing.

"Grant, I'm not asking you to risk anything. I know what awaits us inside Violent's Prison." Her words stirred something familiar inside Grant. She knew what she was talking about.

"What do you mean, Avery?"

"What I mean, Grant Justice, is this," he watched her lips move, entranced with each syllable. "I know Violent's Prison. I was there for two years before the Minith took me as their slave."

Silence followed Avery's matter of fact statement and the three men stared at her, too surprised to speak. No one was more surprised by the words than Grant.

"I'll be damned." Amazement coursed through his body. "Beautiful as well as violent. And I thought they didn't make 'em like that any more."

The disclosure did not change his mind, though. He needed her here, not in the prison.

\* \* \*

For the next three days Grant learned everything he could about Violent's Prison. He studied the material Tane provided and had numerous conversations with Avery.

Used by all Cultures as a place to deposit their violent miscreants, the prison was huge. The four outer walls, each nearly a half-mile long, formed a giant square. The prison held upwards of twenty thousand inmates. Men, women and children were sentenced to life within the prison's walls for offenses ranging from rock throwing to mass murder. Outside of the mainstream social atmosphere of the rest of the world, the prison had its own laws and codes of behavior. In short, it was a brutal piece of hell among a world of Peace loving humans.

The social pecking order within the walls of Violent's Prison was established by the not-so-complex method that Grant labeled "King of the Castle". The strongest, smartest, most feared inmate was king. Fights for dominance inside the prison were constant as inmates sought to improve their standing within the hierarchy. Most of those sentenced to a life within the walls of Violent's Prison were not generally violent, at least not when they first entered the walls of the prison. They were mostly victims of their own inability to conform to the rigid social norms of the world and its strict pacifist code. Once inside the cold gray stone walls, however, they were forced to fight for their lives or submit to the dominance of those around them.

In all of their conversations, Avery never said why she had been banished to the prison and Grant, sensing her discomfort, did not ask. She was adamant, however, that life inside the Prison's walls was preferable to living with the Minith.

After much debate Avery relented to remain at the hospital while Grant went to the prison alone. Two of Grant's arguments won her over: her blindness and his need to have the Minith language recorded onto one of the transference educators.

"I am staying here because it *is* needed to defeat the Minith, Grant," she told him, still unsure if she was doing the right thing by not going with him. "But you must promise me you will be careful! It is dangerous there."

"I promise, Avery. Believe me. I don't have a death wish. But I've gone over this a hundred times. The only chance we've got of defeating the Minith requires the help of the people in Violent's Prison."

Avery sat on a bench in Grant's workout room while he pushed iron plates over his head.

"When do you leave?"

Grant stopped lifting, his breathing heavy from pushing his new body to its limits. So far, it had not disappointed him in its capabilities, though he still grieved the loss of his own arms. His own legs. The initial pain, which had been every bit as punishing as Tane had promised, had dulled. He ached constantly, but it was the ache of sore muscles after being pushed to the limit. It was no longer a pain inflicted by recuperation. It was pain inflicted by muscle growth.

"Tomorrow morning, Avery. I'm going in just like a new prisoner would."

"But Grant! That is the most dangerous way! The new ones are always treated harshly and must fight well or be made a slave!"

"Then I will fight well," he told her calmly. Her concern was moving, but Grant was not overly worried. He knew his own capabilities and had over six hundred years to mentally perfect his fighting techniques. What concerns he did have about entering the prison were wiped away by one stark reality: If he was to win the support of the inmates of Violent's Prison he would first have to win their respect. It was a soldier's rule.

"I hope you know what you are doing, Grant Justice," Avery said. She reached for his hand and brought it to her cheek. "Since you do not leave until morning, would you spend the night with me?" She cast her sightless eyes toward the ground and her cheek flushed beneath his hand. Her sudden shyness disguised the courage it had taken for her to ask the question and Grant pulled her close to his chest.

"How could any man resist, Avery?" He wrapped his arms around her and held tightly, the closeness of her body doing marvelous things to his.

"I was afraid my blindness would...would..."

"You are beautiful, Avery," he reassured her. He understood her feelings that her handicap might put him off but there was nothing farther from the truth. She held an inner as well as an outer beauty that astounded him. Had astounded him since he first saw her.

"But my eyes are disfigured. The Minith had the lids removed when--"

"Shhhh. It's okay, Avery. I don't have secondary lids, either," he explained. She drew away slightly and turned her face up to his, unsure of what he meant.

"But you are not blind, Grant! Even in the light you can see!"

"It is a long story, Avery. Tomorrow, ask Tane to explain it to you." Grant bent forward and kissed her. The light touch was fire upon his lips. "Tonight, we have better things to do than discuss our eyes."

He led her to his small room and they turned out the light.

To his surprise Avery could see as well as he could in the dark. "Yes, I can see when the lights are low. The secondary lids only work to filter out bright lights."

"Well," he asked her, afraid she would find some fault with his features now that she could see him, although dimly. "Do I look anything like what you'd imagined?"

"Oh Grant," she whispered, nuzzling her face into his chest, "you are handsome as well as brave. I did not think they made men like that anymore."

They laughed. Then turned to other pleasures.

## CHAPTER ELEVEN

Grant watched farms and cities pass as the carrier sped westward across the morning sky. From the carrier's height of two thousand feet, the people below looked like ants. How many were toiling away, trying to keep up with their work, just so their fellow humans would not starve? Grant didn't know for sure, but there were not enough. The Minith quotas had forced millions to redirect their work efforts away from farming and towards the mines of Africa, South America and Asia. Old names now.

He thought about the Minith. He thought about his past. He thought about Violent's Prison. And he thought about Avery. Their night together had been wonderful. Sensual. Better than he deserved. She was the most beautiful woman he had ever known and he wondered if he was in love. He had no experience with that particular emotion. His previous life as a soldier had never allowed him the luxury of a close relationship. Sure, he had encounters with women but nothing left him feeling the way he now felt. A warm kernel burned in his stomach. It popped when he saw her. That had to be love. If not, what would the real thing feel like?

"The prison is just over the horizon, Grant. We will be there in ten minutes." Tane brought him back to Earth. The young scientist sat in the back of the carrier with Grant. One of Tane's junior scientists was at the controls of the carrier

"Tane."

"Yes, Grant?"

"The surgery that you did to me -- the regeneration of tissue?"

"Yes, what about it?"

"I've been thinking. If it worked for me, do you think it

might work for others as well? I mean, if it was required?"

Tane nodded his understanding. "You mean Avery? Her eyes?"

"Yes. Can it help her?"

Tane smiled.

"I've already begun the process."

Their discussion was interrupted by the pilot. "Violent's Prison, straight ahead!"

Grant recognized the fear in the pilot's voice and turned to look. The gentle greens of the sub-farms were gone. They had been replaced by the dead tans and browns of scrub and desert. The land below was flat, but mountains were visible in the distance. The prison was located in the southeastern part of what Grant had once known as Idaho. He did not know if the name still held.

At first a speck in the distance, the prison grew larger and more imposing with each passing moment. It rose from the desert rapidly – an immense stone structure. Grant knew the outer walls of the prison were a hundred feet high and ten feet thick. There were no guard towers, no guards. Instead, there was The Channel.

The Channel was a 100-foot wide man made river that surrounded the entire prison. Filled with a thick soup of deadly acid, the channel provided an effective barrier against escape. According to the records he had seen, no one had ever escaped the prison and, seeing the width of the deadly moat, Grant believed it.

The carrier pilot circled the prison at a height of three hundred feet and Grant studied it from above. The giant structure was actually a series of five stone buildings set within the outer wall. Inside the outer wall and courtyard, the five squares of the prison formed a box-within-a-box design and Grant thought of the Pentagon in what used to be Washington, D.C. This prison, although only four-sided, was set out in a fashion similar to that ancient structure, except that there were no corridors connecting the separate buildings. Instead, there were merely four doorways on the inner and outer side of each building, leading to the next courtyard. Each building was separated by a courtyard of hard-packed dirt. Grant saw thousands of inmates in the outermost space between the outer wall and the first building. Some looked up at the circling carrier, others seemed oblivious or unaware of the vehicle.

Grant directed the pilot to fly over the center of the prison. The pilot groaned, but complied. In each successive courtyard, there were fewer people visible. At the innermost courtyard that made up the center of the prison, Grant saw only four men, one at each door of the innermost side of the Fifth Square. Grant knew that food, clothing and supplies entered the prison through that inner courtyard on a regular basis. From there, it was distributed to the outermost squares. Grant also knew that the farther a prisoner was from the inner square, the less of those supplies he or she would ever receive.

Unlike supplies, new inmates were dropped into the prison near the southern door of the outermost, First Square.

Grant gave a nod to the pilot. He was ready.

The carrier left the prison and circled around to the south. As they approached the southern wall, Grant checked his communications gear a final time. He would use the small transmitter and receiver to contact Tane only when he completed his mission inside the prison. He carried no weapons.

He stretched his muscles as the carrier vehicle crossed over the outer wall and swept down toward his destination – the courtyard that separated the outer wall from the First Square.

Grant looked down at the crowd gathering around the space where he would be dropped and got ready. New inmates were dumped unceremoniously from an open cargo door and the pilot paused briefly at a height of ten feet. Grant hung from the open door as he had been instructed, then dropped to the hard packed earth below.

It was a fall of less than four feet, but the pilot was

pulling away before Grant hit the ground.

Several forms rushed forward and Grant rolled, ready for what was to come.

He narrowly dodged a vicious kick aimed at his head and leapt to his feet as another, weaker kick caught him in the stomach.

Grant easily grabbed the offending foot and twisted sharply. The bone snapped and the man, dirty and dressed in little more than rags, fell to the ground screaming. Grant spun around, prepared for another attack and found himself facing dozens of raggedly dressed men. They circled him warily, unsure. He saw no women or children.

The outer courtyard, he had been told by Avery, was occupied by the weakest of the inmates. Those who were not strong enough to fight their way into one of the inner squares lived here. These men were restricted to the outer courtyard, denied even the small pleasure of a roof over their heads.

He crouched in a defensive stance and waited patiently for the men to decide on how to proceed. Grant thought his initial effort might be enough to scare the others away, but it was not to be. Two of the men rushed him at once, from opposite directions. He stepped quickly toward the man coming from his right, dodged a looping punch and delivered a clothesline blow that slammed the attacker to the ground.

Grant spun toward the other attacker and barely managed to snap his head back, dodging a quick slash from a small bladed weapon. He grabbed the man's wrist and twisted as another of the prisoners rushed from his left. The man holding the knife howled. Grant quickly twisted the arm a second time and snatched the blade from the air as it dropped from the man's grasp. He flashed the small knife to the left and the attacker pulled up short, suddenly afraid to press his rush. The knife's previous owner lashed out with a weak knee strike that Grant easily blocked. The man hesitated, his right wrist still held tightly in Grant's right hand. Grant saw that he was unsure of whether to keep up the attack or give up.

"Better not try it," Grant cautioned the man in Earth standard.

He let the man's wrist go as a sign of good faith and rose to his full height. He dropped his arms to his side and hoped the other would take the hint and back off.

The dirty convict looked right and left at the other men around them. He was obviously judging the level of support he had against Grant but no one rose to the invitation. Angered by the turn of events, and the loss of his knife, the man roared at Grant and rushed forward once again. Grant stepped easily to the left and stuck out his foot. The man tripped and landed face first next to clothesline guy, who was gasping raggedly for breath. Nearby, one of the observers was helping the man with the broken leg.

Grant scanned the watchers around the square and saw no immediate threats. He then turned back to the man on the ground and put out a hand to help him to his feet.

The man stood up without assistance and looked at Grant defiantly, unwilling to cower. To the man's – and the rest of the crowd's – surprise, Grant turned the blade around and handed it out to the man, handle first. The man hesitated the barest moment before plucking it sharply from Grant's hand. He looked to Grant for an explanation but Grant merely shrugged.

"It's your knife, friend. I don't need it."

A murmur coursed through the crowd of onlookers. Grant guessed from their reaction that this was not expected behavior and that pleased him. He was not here to accomplish the expected. The man with the knife nodded and tucked the weapon beneath his belt. He faced Grant squarely and spoke in Standard. "My name is Pound. If you need anything within this square, you see me. I will help you."

Grant was mildly irked to hear that Standard was also spoken in a place like Violent's Prison. He recognized the man's accent as Urop'n, though, and responded in that Culture's primary language. "Very well, Pound. I desire access to the next square."

Pound smiled, and the crowd murmured its surprise at this request as those that spoke the Urop'n language translated Grant's words into Standard.

"We shall see if you desire it badly enough, my friend," Pound said. "We shall see."

## CHAPTER TWELVE

Grant and Pound sat in front of a blazing fire. It was dusk and others crowded around them until the space around the fire was gone.

Food was shared among the men in an ordered fashion. Two teen-aged boys served the men closest to the fire first. Grant and Pound received the first helpings of a stiff cornmeal-like substance. It was dished onto flat metal plates. Cheap tin spoons and small cups of stale, tepid water were passed out. Grant considered passing on his portion but the men around him spooned up the gruel with such fervor that Grant forced himself to join them. He had no desire to humiliate these men by turning down their offer to share what little they had.

Pound recognized Grant's hesitancy with the food and nodded.

"I am sorry that we have nothing better to offer, but this is all that the inner squares allow us. All food is delivered to the Inner Square. By the time we receive ours, everything of value and sustenance has been taken."

"Why do the other squares allow you any food at all?" Grant asked.

"Because they need us, my good friend. We weed out most of the newcomers and save the other squares the trouble. And we are no threat to them. Anyone who has been forced to eat this mush for a month is no longer able to challenge them for dominance."

Grant considered the implications of Pound's statement and saw the truth in the words. Men who lived on nothing but damp oatmeal and rancid water would not remain strong for long.

"I guess I should make my challenge soon then, eh?"

Pound squinted sideways at Grant, appraising him for weaknesses and strengths. Apparently, Grant met with his approval for he said, "I would not wait at all if I were you, friend."

"Very well. In the morning, I begin."

"Take care, brave one! The next square is difficult. Should you get past their door guard, be wary. They are armed in there. Oh, not quite so well as further on, but they are armed with more than a knife." Pound's eye twinkled with the mention of his knife and Grant was glad the man did not hold a grudge. He rather liked the grubby man.

"What kind of weapons do they carry, Pound?" Grant was not overly concerned about the next square, but wanted as much information as possible before proceeding to the Inner Square.

"Oh, chains and sticks mostly. And many knives."

"One more question, Pound. Where are the women and children?"

"Hah! There are no women here in the Outer. No, no! They are too valuable, as are the children. As soon as a female or child is dropped, the First Square's door guard summons his mates. They are taken inside and who knows what becomes of them? Certainly, not I!"

"Why is it that you've never challenged the First Square, Pound?"

"Have you not reached your limit on the queries, my friend? Ah, well, never mind! I shall tell you why. I would much rather be a large fish in a small pond than a small fish in a large one." Pound indicated the area around the fire. The space was twenty meters square. "This is my pond. Through the First Square door, who knows what exists?"

Grant nodded and checked the security of the radio he carried; he did not want it stolen in the night.

"Wake me at first light, Pound," he said and curled up next to the fire and closed his eyes.

Pound stared at Grant, as if weighing his chance to kill the other man. He must have thought better of the idea. He passed an order about the fire that no one was to harm the stranger during the night and curled up for sleep himself.

It was well that he had done so; for Grant feigned sleep long enough to be sure that Pound's order was not ignored. Long after the fire grew dim, Grant finally gave in to sleep.

He awoke the next morning before the sun crept over the wall. He was the first up and scanned the top of the First Square wall for anyone who might be standing watch against the outer courtyard. He doubted that a guard existed and his search showed no one. Satisfied that he was as well prepared as he could be, he stepped carefully across the scattered forms of the sleeping prisoners. He reached the wall of the First Square without trampling anyone. He followed the wall to the doorway, nearly a quarter mile away.

Each square held eight doorways. Four along the outer wall and four along the inner. Avery had informed him that one of the square's most formidable fighters guarded each door at all times. To make it to the inner, Fifth Square, Grant had to successfully defeat each square's outer door guard and each square's leader. Pound was the leader of the Outer Courtyard, and his defeat had ensured his loyalty. If Grant had wished to stay in the courtyard on a permanent basis, he would have become the new leader. In this manner, the survival of the fittest was accomplished. It was a brutal form of succession.

Grant reached the southern door of the First Square and prepared himself mentally. When he was ready, he stepped forward.

"I demand Challenge!" he yelled.

Grant had but a minute to wait. The guard from the First Square summoned another of his comrades to stand watch over the door while he responded to the challenge. The customs of Violent's Prison forbade the new guard from interfering with the contest. His only task was to prevent any of the other Outer Square men from entering his square while his comrade responded to Grant's challenge.

Once the doorway was secured, the challenged guardian stepped from the darkness of the First Square building. Grant noticed that the man carried a long stick made of hardened wood. It appeared comfortable in the man's grasp. In turn, Grant crouched, prepared to defend against the weapon and waited for the guard to attack. The guard did not let Grant down and covered the five meters that separated them at a run. He swung the two-meter long stick and Grant reacted by stepping to the right. Almost too late, Grant saw the move as a feint and barely managed to duck the stick as the guardian changed its direction expertly in the middle of his swing. The staff whistled by Grant's head.

The guard was well trained but the surprise of his miss showed clearly on his face. The surprise was quickly replaced with determination and he gripped the staff securely, readying himself for another pass at the challenger. Grant circled to the left, more cautious in his defense now that he had seen the man wield his weapon effectively. They circled for a moment, each eyeing the other carefully.

Grant was dimly aware that a crowd had gathered around them and, from the corner of his right eye, noticed Pound watching the contest. The man appeared ready to join in the fight against the First Square guardian and Grant prepared to warn him away. Before he could do so, the guard thrust the weapon viciously, the point of the stick aimed at Grant's chest. Grant dodged left, seized the wooden rod with his left hand, and yanked the guard off balance  He kept his grip on the weapon and, using his left foot as a pivot, spun toward the guard and delivered a brutal roundhouse kick to the side of his head. The guard dropped like a stone.

Grant entered the First Square door carrying the heavy wooden rod. His victory over the guard had been easier than his win over Pound. He turned back toward the Inner Square. Grant raised his hand to Pound and the other man waved back, smiling.

"Good journey, oh, brave one!" Pound called. "And beware of Titan!"

Grant waved again and continued into the building of the First Square. He briefly wondered who Titan was, but had no time to dwell on the message. Inside the First Square, he was met by a score of men, all armed with sticks and chains. These men, he saw, were better fed than the men of the previous courtyard. Pound and his group depended on these men for everything, including food and the fuel to light their nightly fire. Grant watched the men appraise him. He had just defeated the guard at the door but that meant little now that he was inside. Grant nodded and walked.

The men of the First Square followed him, silently watching his progress toward the far side of the building. Grant was alert and watched every move the men made. As with the outer courtyard, Grant saw no women or children, and guessed that they were immediately taken from here by the men of the Second Square.

Grant arrived at the far wall of the First Square without incident. The door was guarded by another stick wielder. Apparently, from the actions of the guardian and the men around him, he was required to fight his way out of the building if he wished to proceed into the space beyond. Why waste any time, he decided with a sigh. He stopped a few meters from the door and faced the man standing there.

"I call Challenge!"

"For what purpose do you desire to cross this doorway, newcomer?"

The question caught Grant by surprise. Avery had mentioned nothing that would indicate he would be questioned when trying to proceed to the Inner Square. The cry of 'challenge' was supposed to be sufficient.

"I've got my reasons. And I don't need to share them with you," Grant answered. The guard considered Grant carefully, apparently weighing the response. With a nod, the guard stepped aside.

"As you wish, newcomer. You may pass."

There was a disappointed hum from the watchers inside the building, quickly silenced by a glare from the guard. They obviously feared and respected the guard of this doorway for they quickly dispersed from the area. Grant found himself alone with the guard who stood to one side of the door permitting passage.

"Why are letting me pass unchallenged?"

"For reasons of my own, and for which I choose not to share with you, newcomer." Grant laughed and held out his hand.

"My name is Grant. I'm honored to meet you, guardian."

The man eyed Grant with some suspicion of his own but accepted the proffered hand. "I am Davis, Leader of the First Square."

Grant stepped through the door into the space beyond. He was now entering the area between the first and second square buildings. Several men in the open space turned their heads his way. Within seconds, dozens were headed in his direction.

"Well, Davis," Grant said to the guardian. "Have *you* any advice as I make my way toward the Inner Square?"

Davis eyed Grant. "Certainly. Be careful of the man named Titan."

Grant wondered again at the name, and questioned Davis.

"You may meet him should you be skilled, Grant. That is all I will say."

"As you wish, Davis." Grant gripped his staff tightly and strode out to meet his welcoming committee.

## CHAPTER THIRTEEN

Zal's leathered toes dug into the soft earth as he surveyed the human sub-farm. Little had changed since his last visit and he waved his fellow Minith soldiers into position with much relish. The humans stopped working to stare at the aliens, without exception the largest group of off-worlders they had ever witnessed. Several of the assembled hundreds whispered urgently to their co-workers, a few pointed.

Zal thought it unlikely they would distinguish him as one of the two who had recently killed several of their clan, but did not dismiss the possibility out of hand. Who knew what these humans were capable of, he wondered.

The Minith spread out in a line of twenty, their complete unit assembled for the upcoming sport. Even Lieutenant Treel, normally aloof and distant from the rest of his unit, lined up in anticipation of the game. When the farthest soldier reached his place along the edge of the immense human field, Zal gave the signal.

At a steady pace, the line of huge troopers moved into the green rows of vegetable and fruit. Each was armed with a long blade of polished steel and a length of Minith chain. They were barbaric weapons, but their use would increase the sporting value of the task. The troops had become bored with their duties on the tame planet. Bred to fight and kill with no regard for mercy, an assignment to Earth was a punishment often reserved for the most undisciplined Minith warriors. Zal planned to change the image of Earth as a dull assignment with his reign as Minister, and this would be a good beginning. Soon, the Minith Empire would hear of the sport to be had here. *If only these humans would fight back*, Zal thought, *then this would truly be a planet worth holding.*

The humans stood unmoving as the Minith soldiers approached. Only after the first of them went down, felled by a blow of Minith chain to the head, did the humans realize what was happening and begin to flee. The Minith soldiers, with their increased leg length, easily kept pace with the screaming humans and mowed them down with well-aimed blows and swings of the blades and chains. Sixty seconds after the first human went down, more than a hundred others lay dead or dying. Zal's features contorted with grotesque glee. He reveled in the carnage. He laughed harshly as one of the nearer troops beheaded two young females with a single slash of his long blade. Sharp Minith steel did not tarry long in the flesh of humans, he noticed.

He soon tired of the game and turned back to the carrier where he could await the return of his men in comfort. He passed a contented sigh and dropped to the plush purple cabin seat. He admired the noble color, marvelously pleased with his command of this planet.

The soldiers returned two hours later. They wore the bright red blood of the hunted like a new set of clothes and hesitated at taking their own seats lest some of the crimson dressing be rubbed from them.

"Come now, troopers," Zal reminded them. "Do not fret upon losing your momentary badges of valor. Remember, we have two other such farms to visit before our work is done."

The soldiers cheered Zal. They no longer cared that two of their fellow guardians had been dealt their fates by these humans. This entertainment of revenge more than made up for the passing of two lesser soldiers.

\* \* \*

A final parry of the man's sword and Grant was inside

his guard. He did not want to kill, but there was no choice. With a quick stab to the heart, the ten-inch blade he had won in the Third Square ended the contest. The door's warrior fell and Grant strode silently into the Fourth Square. He began his third day in the monolithic prison by defeating yet another guardian.

The first difference he noticed was the women. They were not beautiful by any means, but they were not the thin, emaciated females that had greeted him in the Third Square. He nodded to one who seemed to be taking an interest in his presence and made his way through the darkened stone interior toward the Inner Square. The woman fell in behind Grant's quickened pace and tagged along three paces behind him for quite a distance before he turned to face her.

"Can I help you?"

The girl said nothing, only stared at him. She was in her mid twenties, Grant guessed. The dirty, reddish-brown hair that hung loosely over her eyes nearly caused Grant to miss the furtive glance over his left shoulder. He ducked to the right and brought out his blade as a length of chain blurred past his head. He turned to face the threat and found himself facing a large black man twirling a heavy chain with an ease and confidence that caused Grant to take great care. From the corner of his eye, he picked up a sudden movement and barely dodged a knife's downward plunge. Grant reached out for the knife's wielder and caught the girl's wrist in a vise-like grip. He broke the wrist with a single twist and the girl dropped to the floor.

The girl's distraction was minimal but almost proved his undoing. The chain pounded across his chest and knocked him backward. He grabbed out and snagged the chain as he fell. He held on long enough to prevent another use of the steel weapon against him and regained his feet. His chest throbbed hotly as he faced the black man again. Grant consciously discarded his previous reservations about killing and set out to fight for his life. His opponent, having had an opportunity to assess Grant's abilities, folded the chain in half to a length of four feet. It gave him more control of the weapon and he twirled the folded metal before him and advanced.

"I don't want to fight with you. Just on my way to the Inner Square." Grant tried to reason with the larger man. The other stood well over six feet tall and must have weighed close to three hundred pounds – and there was no flab on him.

"Inner Square, huh?" The black man's smile showed three gold teeth. Other than those few trinkets of wealth, the man was toothless. "The path to the Inner Square runs right through me."

"Ever considered getting your teeth fixed, asshole?" Grant asked. The flash of anger was brief but more than enough of a distraction. Grant launched himself at the chain's owner. Before the man could react, Grant was within the chain's arc, the weapon neutralized. The large man barely dodged Grant's right hook but managed to catch Grant on the temple with one of his own.

The blow dazed Grant and he fought to stay on his feet. He succeeded, but was clubbed by a powerful left hand. The fist, made much more potent by the chain it held, slammed Grant's jaw. His teeth rattled and he saw the fireflies of his youth dancing around his head. Sheer determination and fighter's instinct kept him erect and conscious.

He felt his opponent wrap him in a bear hug and Grant flashed back to the Minith in the Mother Ship. Reflexes took over and Grant's knee struck home with force. Enough force to make the man cry out and sink to the ground. Grant staggered away from the man and looked at him through blurred vision. The man was not going to get up.

"Ain't that a motherfucker," he said. In his earlier life, the knee had been a devastating weapon but not to this extent. He silently thanked Tane for the ability to do such damage. The new legs that the small scientist was quick to brag about had come through once again. Grant began to feel a new appreciation for the body he had been given.

He shook the stars from his head and took inventory. Roughly two dozen spectators stood about but no one made a threatening move. The girl sobbed quietly and cradled the broken wrist to her body. The black man rocked himself gingerly on the ground, his hands clasped tightly to his groin. He wheezed. Grant retrieved the chain from where the other man had dropped it and tossed it at the man's feet.

"I think you dropped this," he gasped through tired lungs. Several of the crowd laughed and the black man looked up through tear stained eyes.

"Thanks. I've been looking all over for it," he managed hoarsely. The man smiled and slowly uncurled his body. It was apparent he was still in serious pain. He squatted on the floor of the Fourth Square building and grabbed the chain.

"You take it. You earned it." He tossed it to Grant who caught it easily and draped it over his shoulders like a scarf.

"Thanks. Now, can you direct me to the Inner Square?"

The black man smiled and shook his head.

"Yeah. Eastern door is blocked. Been that way for years. Closest door is to the South." The black man pointed to the south and stood up slowly.

"That's some knee you've got there, partner. I've been kneed in the balls before but never like that. Where did you learn that?"

Grant smiled. The man would never believe the entire story, so he told him part of the truth.

"A skinny little scientist showed me how."

"That must be some scientist. Think he'd show me?"

"Next time I see him, I'll ask. Good enough?" The black man eyed Grant doubtfully, unsure if he was joking.

"Yeah. Good enough. I'm Mouse. It's not my real name, but I like it. Supposed to be the name of a fierce animal that lived a long time ago, but who knows?"

Although he had yet to see a mouse, Grant doubted the little critters were extinct as the big man seemed to think. Along with rats and cockroaches, they would no doubt outlive mankind. He considered telling the prisoner what kind of creature he was named for, but decided against it. The irony of such a large man being called Mouse held a certain appeal.

"I think I've heard that too, Mouse. A very ferocious animal, I believe."

Mouse smiled at Grant's agreement, apparently pleased.

"Come on. I'll take you to the southern door. It is a rough journey for one man to make alone."

Mouse bent down and lifted the girl from the ground. She still cried with the pain of the broken wrist.

"Help me with, Sue. She doesn't talk much, but she's the best friend I have. Then we'll begin."

"Of course. My name is Grant, by the way."

Pleased to meet you Grant. Your knee, not so much." He still hobbled from the blow to his groin.

Two hours later, the three arrived at the south door. Standing guard at the door was an even larger man than Mouse and when he saw the small party approaching his door, he stepped forward in challenge. "No further, little ones."

Grant and his escorts stopped short of the door. Grant looked at Mouse who was smiling. "I guess we have to fight this guy, Mouse?"

"Only if you want to proceed toward the Inner Square." Mouse stepped toward the large guardian. I call challenge!"

"What? Mouse, I can't let you do this. This is my fight, not yours."

"Grant, this man and I have been avoiding our battle for too long. I have elected not to challenge him until now only because Sue has asked me not to. I will wait no longer."

"Come, Mouse," the guardian called to the black man. "It

will be a pleasure to choke the life from your darkened skin!"

Mouse looked to Grant once again, his eyes were serious as he said, "Do not interfere, Grant."

Grant nodded. He would not interfere. This place, known to the outside world as Violent's Prison, held its own code of honor and social propriety. Grant took Sue's good hand and led her a distance from where Mouse stood. She struggled silently against Grant's hold and he realized that she was a mute.

"It's okay, Sue," Mouse calmed her. "This won't take long. Then we'll be on our way to the Inner Square. Just like I promised you."

"Not in this lifetime, Darkie," the guardian taunted. He hefted a broad sword and flashed it quickly through the air. The blade cut a deadly path.

Mouse did not appear affected by the man's show. He turned to Sue. "Hon, today is the day." He twirled the chain Grant had returned to him and advanced.

## CHAPTER FOURTEEN

Sue drew the length of thread slowly, expertly through Mouse's skin. She showed little emotion. The splinted joint was swollen and blue but she did not seem to notice it as she worked on her man.

Unlike the girl, Mouse grimaced with pain as his left arm was stitched closed. The door's guardian had almost caught him in the chest with the long blade of his sword, but he managed to duck aside at the last moment. Now, Grant and the two prisoners sat around a fire in the open area between the Fourth and Fifth Squares. It had been Grant's decision to wait until the next day to challenge the final square and that gave Sue a chance to close Mouse's wound.

"Almost done, Sue?"

"A war wound you can be proud of, Mouse. I count about twelve stitches." Grant found the giant's unease at the sight of his own blood somewhat amusing considering his abilities to fight and his status as a feared fighter of the Fourth Square.

Mouse looked at Grant sideways. "What are you about, Grant? What type of man are you?"

" I don't know what you mean."

"Yeah, you do. You're not like the rest of us. And certainly not like those outside of here." He waved to the stone walls around them.

"It's a long story, Mouse. I guess you could say I'm a throwback to an earlier time."

"There! That's what I'm talking about! You say the strangest things. I mean, what the hell does that mean, huh? 'A throwback!' What the hell is that?"

Grant chuckled. His language was six hundred years behind the times.

"Sorry, Mouse. Sometimes I forget where I've come from and where I've been. A 'throwback' is someone who belongs in the past. My time was about six hundred years ago."

"I can relate to that, Grant. I've always felt like a... a throwback. That's why I ended up here, I guess. Nowhere else to go, really." Sue patted Mouse on the shoulder, a signal that her handiwork was finished. He inspected it briefly and smiled at the girl. She beamed at the approval and sat down next to him, content.

"Would you like to leave this place?" Grant watched Mouse's reaction closely. He was met with a cold stare of doubt and suspicion.

"You mean the Fourth Square? My friend, we already left there. Nowhere left but the Inner Square. We'll make that tomorrow."

"That's not what I mean, Mouse. I'm asking you if you would like to leave this place. This prison?"

Mouse's eye drilled holes. He shook his head.

"That is not possible, Grant. Believe me. I have heard it before. No one has ever made it out of here. Plenty have talked about it. I've heard of some who have gone to the Outer Wall and jumped. Thought they could swim through acid. You don't seem crazy like that, though. What kind of nonsense are you trying to sell me, friend? Tunnel out? Build a carrier? A boat that can cross the moat? What? There is no way out of here. Ever."

Mouse spat.

Grant smiled. Put a hand on Mouse's shoulder.

"Let me tell you a story."

For thirty minutes Mouse listened. Grant described his history and his reason for being in Violent's Prison. Mouse asked a few clarifying questions, but remained mostly silent while

Grant relayed his story.

"Well? What do you say? Are you with me?" Grant watched the other man's face. The doubt was easy to see. Before he had a chance to answer, another voice spoke.

"Yes."

Grant and Mouse looked at Sue, their mouths agape. Grant had assumed the girl mute, and from the look on Mouse's face, he had as well. As if to rub their noses in the surprise, she spoke again.

"Yes. We are with you." She returned Grant's stare. Her eyes blazed with determination, courage and conviction.

Grant blinked first.

"I'll be damned, Grant. My lady can talk."

\* \* \*

Grant awoke the next morning to a dead fire and sore muscles. The ground in Violent's Prison was hard. Packed solid by the incessant footsteps of its inhabitants, the ground was a solid stone-like surface. He sat up and looked around.

Mouse was still sleeping on the other side of the fire's cold ashes. Sue sat next to Mouse, quietly and calmly staring at Grant.

"Good morning," Grant said. The dead taste in his mouth made him yearn for a toothbrush. He would be lucky to find a clean sip of water to rinse his mouth.

Sue nodded her greeting, and Grant wondered if the girl had once again fallen into the role of a mute. His thoughts were quickly answered.

"Did you mean what you said? About leaving here?"

Grant glanced at the sky, unsure of the answer. The invitation to leave the prison had been directed to Mouse, not the female who traveled with him. "I can't promise anything," he compromised. "It may not be up to me."

"Who is it up to?"

"The men I told you about yesterday. The scientists and politicians."

"Politicians?" The look on Sue's face told Grant she had no idea what he was talking about.

"Never mind."

Mouse stirred and sat up.

"Is it time to move on?" he asked. He rolled his shoulders and looked down at the stitches Sue had crafted the day before.

"Not yet, Mouse. There are a few things I need to know before going on."

"What?"

Grant stood and stretched. He needed to work the soreness from his body. He arched his back and swung his arms in a circle. It felt good to move and he went through a brief cycle of calisthenics.

"Who is Titan?" he asked as he moved.

"What? Who is Titan? Grant, where have you been for the past fifteen years?" Mouse gave Sue an incredulous look, unable to believe, for whatever reason, that Grant did not know the name Titan. Grant did not miss the same look returned by Sue.

"I've been frozen at the bottom of a fucking lake. Now who the hell is Titan? Everywhere I've been since I entered this place, I hear the same damn name -- Titan. Who the fuck is Titan?"

Mouse shook his head skeptically but answered Grant's question. "Man, Titan is the meanest, most violent Violent in this prison. Damn, this place was built for men like Titan."

"Yeah? What did he do to deserve such a reputation?"

"He flattened about a hundred people for his eighteenth birthday! He went totally off the Violent scale, man! It took about twenty Peace loving citizens to restrain him and even then it was no easy thing to do. The man is huge. You think I'm big? Titan makes me look tiny.

"It took him three hours to make the Inner Square when he ended up here. And he killed every guardian he fought. Not a peaceful Violent, like you or me. He kills because he loves to kill. No other reason. Hell, just a few years ago anyone who went violent out in civilization was called a 'Titan'."

Grant shook his head. Inner Square in three hours. Impressive. He would be a dangerous foe.

"Sorry, but no. Never heard of him." Grant calmly finished his calisthenics and shook the last of the soreness from his muscles. "You ready to go?"

Mouse sighed. Stood up.

"Why not? Hell, Titan's waiting for us."

"He'd better be, Mouse. I didn't come all this way for nothing." Grant turned toward the Inner Square, inconspicuously checking the transmitter inside his belt. Mouse and Sue brought up the rear.

## CHAPTER FIFTEEN

"I want the human returned!" Zal's fist banged the tabletop. "Immediately!"

The puny human male from the Interpreter Corps nodded dumbly. Zal smelled the fear. The human was fearful for his life. As he should be.

"Y-y-yes, Minister. I shall p-p-pass your command along to the Leadership Council."

"If the female is not returned within two days, your race will forfeit three more of its farms. And another for each day thereafter! Is that understood, puny one?"

The interpreter could not find his voice so merely nodded his pale countenance at the newly appointed Minith Minister. He no doubt wished for the return of Brun, the previous Minister. Zal had no doubt that his predecessor would have coddled this one.

"You are dismissed, human." Zal waved the tiny male away and thought of the missing female. How had she gotten away from the ship? She could not see in the light. And who had killed the two guards in the corridor? It was a mystery and he detested mysteries. Zal was certain that the return of the female would allow him to solve the dilemma.

\* \* \*

The news of the Minith Minister's threat was a physical blow to the Leadership Council. Still reeling from the destruction of three sub-farms and the deaths that had occurred, the debate over how to proceed with the Minith Minister was quick and unanimous: Find the girl and return her to the Minith.

The human population could not afford the loss of another sub-farm. Already the cost paid in human lives at the first three farms was too great to bear.

N'mercan Culture Leader Randalyn Trevino immediately passed word to Mr. Blue. "Deliver the girl back to the Minith Mother Ship."

Blue smiled from one of the couches in his apartment as he terminated the call from Culture Leader Trevino. He summoned one of his assistants and promptly carried out his orders.

\* \* \*

Grant and his two companions approached the door to the Inner Square. Mouse was armed with his chain, Sue with nothing but a knife. Grant still carried the wooden staff and ten-inch blade. The guard saw them and stepped forward to meet their unspoken challenge.

"Halt."

Grant stopped six feet from the guardian and motioned for Mouse and Sue to stand behind him. "Good day, Guardian. We desire passage into the Inner Square."

The corners of the guardian's mouth turned up in a parody of a smile. His eyes sparkled.

"Forgive my rudeness, stranger, but that is one request I cannot allow to go unchallenged. What business do you have in this Square?"

"I'm looking for Titan. I have a proposition that I think he'd like to hear. I don't want to fight you for passage. But I will if I must."

"You say you wish to speak with Titan, eh? You are far braver than I, stranger. Go through my doorway and good luck with your journey," the guardian said as he stepped to the side.

The other side of the doorway was dark and uninviting,

and Grant studied it skeptically. He considered it unlikely that this guardian would move aside so easily unless a trap lay just within. Apparently, Mouse was affected by the same apprehension for he whispered to Grant so that the guardian could not hear.

"This is not right. It is too easy."

Grant nodded his head but a fraction. He studied the darkness inside the doorway. Anything or anyone might be waiting for them inside, but it was a challenge they had to meet if they were to reach Titan. Grant observed the guardian for clues but the man's emotions were veiled, ungiving. The man would make an excellent poker player. He turned back to the door and, with a shrug of his shoulders, walked into the gloom on the other side.

"Here we go," Mouse whispered as he pulled Sue close to his side and followed Grant into the darkness of the Inner Square.

\* \* \*

"You're going to do what?!" Tane could not believe what he was hearing. He knew Blue to be a self-serving pompous fool, but he had not thought the man capable of this.

"I am doing as I was ordered by the Council, Senior Scientist! It is my duty to do so, as it is yours not to get in the way. It is beyond my control now," the overweight man said. He studied the nails of his pale, beefy hands.

"But don't you – I mean, doesn't the Council understand what this could mean? All of our work – our efforts to relieve ourselves of the Minith could come to nothing if we send her back to them!" Tane saw the indifference written clearly across Blue's features and he tried another approach, searching for anything that might sway the other's actions.

"She knows too much about our plans. They could

torture her to tell them everything she knows! We cannot allow her to be returned to them. Don't you understand? Doesn't the Council understand?"

Blue raised a hand to stifle a yawn. Tane seriously considered a commission of violence upon another human. His anger was swatted away by a soft voice. It cut cleanly through the tension.

"I will tell them nothing, Tane." Tane and Mr. Blue turned to find Avery standing in Blue's doorway.

"Avery," Tane muttered, suddenly unsure of what to say. He had not meant for Avery to discover what the Council wanted them to do. To send her back to the Minith would mean certain death. But not before an even more certain torture.

"Avery, I know you would never disclose our plans willingly. But the Minith are cruel monsters. They will commit severe Violence upon you."

"Tane. I have served them for years. I know what they are capable of." Tane saw the truth in her words and could almost believe her when she told him, "I will not tell them anything."

The woman's words ended any arguments Tane possessed.

"Have you provided the hospital with a recording of the Minith language, Avery," Mr. Blue asked.

"Yes, it was completed yesterday."

"Good, then your purpose for being here has been served. It is the Leadership Council's decision that you be returned to the Mother Ship. I will arrange your departure within the hour.

"But Blue, she can't --"

"Enough, Rolan! I am carrying out the Council's order! She must be taken back."

Tane sighed, defeated. He had no doubt that by returning the girl to the Minith, their goal to eliminate the aliens from their planet was doomed. The human race had decided once again to ignore long-term benefits in order to sate an immediate need. The Peace that was earned with Avery's return would be short lived. When the Minith discovered what their human chattel were attempting, the repercussions would be severe.

The Minith would squeeze information from Avery. Short of kidnapping or killing Avery, he had no idea how to stop her return. He could not carry out either of those options.

Tane nodded his acceptance of Blue's order and turned to go. He saw Blue smile, apparently pleased with his victory. Tane accepted the failure. It was a short term loss. He was more concerned with long term success. As he departed Blue's apartment, his mind was already considering his next step.

Grant would not be pleased with the Council's latest decision.

## CHAPTER SIXTEEN

They entered the darkness slowly, hesitantly. Grant felt his way forward. He balanced on the balls of his feet and waited for his eyes to adjust. Unlike the four previous squares, this one was unlit. The only illumination came from the doorway they had just entered and a pale light that shined in the distance. The fact that this square was different from the others, coupled with the ease with which they had been granted entry, set off alarms in Grant's head. He was an experienced soldier. One trained to detect slight changes in routine and not-so-routine patterns. His entire being shouted 'danger'.

He suddenly remembered Avery's ability to see in the darkness.

"Mouse," he whispered to the large black man. "Can you see anything?"

"Nothing but that light in the distance," Mouse whispered back from three feet away. The words surprised Grant. He had not realized the other man was so close.

"That's what I was afraid of," Grant replied. He moved toward the light, alert for any smell, sound or movement.

Grant searched the blackness around them as they made their way through the corridor of the Inner Square. He heard rustling and turned to face the sound.

*Beep. Beep. Beep.*

The communicator beneath his belt went off. The tin beeping of the device echoed like thunder in the stillness and Grant fumbled to quiet the sound. The beeping had surely given away their location. He found the button to silence the incoming signal. As he pushed it --

-- light flooded the three figures.

The harsh white light blasted his eyes and Grant lashed out blindly with the staff. Nothing but air.

"Nice trap," Grant had time to think before being slammed brutally to the ground. He fought against the weight holding him down but could not move. Struggles and curses behind him. He had no doubt Mouse and Sue were similarly captured.

"Son of a bitch," he muttered.

"Shut up," a voice spoke from beyond the light. "You will not speak unless told to do so."

Grant was in no position to argue.

\* \* \*

They were marched through the Inner Square corridor by eighteen men. They were boxed in – four guards ahead, four behind and six on each side. All were armed with pikes or swords. And all were pointed at them. The guards did not tie their hands or bind them in any manner but Grant did not fight or struggle. There were too many. And he suspected they were taking him where he wanted to go.

His eyesight returned to normal. Grant took in everything they passed and filed it away for future reference. They passed men, women and children. All seemed amused at the trio being led through the corridor. Many of the women and children threw garbage and stones. Grant ignored the garbage and did his best to dodge the larger stones. Grant opened his mouth to ask their destination and was immediately jabbed in the ribs by one of the guards. The men who escorted them were alert and well trained.

The women were more attractive and better fed than in the outer squares. Sue also noticed. She stared at the women with suspicion and envy written upon her features. There was obviously no love lost between the women here and those in the outer squares. The pecking order appeared to be based strictly on appearance.

Sue also bore the brunt of the taunts and jeers. To her credit, she ignored the words and dodged most of the trash that was thrown. Grant was proud to be in her company. He doubted if many of the women who wielded the garbage and hostile threats would have held up so bravely.

Most of the male prisoners they passed were actively engaged in some type of fighting, sparring or exercising. Grant sensed an army in training. Grant was reflecting on this when the procession turned into a large stone chamber off the main corridor.

A raised stage made up the far end of the chamber. It was two feet high and, on the platform, stood a man. He was easily seven feet tall and massively built. Shoulder length brown hair, pulled into a pony tail. He wore pants and boots, but no shirt. His muscles rippled and flexed as the group approached.

"Titan," Grant said beneath his breath.

The dais increased the man's presence; his sense of height. Grant knew the position was an affected one, chosen for its effect on the visitors to the chamber. The knowledge did little to diminish the man's true size, however. This man deserved the name, Titan.

"Kneel, strangers," they were told by one of the guards. Mouse and Sue immediately dropped to their knees. Grant remained standing.

"I said kneel!" the guard shouted. The end of his spiked bar stabbed into Grant's kidney. He meant business.

Grant staggered. The pain bit, but he did not kneel. Instead, he turned his head and spat at the guard. The incensed guard jabbed the sharpened steel for a second blow. Grant sidestepped the weapon, flashed forward and sent his boot into the man's solar plexus. The guard flew backward, dropped like a swatted fly.

Four of the man's comrades moved toward Grant but a deep voice, resonant with authority, halted the movements with a single word, "ENOUGH!"

Grant faced the four attackers and, seeing them back down, turned to face Titan.

"I'm not kneeling to anyone, pal."

Titan seemed amused by Grant's defiance.

"You may be a fool, little man, but you do not lack courage." Titan stepped from the dais and Grant sized him up. Titan had superior strength and size. No doubt about that. The giant would likely view him as an overmatched opponent. If they fought, it would be the intangibles that made the difference. Speed, cunning, fighting skill. And his newly improved body. Grant was more than ready.

"Bubba, I ain't kneeling. And I'm no man's fool."

Titan's eyes widened slightly at the stranger's affront but he held his anger.

"Who are you? And why have you been looking for me?"

Grant was surprised, but saw how information might travel quickly in an environment like Violent's Prison. There were no distractions from the outside world and anyone with information would surely try to parlay such information into a favor. It was obvious that his rapid journey to the Inner Square had been noticed and communicated to Titan.

Grant had every intention of telling his story to Titan. It was the sole reason for his being here: to enlist Titan into the fight against the Minith. However, Grant had a rule when bargaining with an opponent – never give up anything unless you get something in return.

"How did you know I was searching for you?"

Grant's question was met with a blast of laughter from the giant.

"Ah, little man, who are you, eh? You say you are no

man's fool but you act like one at every opportunity. I asked you a question and you answer it with one of your own! If that is not the act of a fool then you must be a powerful fighter.

"And outside of these walls, there are no fighters. Only inside the walls of Violent's Prison do real men live and die." Titan waved his hand at the stone walls that surrounded them. "Outside... outside there are only cowards who live with their heads hidden beneath the coverlets of their comfortable beds. Men who believe in the lie that they call 'Peace.'

"Are you one of those, little man? Or are you a fighter as your talk and your actions would have me believe?"

Grant ignored Titan's question and repeated his own. He had an agenda and it did not include Titan being amused.

"I asked you once. I don't want to ask you again. How did you know I was searching for you?"

The mirth left Titan's face. He stepped closer, now only six feet away. He glared down, his face flushed with anger. Grant felt a sliver of satisfaction. Piss a guy off and you've got an edge. Piss off a big guy and you eliminate a little of the advantage of his size and muscle. The more they fight with their emotion and not with their heads, the better your odds.

"Alright," Titan whispered. His tone promised violence. His eyes promised carnage. His tightly clenched hands promised a savage beating. "I was told. It is that simple, little man. So I had a surprise waiting for you. And here you are."

Good. Good. Time to poke the bull a little further.

"Very good." Grant added a hint of humor to his words. "Now, what was it you wanted to know, you dimwit? I forgot."

The huge man charged. His face a twisted mask of rage and fierceness. Grant sidestepped. Crouched. Pushed his left leg out. Swept his right leg behind. The slap of head on the hard floor resounded.

Cries of disbelief and anger arose from the guards who rushed forward. Mouse met the rush and dropped the first three. The fourth caught him across the face with a swing of his mace. Mouse dropped. The remaining guards turned toward Grant but were stopped by a shout.

Titan had regained his feet. Blood dripped from his forehead. He was smiling coldly at Grant.

"He belongs to me."

"Sorry, Bubba," Grant answered calmly. "I belong to no man."

"You soon will, little man. Soon, you will belong to me and I will make your life miserable."

Grant countered with another taunt.

"We'll see who belongs to who, Bubba," he teased.

Titan motioned for one of his men to throw him a sword. He caught the blade carefully on the grip. He advanced, carefully this time.

"Choose your weapon," Titan growled.

"I won't need one." Grant was pushing Titan. Perhaps farther than he should. Here he stood, facing a giant with a sword, and refusing a weapon of his own. It must have appeared lunacy to those who watched, but Grant had little experience with maces, swords or pikes. His weapons were rifles, grenades, hands and feet. He decided to rely on the hands and feet that Tane had given him. Better than his own, Tane had said. Well, time to find out how good they really were.

Grant spread his legs. Balanced his weight on the balls of his feet. He was well trained in several martial arts. He wondered briefly if those arts had died along with the rest of his ancient warrior brothers. If so, this would be the first lesson for his new warrior brothers. The martial arts were as much a mental effort as a physical one. His mental abilities were well honed, he knew, from six hundred years of cerebral exercise. He had gone through the movements of the arts countless times during his endless state of suspended animation. He hoped the mental exercises would benefit him now.

Grant breathed deeply and watched silently. He settled into a zone – his concentration deepening as Titan circled left. Blood from the gash dripped into Titan's right eye and he wiped it away. That was in Grant's favor. The blade sliced the air, weaving a hypnotic pattern. The man was good with the weapon. That was in Titan's favor.

Grant circled right. He looked for an opening. Saw none. Gave Titan one instead. Titan reacted and Grant narrowly dodged the sharp blade. The giant was quick and Grant filed the reaction away for later use.

"Take a weapon, little fool," Titan advised.

Grant ignored the words and feigned a kick. The move was meant to appear clumsy and unskilled and Titan fell for it. The slash found air – Grant's leg no longer where it was supposed to be. Grant stepped inside the swing, pivoted and landed a roundhouse kick to Titan's head. The larger man staggered. Regained his balance and staggered again as another boot smacked his right side.

Grant knew the kick did damage – bruised ribs at a minimum. Titan roared. Swung the blade wildly at Grant. The parry sliced his right arm. Drew blood. Grant saw an opportunity. He winced and cradled the wounded limb to his body.

Titan howled with delight. The giant raised the blade above his head. His eyes blazed. His voice roared in triumph. Grant had no doubt the other man would put all of his power into the swing. Grant waited. Watched.

The blow never had a chance. At the apex of the swing, Grant drove his left foot forward. The impact of his foot to the larger man's solar plexus echoed around the chamber. The blade left Titan's hand and he was thrown backwards. He landed in a heap atop the raised platform. Unmoving.

Grant spun towards the guards, prepared to defend himself from another attack. They did not move on him. He had defeated their leader, therefore they were also defeated.

Grant nodded to one of them and then pointed to Titan, who still had not moved. "See if he is alright."

The man moved without hesitation.

"He's still alive!" the man reported. Grant sighed with relief. He did not want to kill the man. He needed his help.

"Grant, that leg is going to kill somebody one of these days," Mouse exclaimed. Grant looked over at his friend. Blood dripped from a split lip and his nose was starting to swell. Otherwise, he seemed unfazed.

Grant flexed his legs. Gave them renewed respect. Tane had done well. He would have to thank him when he saw him again.

He remembered the call that had come in on the communicator just before they had been captured. Wondered who would be contacting him and why. It was agreed that no calls would be transmitted to Grant while he was in the prison. Only outgoing calls would be permitted. Only one thing could be behind the transmission – the Minith.

Grant retrieved the communicator from one of the guards. His guards now.

"No, Mouse. I won't kill *someone* with these legs. But I sure as hell will kill some *thing*."

## CHAPTER SEVENTEEN

Grant called to the hospital on the tiny communicator. Tane answered his signal almost immediately. His voice held an edge and Grant knew something very important was going on out in the real world.

"Sorry it took so long. What's going on, Tane?"

"It is bad, Grant. The Leadership council has ordered us to return Avery to the Minith!"

"They what? Are they insane? We can't do that!" Grant spoke from two points of view. One wanted Avery kept from the Minith for security reasons, if she told them what she knew about their plans, they were as good as finished in their fight. The other point was more personal.

"I'm sorry, Grant. I tried to stop them, but..."

"You mean she's already gone, Tane? They've taken her back to the Minith?" Grant could not believe the idiocy of the Leadership Council. Avery knew what they planned. She knew about Violent's Prison. She knew about Grant.

"Grant, the Minith threatened to destroy more of our farms if she was not returned. They have already destroyed three as retribution against your attack on their Mother Ship."

"I didn't attack their ship, Tane. I merely defended myself against two of their guards." It was a weak argument. He *had* attacked the ship and the guards. But he was angry. Avery's face flooded his mind and clouded his thoughts.

"Grant, what do we do now?"

Grant struggled to clear his mind -- to think rationally. He rushed through the possibilities, searched for the right course of action, one that could save Avery and their fight against the Minith. He quickly settled on perhaps the only one that could accomplish both and whirled into action.

"Tane, arrange a pick up at the Outer Square where you dropped me. Get here as soon as you can. There will be two additional passengers."

"But, Grant...won't that be dangerous? I mean, we will have to land."

Carriers never landed inside the prison. They hovered long enough to toss out their cargo, then flew away as quickly as possible. Getting a pilot to land would take some doing.

"Don't worry about the prisoners, Tane. I'll take care of them. Just convince the pilot there's nothing to worry about."

"I'll pilot it myself, Grant." Grant wanted to hug the brave little scientist. Tane would come through.

"Get here as soon as you can. If I'm not waiting when you arrive over fly the area. Do not land until you see me personally."

Across the room, Titan stirred, sat up slowly. He wiped a stream of blood from his face. Grant wondered if he would be a problem.

"Hey, gotta go. Something's come up that I need to deal with."

"Good luck, Grant," the scientist added. The communication link dissolved.

\* \* \*

Titan shook his head to clear it and looked about the room. His eyes settled on Grant and he slowly rose to his feet, the gaze unwavering and steady. Grant steeled his stance, ready for another attack.

Instead of violence, he was met with a fierce smile. The giant shook his head and stepped forward, his body still as ominous in size but less intense in its overbearing presence.

"No, Stranger, I have met a valiant opponent and desire

no further violence with you." Titan held his arms in front of his body, his hands turned palm upward.

"I defer to your superiority as a fighter."

The guards passed a collective gasp at the large man's words and actions; they had obviously never expected this man to be in such a position. Grant was moved by the other man's action and stepped toward Titan's outstretched arms. He reached out his right hand and grasped Titan's hand firmly.

"Titan, where I'm from, this is how fellow warriors show respect when they meet."

The two shook hands for a moment and released the hold. The smile on Titan's face changed to a grin. It was going to be okay. Grant had made a respected acquaintance, if not a friend.

"You are indeed a mighty warrior."

"I am a warrior at your service, then, stranger. It is the way of this place."

Grant understood well enough how this place called Violent's Prison operated. He was now in charge of the Inner Square and, as a result, the entire prison. He had not set out to conquer the leader of this square, the man named Titan. He had only wanted to enlist the man's services and those of his lesser warriors in the cause against the Minith. Nevertheless, the fight had been pressed and he had escaped as the victor. Now, he held the allegiances he desired. And he was not unwilling to use them in the success of his plan.

"I'm honored, Titan. I... No, not I, but the world. We need your services." Grant waved at the men assembled in the chamber. "Indeed, we need all of your services."

Mouse smiled and stepped forward from the back of the room where he and Sue had retreated.

"Men, you are not going to believe what this man has in store for us," he joked. "It is difficult to believe. But apparently the Leadership Council has approved it."

"What do you need from us, Stranger," one of the guards asked.

Grant saw no need to withhold anything from them.

"My name is Grant Justice. And we are going to drive the aliens from the planet."

"Do not play with us, Stranger." Titan's words were hushed but clear. He closed the distance between them. "I will quickly take up my weapon against you once again if you joke with us. I have no patience for pranks."

Grant wondered how the Minith had hurt this man so horribly to make him act in such a manner. He put a hand on the larger man's shoulder.

"No joke, Titan. I've come here to recruit warriors." Grant paused. Searched the faces around him. "Are you with me?"

Titan snaked Grant into his embrace, lifted him from the ground and hugged. Grant gasped for air as the crowd cheered and whooped.

## CHAPTER EIGHTEEN

Grant did not greet Tane. He merely flopped into the rearmost seat of the carrier and checked his weapons. The wooden staff was added to the pulse weapon, shurikens and boot knife that Tane had delivered.

Tane lifted off from the cleared area and waved hesitantly to the men outside. One of the Violents lift a dirtied hand in return, the glint of a knife's blade held in the hand was recognizable. The climb took him above the prison's walls and out of sight. He pointed the vehicle to Bst'n and programmed an automatic flight.

"What happened, Tane?" Grant asked, ignoring the social nicety of introducing his two companions. The edge in Grant's voice would have concerned any other Peace loving man, but Tane knew the other man well enough now to dismiss his inadvertent violent tendencies.

Tane checked the flight plan for accuracy before turning to face his three passengers. He glanced warily toward the black man and the white woman with him before telling Grant what little he knew. Avery had displayed her own slightly violent tendencies earlier by refusing to leave Bst'n until Tane had her message memorized word for word. The message included directions inside the Minith Mother ship, directions designed to assist Grant in finding her should he choose to do so. He repeated the words now and watched as Grant turned them over in his mind. Tane wondered if Grant was aware that he could be read so easily when he was planning violence.

"What are we going to do, Grant?"

"We're gonna get her back, scientist," the large black man answered and Tane felt an involuntary shiver pass through his body. Other than Grant, he had no experience with Violents and the proximity of these two convicted Violents was disturbing. The fact that one of the convicts was a woman did little to soothe his fear but he did his best to swallow it away.

"He's right, Tane," Grant agreed. "We've got to get to her before they can hurt her. She knows too much." Tane knew there was more to it than that for Grant. It was not only an operational necessity to rescue Avery; it was an emotional one as well. He suspected the two had deep feelings for each other. Grant was starved for emotional input after his period of suspended animation and he had rescued Avery. Those were two strong reasons for the immediate attachment, but Tane wondered if their feelings for each other would stand up through time. He dismissed the thought and concentrated on their situation.

"If you go to the ship and try to get her out," Tane argued, "will not the Minith know that we are able to resist them, and are perhaps planning to do so?"

"Yes, Tane," Grant answered. He spoke as if explaining a simple arithmetic problem to a child who should already know the answer. "But if we do nothing, they will also know that we are able – and planning – to resist them. They will also know where our headquarters is located and that we plan to somehow use the men and women of Violent's Prison. In other words, Tane, they will be able to crush us before we ever get started."

Tane nodded and felt almost ashamed. He, one of the brightest men on the planet, should have known that. He also knew he should have done everything in his power, regardless of how violent it may have seemed at the time, to have prevented Avery's return to the Minith when he had the chance.

"So what can we do now?"

"We do the only thing we can do, Tane. We turn this thing around and head for the Mother Ship. We get her back. Now."

Tane did not speak. He did not argue. He simply turned around, faced the controls and changed their course.

Thirty seconds later, one scientist, two Violents and one six hundred year old soldier were headed for the home base of the Minith.

*   *   *

"Take her to the Zone. We shall hear what she has to tell us."

"Yes, Zal. It shall be done." The guard left to follow out his orders.

Zal smiled. The answers were at hand. This human would tell him what he suspected – that these tame creatures were straining at their bonds like oxen to a plow. The yoke of slavery gets more uncomfortable the longer it is worn and these humans had chafed under that yoke for over a decade. It was time they fought back.

*It is time to show them what slavery really is*, Zal decided. *Only when slaves rebel against their masters can they begin to learn that lesson.*

He strode to the Zone, eager to watch the demonstration that waited.

*Will she resist?* The thought stirred his body. A pleasurable sensation. *Moreover, if she does resist, how long will she be able to keep her silence?*

"Let us hope she is a strong female," he muttered to himself as he entered the Zone.

*   *   *

The Mothership loomed in the distance. Even from the height of the speeding carrier vehicle, the barren earth that surrounded the ship seemed to extend forever, a blackened circle of earthly protection for the aliens. Although the sight was not new to Grant, the implications of the burned earth still affected him.

The flight had taken a few hours and Grant had spent the time planning the assault and briefing the others on their responsibilities. From the information Avery had relayed through Tane, and his own knowledge of the ship's layout, Grant had a good idea of where they would have taken her.

The 'Zone', as Avery had called it, was where the aliens tortured their human captives. Every human slave who entered the ship was taken there first to have his or her secondary lids removed by the Minith. Their blindness made them more trustworthy but Grant wondered how these people could ever be considered untrustworthy when they practiced no violence whatsoever. *And see where it got them*, Grant thought.

"Entering Minith detection range, Grant," Tane informed the man. Grant looked to Mouse who nodded and checked his weapons a final time. Their plan was simple and straightforward. Get in, get Avery and get out.

"We're ready, Tane. Go for it!"

Tane stopped circling beyond the range of the alien's listening devices and pointed the vehicle's nose toward the ship. They approached the alien ship without any indication that its owners were aware of their presence.

"Okay, Tane, drop it here!" Grant and Mouse opened the carrier's door and waited for the vehicle to descend. Grant jumped before the craft touched down and sprinted for one of the ship's doorways, twenty feet away. Mouse was right on his heels, his length of chain already swinging. Tane and Sue waited in the carrier.

Grant reached the door and turned the handle. His prayers were answered and the frame swung inward, opening into the interior of the ship for their convenience. He rushed in and turned left at the first corridor, as Avery had instructed.

Mouse was right behind. The corridor ahead was clear but Grant knew it would not stay that way for long. These aliens were well trained and had to have heard their landing. He sprinted for the nearest corridor and turned right.

They passed three other corridors before making a final left turn. As they made the turn down the final hallway, Grant spotted two Minith guards in front of a doorway. Grant knew that the door opened into the Zone. The two aliens looked in their direction. Their attention, but not their weapons, drawn by the sound of the approaching humans. Grant took advantage of their initial confusion and hit each with a short blast from the pulse weapon. The two guards crumpled in the hallway. Their bright purple blood splashed freely across the width of the ship's corridor.

Grant and Mouse hurdled the bodies and the spreading pools of purple and stopped in front of the doorway.

"This is it, Mouse. Ready?" The other man grinned and hefted his chain. "On three. One.. .two.. .thr—"

Before Grant reached three, Mouse was through the doorway and into the room on the other side. Grant wasted no time in following and leveled his weapon as he did so. The warm metal barrel sought targets and quickly found several. He took out two of the aliens before others scattered for cover.

From the corner of his right eye Grant saw Mouse take on one of the Minith with his chain and then, as if in a dream where everything moved in slow motion, he saw Avery. She was strapped to a long metallic table in the center of the room. Wires hung from several places on her body but she appeared unharmed.

With one eye, Grant saw her smile weakly. The other eye saw Mouse drop the Minith with a well-placed swing of the lethal metal chain.

Grant rushed to the table but was grabbed around the ankle by one of the aliens who had ducked for cover only seconds before. Grant fell but got a shot off as he was falling. The hold on his foot was relinquished but two more aliens charged into the room. He took the lead alien out with a shot to the head and, before he could swing the barrel to the second, Mouse attacked with his chain. The second Minith went down. The situation under control for the moment, Grant turned to Avery once again. Undid the straps and wires.

She was weak from whatever the Minith had done to her but she seemed whole; even smiled when Grant asked her how she was. She did not answer so, taking a chance that she had no broken bones or internal damage, Grant picked her up and tossed her over his shoulder. He turned toward the door, stepped over one of the dead Minith and nearly slipped in the alien's blood as he did so.

"Mouse, let's go!" he shouted to large black maniac who was pummeling another of the aliens without mercy.

Grant was glad the other man's anger was not turned upon him and stepped over another of the aliens.

The Minith moaned.

Grant calculated. Kill the alien or make haste? They needed to get back to the carrier as quickly as possible and he had no time to check how much charge was left in the pulse weapon. He elected to forego another shot at the injured Minith. He was down for now and there could be more in the hallways.

He turned to the door, and Avery groaned. She couldn't be comfortable over his shoulder but it couldn't be helped. Mouse gave his latest victim another lash then followed Grant into the corridor.

They met one other alien before reaching the waiting carrier but Grant's weapon eliminated the danger. Seconds later, Grant had Avery stashed in the back of the carrier and they were speeding away from the alien ship as fast as the machine would take them.

* * *

Zal came to minutes later.

Several guards had arrived since the humans had left and two were trying to assist their leader. He stared up into their Minith faces and slowly remembered where he was. His first rational thought was a personal denial that two humans had actually entered his ship and nearly killed him, but the pain in his left side brought the reality of the situation close enough to spit upon. Two humans had entered the Zone and nearly killed him! And they had killed several of his soldiers!

"The female?" he whispered to the assembled guards.

"Gone, sir."

Zal pushed himself slowly from the ground. His head pounded. He recalled the sound of the metal chain as it blurred through the air toward his head. A flash of pain and then… darkness. He raised his hand and felt the gash. The bleeding had stopped and the wound had already begun to close up. He was greatly relieved that he was in no danger of losing his command because of the injury.

With his body taken care of, his first thought was that he had been correct in his previous assumption. The humans were beginning to resist!

The idea of a rebellion on this weak world was like a drug in Zal's system and the power of the drug flowed like lightning through his veins. Now he could fight these humans more as equals and less like the sheep they were. Once he described this act of rebellion to his superiors, they would not prevent him from making the appropriate decisions. Rebellion was never allowed on a world ruled by the Minith. That was the most important rule by which his race lived.

Zal considered his next moves carefully and noted with some satisfaction that he could have great fun with these humans. Free reign to prevent open rebellion was every Minith Minister's fantasy and he was about to live it. It was this thought that caused Zal to reconsider his decision to inform his superiors of the humans' actions. He could handle this without their interference and, when he informed them of how he had handled the situation, they would certainly be pleased with his resourcefulness and leadership abilities. Zal could almost taste the sweetness of that moment.

As an afterthought, and certainly without serious consideration that it would ever come to pass, Zal recalled the second most important rule by which the Minith lived: If a world cannot be dominated, it must be destroyed. He waved off the thought.

"Bring me Lieutenant Treel."

## CHAPTER NINETEEN

They landed outside of the hospital. The flight from the Minith ship was without incident. They were not followed and Grant suspected that the Minith leadership had been unable to counter their assault with any coordinated effort of their own. Still, the flight had been tense, especially for Tane who, in between checks to the rear for sign of being followed, babbled incessantly. The words he muttered were an attempt to allay the fear he felt in his stomach, Grant knew. It was a common occurrence among new soldiers or those not used to fighting for their lives. Grant suspected that many more of these present day humans with their lidded eyes would be following in Tane's example soon.

"Will they be able to locate us, Grant?"

Grant shook his head at Mouse's question but was not wholly sure that he was right. He did not know what sophisticated equipment the Minith might possess and the ability to track a specific vehicle that had undoubtedly been recorded on the alien sensors was probably not beyond them.

"Tane, make sure this vehicle is taken away from populated areas and destroyed," he said, indicating the craft. Tane looked at him quizzically but a mask of understanding quickly replaced his confusion and he nodded.

"It will be done at once."

The five humans left the carrier and entered the hospital. Grant carried Avery who was sleeping. He followed Tane who led them to the secure portion of the building that had been used for his experiments with Grant. Mouse and Sue followed quietly, their eyes taking in everything they passed. Grant felt they were holding up well for two people who had been freed from Violent's Prison only hours before. They, like everyone else on the planet, had believed that no one ever left the prison alive. Their presence here was a first and they showed very little sign of undue stress or pressure in the fact. It made Grant realize what a unique place the prison was and what effect being sentenced there could have on a person. They showed flexibility, endurance and a marked ability for survival. Mouse's actions inside the Minith ship validated Grant's decision to use the men and women of Violent's Prison. Three hundred more men like Mouse and they would have a fighting chance against the aliens. There were thousands of prisoners. Finding a few hundred who might like a chance to fight the aliens should not be too difficult, Grant decided. He wondered how Titan was coming in his assignment to develop the inmates of the prison into fighting units.

Grant followed Tane into a small room exactly like his own and placed Avery gently on the bed. Grant's thoughts left the Minith and the inmates of Violent's Prison as he recalled the night he had spent with Avery in his own room just down the hall. He reached out to touch her face and brushed an errant strand of hair from her cheek. She was more beautiful than any woman he had ever known and prayed she would be all right.

Tane must have understood his feelings for he placed a hand on Grant's shoulder. "She is fine, Grant. All she needs is some rest." Grant nodded and allowed himself to be steered from the room.

Mouse and Sue were waiting in the corridor, questions written clearly across their faces. Grant recognized the look of subordinates waiting for their leader to tell them what came next and, for the first time in his life, regretted his decision to become a soldier. The burden was more than what he cared to hold right now, but like the professional he was, he did not shy away from his responsibilities. He knew that action followed decision and quickly decided that they had to get back to the prison.

"We have to return to the prison to help Titan." He then turned to Tane who stood quietly, almost comfortably, to the side.

"Tane, it would be wise to inform the Leadership Council of what's happened. The Minith will waste no time in striking back. Try to make them understand that what we did was necessary and that more of the same will be coming. No fight is without casualties and they should know that up front. They have to get the word out that violence is necessary against the Minith. They have to alert the population that violence is not only necessary but also expected."

"They will not like it, Grant."

"Hell, Tane, I don't like it either, but it has to be done."

Grant saw the resolution in Tane's face and knew that the scientist would do everything in his power to make the Council understand. He only hoped that Tane would succeed. "The Minith cannot be defeated without violence. Peace has its place in every society, but so does violence."

"I will leave immediately, Grant." Tane turned to go, but stopped and turned back to Grant. "And do not worry," Tane said, tilting his head toward Avery's room, "We will take care of her." Grant nodded his gratitude, glad that his friend understood.

"Mouse, Sue, are you ready to go?" The two ex-prisoners nodded and followed Grant toward the exit.

"Hey, Grant?"

"Yeah, Mouse?"

"We ain't gonna have to stay this time are we?" Grant realized that Mouse was planning to stay an ex-prisoner and had to smile at the large man.

"No, Mouse. We've got too much to do outside those walls to ever make you go back against your will."

Mouse smiled broadly, his few teeth shining brightly. "Sounds good to me, boss."

* * *

Mouse piloted the carrier vehicle as if he was born to it and explained to Grant that his experience came from his 'pre-violence' days. He had studied hard in school and had been one of the fortunate ones in his post-education assignment as a shuttle pilot for N'mercan dignitaries. Surprised by the insight into the other man's background, Grant asked for more information and found out that Mouse, whose real name was Bryan Rogerson, had been sent to Violent's Prison nearly six years before.

Mouse explained how he had been piloting a routine shuttle flight between Lanta and Washt'n for one of the N'mercan Culture's dignitaries when his problems began. Midway through the flight his attentions had been drawn to the rear of the carrier by a scream from the dignitary's female companion.

At first, as his training demanded, Mouse made no attempt to move from his pilot's chair. He ignored the sounds of the struggle in the rear but his judgment would not sit still for long. Sure that the woman had hurt herself in some manner, Mouse placed the vehicle on automatic flight and opened the door that separated the flight cabin from the passenger's compartment. His naiveté at believing the sounds coming from the rear were the result of an accident was quickly wiped away.

He stopped with barely one foot through the door. The scene before him was the first incident of Violence he had ever witnessed and he found it nearly impossible to believe it was really happening. The woman was on the floor of the carrier with her neck held securely in the grip of the dignitary's clenched hands. The woman struggled feebly beneath the man. Her clothes had been torn from her body. Mouse stared at the scene, at first unsure of what to do. Then he noticed the woman's face turning blue.

With no conscious thought regarding Peace or violence, Mouse hurled himself at the man he had been hired to transport. Because of his size, he easily toppled the man and had him restrained in less than a minute. After securing the Violent, Mouse checked the woman, but could find no pulse. She was dead. Sickened by what he had witnessed, and distraught that he had acted too late, Mouse flew the remaining miles to Washt'n, relieved that he would at least be able to turn in her killer.

"To make a long story short," he continued, "the guy convinced everyone that it was me who killed the woman."

"So you ended up in Violent's Prison?"

"Sounds like a bad dream, doesn't it?" Grant had to agree that it did and shook his head that even now, six hundred years after his own time, such injustices could still occur.

Grant felt that Mouse wanted to be alone with the controls he had not operated for over six years so he retreated to the rear. He used the remainder of the flight to learn the Minith language from the tapes Avery made before she had been returned to the aliens. He had a clear understanding of the alien language after ten minutes. It was easier to pick up than most of the Afc'n Culture Languages and all of the As'n ones. An hour later, the carrier landed on the ground at the Outer Square and Grant could speak near-fluent Minith.

Pound met them as they exited and Grant shook hands with the man he had faced upon his initial arrival at the prison. He looked better now than he had before and Grant suspected Titan had already begun spreading the food among the outer squares. He looked around and his suspicions were confirmed. He saw meat cooking over several fires and heard his stomach rumble as his nose quickly picked up the scent. He had not eaten in more than 24 hours.

"How about some food, Pound?" he asked the other man, who smiled at once. Pound was obviously pleased with the turn of events since Grant's arrival days before.

## CHAPTER TWENTY

Tane arrived at the World Building of Cultural Leadership and Peace an hour after the Minith left it.

The building that housed the Leadership Council was chaos incarnate as people ran in and out of the building unimpeded by the usual access controls that governed entry to the hallowed halls of mankind's most important structure. There was blood, still wet and bright red, splashed across the granite steps that led into the building. Tane worked his way around the larger pools of red, fear etched deeply in his nerves. There were no bodies, but he knew what waited inside. Death.

He quickened his pace and passed deeper into the building, heading for the Council's chambers at the center. He passed more tracks of red in the outer hallways of the building and followed them. They seemed to lead inward, toward the core of the building. Still, there were no bodies.

He reached the solid wooden doors of the Council's Chamber and hesitated, suddenly afraid to proceed. With a deep breath to steel his ragged nerves, he pushed the heavy oak barricades open. He stepped into the chamber and froze.

Inside, seated quietly around the table, were the six Culture leaders. Alive. Unmoving. Staring.

On the Council Table in front of them, piled like sticks of fallen timber, were dozens of human bodies. The bloodied corpses had been tossed upon the wooden surface by the Minith who had dragged them there. Their message was clear. They were a warning to the Council, and to the World, that the Minith would not accept rebellion by its subjects. At least, not without a price.

"Peace be with us." Tane croaked. Without warning, the

contents of his stomach rose like lava and splattered across the crimson-stained floor. His stomach emptied itself of the bile but his mind could not. The sight of the broken corpses piled upon the table soaked through his tightly closed eyes. He lost track of time as his body rebelled against the horror.

An eternity later, Tane opened his eyes to the reality that would forever haunt his days and nights. It was unchanged, as he knew it would be, and he looked away from the tangle of limbs and blood as quickly as he could. His eyes landed on Randalyn Trevino, his own Culture Leader. She met his look without flinching. Tane saw the hatred that toiled behind the other's seemingly calm exterior.

"The Minith?" It was a pointless question, but one Tane could not contain. He had to hear the confirmation.

"Yes." Primo Esteval spoke, his Standard language tinged slightly with an accent of his S'mercan Cultural accent. This lingual slip was more than enough for Tane to realize how deeply affected the Leader Elect was by this madness before them.

Tane held his voice with some difficulty. Like the others, he was not accustomed to Violence but, unlike the Culture Leaders, he knew that his own race had done recent, similar damage to the Minith. He owed each of the Council Leaders an explanation but did not know where to begin. He was spared from his discomfort by an unexpected source.

"We must resist against the aliens. We have been complacent for too long."

Tane, along with the member of the Council, turned toward Sabatina Sabontay, the Urop'n Culture Leader. An outspoken Pacifist, she surprised everyone at the table with her bold statement. In the seven years of representing her Culture, she had never done less than everything in her power to preserve Peace. At whatever cost. Now, turning completely around in her behavior, she was espousing retaliation against the aliens.

Quasan Alla, the Musl'n Culture Leader, was not so contradictory to his past stance against any form of violence. "No! We must not lower ourselves to their level. Peace is the only way!" Tane opened his mouth to speak, but was beaten to the moment.

"Bah! You fool! There is no place on Earth for Peace now," the N'mercan leader spat. The anger Tane recognized a few moments before was raising its head now for all to see. Randalyn's face churned with the emotion she felt. Her lips curled into an enraged snarl and spittle flew from them as she spoke. Tane was saddened to observe his Leader, who had served his Culture so well for so long, succumb to the madness that gripped her.

"We must fight! We have prepared for this through Senior Scientist Rolan's experiments and we cannot back away from it now! We must destroy the Minith!" Her fist pounded the table and the stacked bodies shifted. One of the topmost bodies, that of an older man dressed in the robe of a scholar slid sideways; threatened to topple of the stack. It held and Tane felt the breath he had been holding leave his chest. To his surprise, none of the Leaders pushed away from the table. Instead, they continued to look toward Randalyn.

"We must fight," Randalyn repeated. "We must remove the Minith from our planet"

Esteval, Sabontay and Diekela Mamun, the Afc'n Leader, nodded their heads in agreement.

"But Peace is the only --"

"Enough!" Primo Esteval, in his role as Leader Elect held up his hand to stop the Musl'n Leader's arguments. "These are not ordinary times. We are at war whether we wish it or not. We must vote on how to proceed. As I see it there are two choices."

The Leader Elect looked around the table, pausing briefly to meet the eyes of each Culture Representative. He had to look around the piled bodies to see Suyung, the As'n Representative, but his look lost none of the emotion it carried and Suyung nodded.

"Option one: We succumb to the violence of the Minith and relegate the preservation of our world and the security of our Cultures to the Minith.

"This option, as we have all known for some time, will lead to the death of our world. There will be nothing left for our race, and we will die."

Quasan opened his mouth to speak but Esteval's glare quickly halted the attempt.

"The second option," he continued, "and the one I will vote for is this: We allow Senior Scientist Tane Rolan, with the assistance of his experiment, continue with the mission for which we have planned. This is no time to turn our backs on this chance. It is our only hope."

Esteval, no longer displaying any trace of S'mercan accent, posed the final question before the Council. "What option do you choose, Culture Leaders?"

Tane left the chamber a few minutes later, shaking his head. The vote had been unanimous and he had plenty of work ahead.

\* \* \*

"We are prepared to fight!"

Titan raised his hands triumphantly over his head and the crowd of men around him shouted in agreement. Their chorus swelled to a din in the building between the Second and Third Squares and quickly became a deafening roar as the shouts and screams echoed and bounced through the enormous hallways. Grant nodded at Titan through the tumult, pleased that they were prepared to do battle with the Minith. Eagerness for the fight was half of the preparation needed for the war. But it was not the only preparation needed and Grant had no desire to go up against the aliens with a gang of thugs. He wanted an army and, as soon as the noise died down, made his point with Titan.

"Good, Titan. Now all we need is a few days of training and we'll be ready."

"Training? A few days? We want to fight now!" Titan was upset by the statement, as Grant knew he would be. Eager fighters never wanted to train. Instead, they wanted to begin the battle, certain in their ability to overcome their opponents through sheer desire and will power. Grant did not know how to tell these men that such determination quickly fades when the battle begins but good training sees an army through to victory. It was a tough lesson to learn and he had been fortunate. Many young soldiers never learned that lesson, their determination and spirit for the battle long forgotten as they lay dying from a stupid mistake.

"Eagerness is one thing," Grant tried to explain, "but there is no substitute for training. There are some things about the Minith that we need to discuss. Strategies and plans we need to work on."

"But, Grant," Titan pleaded, his desire to fight the aliens a visible thing, "we want to fight now." The men gathered around them listened intently to what was said. It was plain to Grant that they wanted to leave this place as soon as possible, and were willing to go up against the Minith if that's what it took.

"I know, Titan, I know. But we must plan this carefully if we are to win. The Minith are well trained as a fighting force. If we meet them with anything less than the same, we, and the rest of the world, will fail."

Titan held his tongue while he considered Grant's words. Finally, almost reluctantly he said, "All right. We'll wait for you to decide when we're ready."

Grant smiled, and the men around them murmured their reluctant agreement.

## CHAPTER TWENTY-ONE

Tane arrived at the prison and immediately sought out Grant. He had to inform him of the Council's decision.

Grant received Tane's news from the Council with little emotion. He had decided already that, with or without the Council's blessing, he and those volunteers he could gather would wage war on the Minith. This world, although not of his era, was still of his race, and very much worth fighting for. He would not relinquish its control to another race, no matter what his own race's leaders decided. In fact, with the help of Titan, Mouse and Pound, he had already begun the work of building an army from the men and women of Violent's Prison.

"It is good to have the Council behind us, Tane, but it means little. Our problems with the Minith go beyond the Council. Every man, woman and child of this planet is affected by the actions and orders of those aliens. They have to be driven away. No matter what it takes."

"I understand what you are saying, Grant. But I feel greatly relieved by the Council's decision. The Minith will never leave of their own volition. Force is our only recourse and I am pleased to know that the Council did not waiver from this difficult decision."

Grant nodded. "I guess you're right, Tane. It's good the Council understands that violence and armed aggression, when used for the benefit of all humankind, have their place. The time for Peace ended with the arrival of the Minith."

"What do we do now, Grant?"

Grant looked at the small man who had given him a second chance at life and who had freed him from an eternity of endless memories. His answer to Tane was simple. "We train, we fight and we win."

For the next three days, Grant and his cadre drilled the men and women of Violent's Prison in the art of soldiering. Mouse, Titan and Pound taught the fighting styles they had been forced to learn in order to survive the brutality of the prison. Pound taught the knife, Mouse the chain, and Titan instructed the soldiers in a variety of other weapons. Other prisoners displayed their own unique skills and contributed where they could.

Grant oversaw the training and gave crash courses in hand-to-hand, cover and concealment, and squad-sized tactics. To the extent possible, he explained what he knew of the weapons used by the Minith and gave in-depth discussions on the human arms of earlier, pre-Peace times. Tane had been sent to gather what weapons he could from museums, ancient armories, or private collections. Avery visited the prison to teach the men and women the intricacies of the Minith Mothership, as well as anything she could about the aliens' physical and psychological make up. It was a grueling period, stuffed with non-stop lessons, and everyone worked hard.

While teaching the prisoners, Grant took the opportunity to talk with the inmates and increase his library of languages. He recruited more than a hundred men to their army simply by conversing with them in their native tongues. For several, Grant's words in their language were the first they had heard from another human since being sentenced to the prison. The prisoners soon looked up to him and welcomed his leadership.

Grant spent most of his nighttime hours planning their assault on the Minith ship. He knew their only hope for defeating the Minith was in taking them at their ship. The aliens' spaceship served as both headquarters and living quarters. Except for those aliens who were out of the ship when they attacked, all of the Minith would be there, located in one place.

Grant was certain the Minith had grown complacent and his previous successes at entering the ship were a direct result. He had penetrated their perimeter twice now without so much as a locked door, and suspected it would be more difficult the next time. The element of surprise was gone and he set his mind to finding a way of regaining it. The daily training continued uninterrupted but the problem was never far from his mind.

At the end of each day, Grant watched the men and women of Violent's prison stumble back to their places of rest. Forgotten now were their arguments over territory or their positions within the prison's squares. They were brothers in arms, forged into a single force with a single goal: Liberate Earth. It was a good rallying cry and Grant heard remarks from several soldiers – for they were shaping up into good soldiers – about how the Earth and its citizens, who had locked them away from their society, now needed them to act as saviors of their world.

The prisoners had been informed of the Council's decision and they accepted their newly found responsibilities with a pride many of them had believed lost forever. Grant was honored to lead such a group and praised whatever fates had elected him to be in such a position. No longer was he angry with the gods for robbing him of his world or his place in time. It no longer bothered him that the legs, arms and whatever else had been replaced by Tane, were not his own flesh and blood. They had come through when he needed them and they were now his as much as his own extremities had ever been.

And Avery.

His mind relaxed, as it always did, when he thought about her. He loved her; there was no denying that now. And, as if his thoughts had somehow magically summoned her, she appeared from around the far corner of the square and made her way toward him. He watched her sightless approach, her left hand reaching out to the stone, her fingers never leaving the wall as she made her way. Several times before reaching him, others moved away from her path in deference to who she was and what she had been through. She was accepted as one of them, as well she should have been. Though she still refused to tell him how it came to be, she was once a prisoner here herself, Grant mused.

Grant waited quietly and Avery stopped only a few feet away from him, her unseeing eyes seemed to look right at him.

"Grant, how is the training going?"

*How in hell does she do that*, he wondered. "It's going fine, Avery. We'll be ready soon."

"Do we stand a chance, Grant? The aliens have well-armed soldiers who have been trained since birth for war. It hardly seems fair."

"Yes. We have a chance, though not a good one. If we are to beat the Minith, we're going to need every soldier we can train and a hell of a lot of luck. It won't be easy, but we have to try."

She stepped toward Grant and their hands met, held tightly. He pulled her to his chest and breathed in the scent of her hair. Holding her felt good, felt right. More right than he had ever felt.

"It's as if they were put here for this, Grant. The men, the women, even the children whisper to each other that they will be heroes for fighting the aliens." Avery stepped backward, away from Grant's embrace and turned her face up to his.

"What will happen to them, Grant? I mean, if we win... after the fighting is over? What will they do then?"

Grant looked away from Avery, unable to face her blind stare. How could he tell her what he did not know? Would these men and women live through the battle they faced? And if they did, would they be returned here by the society they were fighting to protect? It was an age-old problem shared by every army in history. What happened to the soldiers after the war? He had no good answer and said as much.

"But, Grant, if the Minith are defeated, they will have earned their freedom. Most of these people have been here for years. Some for their entire lives. Grant, some were even born here."

The way that Avery shivered when she made the statement cued something in Grant's brain. Had she been born here? Was that how she had come to be in this place? He wanted to ask, but knew he could not. She would open up when the time was right.

Avery hugged Grant even tighter than before and he felt the strength of her conviction in the problem they faced. "We've got to change it, Grant. If we can, we have to change it."

"Avery, things can never be the same. Not after this."

He meant the words, and Avery seemed comforted by them, but Grant withheld telling her that, although things could never be the same, he did not know how the changes would affect the people of Violent's Prison. How would the rest of the world treat them, knowing that they were perpetrators of violence, even though the violence they committed was for the good of their race? Only time would tell. But first and foremost, they had to fight and win.

"There's something else no one has considered, Avery. Something that may not allow the world to remain at Peace, whether we want to or not. The Minith are from out there," Grant explained. He pointed at the sky and, even though Avery could not see the motion, she nodded.

"What's going to happen if we run these aliens off our world? Will they return with more soldiers and larger, more powerful weapons? By defeating the Minith now, will we be killing our world in the long run?"

Grant paused. Breathed.

He had not realized just how deeply he was being affected by his role in all of this.

"Sometimes I ask myself, 'Are we doing the right thing?'"

"Grant, you know the answer to that."

He sighed heavily. The responsibility was a giant boulder that had been shoved uncomfortably onto his shoulders.

"Yes, I know. We have to fight. There's no other choice except to die a slow death at the hands of those damn monsters."

"Exactly. At least this way, even if we lose, it will be because we tried. It won't be because we rolled over and let them kill us."

They stood silently for a few long minutes, holding each other. Grant felt some of the tension drain from his body with the embrace and he knew that whatever happened tomorrow or next week, or even next year, they had each other now, and that was enough.

"Come on," Grant said, breaking the silence. "Let's get some rest." He took her hand and led her toward their small room in the Outer Square. The night was young enough for what he had in mind and the Minith could wait.

\* \* \*

Grant dreamed of the frozen lake. In the dream, the enemy shot him long before he reached the hole in the ice and he lay unable to move, at the mercy of the men above. The enemy soldiers took shot after shot, laughing all the while, and Grant cried in horror as his arms were erased from the rest of his body piece by bloody piece. Grant would have looked up in defiance of his tormentors but his face was frozen securely to the lake's icy cover. Unable to move, he shut his eyes tightly against the only sight his frozen countenance allowed: the ice in front of him. The ice was littered with bits of his own flesh and large splashes of his dark red blood.

CRAAACK!

A cackle of laughter erupted from the watchers above with the latest shot as another chunk of Grant's body was wiped away.

CRAAACK!

Another shot, another burst of laughter.

CRAAACK!

More laughter, but Grant sensed a change in the sound, a change that seemed somehow sinister and terrifying.

CRAAACK! Although the joy of the sport was still in the laughter, the voices were not as abundant or as boisterous as before.

CRAAACK! Grant's body jerked with the impact of the shot and the laughter came again, even stranger than before. It was a 'whispered' laughter, heard only because it was carried on the wind.

CRAAACK!

No laughter. A minute passed without another shot. Five minutes and still no shot rang out. Grant wondered if the soldiers had grown bored. His thoughts were interrupted by the sound of footsteps on the ice and his hopes fell, crushed like a newborn kitten beneath the treads of an ancient tank. The animals had descended from the road above, had come to collect their reward.

Grant pried open his near-frozen eyes and saw the feet of his tormentors not three feet away. To his horror, they were not the booted feet of his human enemies. They were the misshapen, leathered feet of the Minith.

Grant opened his mouth to scream --

-- and awoke next to Avery, the scream still on his lips. He bit back the panic and swallowed the sound. His heart thundered with the fear he had felt and he tried to slow its beat while his mind raced. Something had caused him to wake up and it had not been the dream.

Grant looked quickly around the small room. He saw

nothing out of the ordinary in the dim light of early morning but heard steps in the corridor outside. Within seconds, the dream was forgotten and Grant was out of bed. The sound of footsteps approaching had replaced those of the soldiers in the dream. He grabbed his boots and found Mouse waiting outside the door.

"What's wrong, Mouse?"

"Nothing is wrong, my friend. But Tane just arrived at the Outer Square and he asked me to bring you there."

"Tane's back? I didn't expect him for a few days. Did he get what I asked for?" Grant pulled his boots on and laced them quickly.

Mouse shrugged. "Perhaps. He arrived in a cargo carrier."

"Yes, well, he'd better if we're to have any chance. Those damn monsters are better equipped than we are."

Grant re-entered the small room while Mouse waited patiently outside. Avery was still asleep on the small pallet they had shared for the past few days and Grant smiled lovingly down at her peaceful form. He kissed her lightly on the forehead and left the room.

"How is she?" Mouse asked, his voice quiet so as not to wake her. Everyone had come to care for Avery, both for who she was as a person and for what she had been through. She stood as a symbol to the men and women of the prison that freedom was possible... freedom from Violent's Prison and from the Minith.

Grant understood how Avery was viewed by those around him. But to him she was more than a symbol of hope. She represented everything about humankind that was worth saving. He tried not to let his emotions interfere with his responsibilities but it was difficult, more difficult than he would have believed. He had never been in love and the emotions he carried inside were like a puzzle he could not figure out. He wondered how long the confusion he felt would last.

"She's fine, Mouse. The work tires her out, but she keeps going when others couldn't. She's very strong."

"Yeah, she'd have to be to make it through what she has."

Five minutes later, Grant and Mouse stepped into the Outer Square. Grant saw the scientist leaning against the large cargo vehicle. Tane had his eyes closed. Fatigue was etched clearly across his features.

The rest of the Outer Square was empty. The men who had previously occupied it had gravitated toward the inner squares once the prohibitions against doing so had been eliminated. Now that the prisoners possessed a common enemy, they no longer had to commit violence upon each other. Their preparations against the aliens provided an effective outlet for any aggressions they felt.

Grant shook Tane gently. The scientist opened his eyes slowly and smiled when he recognized Grant.

"Grant. How are you," he asked wearily.

"Very well, thanks to you. Did you get what I asked for?" Tane smiled even wider and Grant knew the other man had been successful.

"Look inside."

He nodded toward the rear of the carrier and followed as Grant made his way around to the cargo doors. Grant opened the large compartment and looked in on several large metallic containers. He looked at Tane and laughed.

"Tane! My friend, you never cease to amaze me!" Grant hoisted his large frame into the vehicle and ran a hand over one of the containers. "Did you get everything?"

"Just about. What I couldn't get, I substituted for, but I think you'll be pleased!"

Tane was obviously pleased with his accomplishment and justifiably so, Grant thought. He took a deep breath, released the two latches on the first crate, and raised the lid. He gazed into the container and whistled. Mouse, his curiosity piqued stepped into the carrier and peered into the container.

"Damn! Grant, is all this for us?" His voice carried the excitement he felt at the contents of the container.

"Fuckin' eh, Mouse! Fuckin' eh!"

Grant reached into the metal crate and removed one of the items from inside. He hefted it in his hands and caressed it like a long lost love. It was one of many in the crate; and exactly like the one that had taken his hands and feet from him over six hundred years before.

Like a deer catching wind of the hunter's scent, Grant remembered the previous night's dream and dropped the weapon like a red-hot poker. It clattered noisily and came to rest beside the others. He wiped his – not his really, he thought, but Tane's – hands on his pant leg but the unease left by the touch of the rifle remained.

"Oh, Grant. I almost forgot," Tane said, oblivious of Grant's sudden discomfort. "There was plenty of special ammunition available for these. I brought it along also."

"Really? What kind?" Grant asked, already knowing what answer he would get.

"The literature with it described it as 'explosive'. It's supposed to be the best for..." Tane swallowed the unease he felt. Violence was still an uneasy concept for him.

"...for killing," he finished.

Grant turned away from the weapons and left the interior of the carrier.

"That's great, Tane." Grant's voice died off and neither Tane nor Mouse heard his final words. "It's good for maiming, also."

Mouse and Tane were clamoring over the other boxes like children on Christmas morning as Grant walked away. He suddenly wanted to be with Avery and hoped she was not yet up.

He began the slow walk through the square, his mind once again drawn to the problem of regaining the initiative against the enemy. He marveled at the architecture of the prison as he walked and wondered at the men who had conceived this place. Without a doubt it was a marvel of stone and mortar, but the more Grant walked its halls the more convinced he became that the place was initially designed to be a castle or fort of some type. Whoever had turned it into this prison had used its strengths and eliminated its weaknesses. It was now the perfect prison.

He reached his room and found Avery still asleep. He lay down beside her and stretched. The bones and joints in his new limbs did not creak and pop as his old ones would have and he rued the loss briefly. Avery stirred but did not awaken and Grant rolled over to hug her. Her back was to him and he pulled her tightly to his body where she snuggled against him warmly. Grant, aroused by her closeness, became hard quickly and Avery could no longer sleep as his erection pressed against her back. She moaned softly and turned to face him.

"You left me," she mumbled sleepily as she reached down, grabbed his hardness.

"Yes. But I'm back now." The pleasure her hand created made him close his eyes and he kissed her deeply as his hand sought her breast.

"So I see," she managed between their urgent kisses.

"What else would--"

Grant bolted up into a sitting position so quickly, his head began to spin. "Grant? What's wro--"

"Shhh!," he interrupted. The revelation had come to him unexpectedly, like a bolt of lightning from a cloudless sky, and, except for the bad timing, he welcomed it without hesitation. He examined the idea for a few brief seconds before knowing that it was possible. He knew what they had to do.

"I'm sorry, Avery," he offered, unsure of how she would

react. "I've got to go."

"You're leaving? Now?" she asked incredulously. Grant merely nodded an unseen apology and began to get dressed again.

"Is it what you've been struggling with these past few days?"

Grant looked at her and marveled once more at her ability to see to the heart of things.

"Yes. It is," he answered.

"Okay. I understand," she said, and Grant knew that she really did understand. "As long as it's not me that's driving you away," she added playfully.

"Never, Avery. Never." He knelt to kiss her goodbye and was quickly off to the Outer Square.

## CHAPTER TWENTY-TWO

The Minith commander heard the muted sound of boots approaching and fumed at the guard's inability to approach his quarters in silence. The idiot's attempt at stealth failed miserably and Zal snarled. His soldiers had been pussyfooting around him since the human's attack on his ship and their efforts to keep out of his way only served to anger him further. The soldier stopped just outside his door and the Minith leader waited impatiently for the guard to find the courage to announce his presence. Finally, there was a soft tap on the door.

"Enter!" Zal commanded brusquely. The command seemed to shake the large purple room. The guard entered his commander's quarters, the shout ringing in his overlarge ears. He kept his eyes on the floor as he waited to be addressed.

"What do you want?"

"Sir, there is a message from General Brun," the large guard offered as he handed a folded sheet of paper to his commander. Zal saw that the message was printed on Priority One leaf and took it with some hesitation. He had no idea why his predecessor, who was now his superior, would transmit a priority message to him...unless word of the attack on the ship had somehow leaked out. He cursed the fact that he had not had sufficient time to seek out the spies Brun had undoubtedly left behind. He searched the messenger's countenance for an indication of the page's contents but the other showed no emotion other than the fear he had entered with.

He turned his back on the guard and read the message silently.

BEGIN PRIORITY ONE MESSAGE

ATTENTION: COMMANDER OF MINITH FORCES, PLANET EARTH ZAL: THERE IS RUMOR OF REBELLION ON EARTH. I HAVE CONFIDENCE IN YOUR ABILITY TO RESOLVE THIS MINOR INCONVENIENCE. I WILL ARRIVE IN THREE DAYS TO OBSERVE. GEN BRUN

END PRIORITY ONE MESSAGE

*If the idiot had confidence, why was he coming?* Zal crumpled the message angrily, thankful only for the fact that no one on earth other than he and this guard had seen the message. All Priority One messages were delivered directly by the operator on duty and no eyes other than the Commander's were allowed to see it. Even with spies on board, this regulation would never be broken. Allegiance to a former superior was allowed and to communicate ongoing events to such an individual was not questioned, but to disobey a standing order or regulation was unheard of among the Minith posted to captured worlds.

"Forget you have seen this message," Zal commanded, remembering the presence of his underling. The other nodded and, recognizing his dismissal, left his commander's quarters.

Zal cursed beneath his breath. Brun had no confidence in his abilities to handle this weak uprising among these weak creatures.

"Well," he muttered, "I'll just have to have this settled before the fool arrives." He summoned one of his personal guards, a soldier he knew he could trust. A few minutes later, a tap announced his visitor's arrival and his leathered lips turned upward in a smile-like fashion. Unlike the messenger, he had not heard the other's approach.

"Enter."

Lieutenant Treel, the lieutenant who had been with him for blood sport at the human farm and who had been sent to "warn" the human Leadership Council entered the room and bowed.

"Sir," he announced.

"Lieutenant," Zal addressed quietly. "We have to stamp out the pests among the humans. Quickly."

"Yes sir. My soldiers have been working on locating the beasts who dared to stand up to their masters."

"And have you had any success?" Zal asked. He displayed none of the anticipation he felt to his subordinate. It would not be wise to show any fear or hesitation to one who was pledged to obey his orders.

The lieutenant wavered for a fraction of a second before answering and Zal knew before the words left his mouth what the other's answer would be.

"Sir. We have been unsuccessful in locating them, however –"

"HOWEVER WHAT?!" Zal shouted. The shout resounded about the room causing the lieutenant to stagger backward a step. "Are we so incompetent that a few sheep can hide from us? How can that be, Lieutenant?"

"Sir," the large Minith soldier offered weakly, "we are trying."

"Well try harder! I want these sheep found within two days, Lieutenant. I don't care how you do it, but do it!"

Zal trembled with rage. He was unused to the feeling of impotence that ran through him. To think that a few weak humans were trying to discredit him to his superiors and his warriors – and succeeding! It was more than any Minith, regardless of status, could tolerate.

"Yes, sir." The lieutenant bowed and began backing out of his commander's presence.

"Lieutenant," Zal said, interrupting the other Minith's

departure. The lieutenant stopped and looked expectantly at Zal.
"Sir?"
"Destroy ten more human farms."
"Yes, sir."
"And see if any of our human 'friends' have any knowledge of what their more courageous brethren are up to. It is unlikely that they will know anything, but we cannot overlook the possibility."
"Yes, sir."

\* \* \*

The plan was put into motion and the time had come to play it to the end. The Outer Square was now crowded with people as the group of fifteen prisoner-soldiers prepared to leave.

"Everything's ready, Grant." Mouse said as he loaded the last pack into the large carrier vehicle and turned to face his friend. Tane, Sue and the others were already on the vehicle and ready to go. The excitement among the group was palpable. With the exception of Sue and Mouse, this was the first trip out of the prison for all of them since their initial arrival.

Grant hugged Avery a last time and turned to face Titan. The huge man, who had once controlled the entire prison, towered over the soldiers gathered in the Outer Square to see Grant and his party off.

"You know what to do." Grant said, the words not a question but a statement. Titan nodded.

"We will be fine, Grant. It's you and the others with you that I'm worried about."

Avery turned away from the group and walked away shaking her head. She had argued against Grant's plan, saying that it was suicide to return to the Minith ship.

Grant, knowing that Titan agreed with her, told the other

man, "It's the only way. We have to destroy the ship."

"I know that, Grant, but let us do it together, in force." Titan waved to the crowd gathered around them. They were well armed with the weapons Tane had brought and had been trained in their use. "We have an army to use."

"And we'll use it, Titan, I promise you. But we cannot fight them on their terms."

Grant did not want to get into the discussion again. They had already hashed this out and reached a decision. Fortunately, Titan did not press the subject again. He, like Grant, was probably tired of it.

"Very well, then," Titan sighed. "Good luck to you."

"Yeah, thanks. You too."

At a nod from Grant, Mouse started the carrier. The six-hundred year old soldier looked around the Square a final time at the army he had helped create and, with a wave to the men and women standing there, he entered the carrier and closed the hatch. Thirty seconds later, they lifted into the air above the prison.

Grant looked down. He saw Avery framed in the doorway to the First Square and waved. Either she did not see him or she was still angry, but she did not return his wave and he let the hand drop.

"Let's go, Mouse," he said and quickly turned his thinking towards what they had to do.

They traveled away from the prison barely ten feet off the ground and held that altitude until well away from the place. When the carrier was far enough away from the prison to prevent anyone who may have seen them from identifying the lone vehicle's point of origin, they rose to a normal altitude of a thousand feet and kept to it for nearly three hours. Then, when they neared their destination, they again dropped to a frighteningly low level and continued. A trip that could have been covered in just over an hour under top speed, took them almost five hours. The adrenalin they had felt upon leaving the prison, but that had waned during the flight, returned at full throttle when they finally touched down.

"Okay, folks," Grant pronounced, "this is where the fun starts. Everybody grab your pack and get out."

The group did as they were instructed and lined up outside the carrier. Most waited patiently for Grant to tell them what to do next. Several busied themselves with checking and rechecking their weapons and equipment, and Grant recognized the signs of nervousness. Most new troops entering their first combat situation acted this way. Some acted outwardly calm, others were nervously busy. All were uncomfortable.

He was not surprised by their reactions to the situation. Instead, he found the situation somehow soothing in its familiarity. He knew what was expected of him and did not hesitate. He gave no unnecessary commands, made no unnecessary speeches. He merely led.

"Tane, did you deliver the Council's orders like we discussed?"

"I did, Grant."

"And?"

"It went as well as you might expect. But there will be no problem. The orders will be followed." Grant wished he could be as confident as the scientist. A key part of their plan was in someone else's hands.

"Well, it can't be helped now. Take the craft and find a location a few miles away. Make sure it can't be seen from the air. Wait for us to signal you on the radio. When we do, we're probably going to be in a hurry, so be ready."

"Got it, Grant. I will be ready." They shook hands and Tane returned to the pilot's seat. A few minutes later, he and the carrier were traveling away. Ten feet off the ground.

"Mouse, take the rear. The rest of you, follow in single file. Don't get closer than five meters to the person ahead of you. And one more thing--" he said, hesitating to make sure everyone heard his next words clearly.

"Make as little noise as possible."

The men and women looked at each other knowingly. All were well aware of the Minith's superior hearing ability and their lives depended on not being heard. The implications were simple: they would be quiet, or they would die.

An hour later, Grant led them to a dry, narrow arroyo that he had spied on his previous hike to the Mothership. Though no more than ten feet across, the embankments on each side of the dry creek bed were almost six feet deep. The group scrambled down into the depression and, at a signal from Grant, sank quietly down.

Ahead of them, not a mile distant, sat the immense Minith ship. For most of them, this trip marked their first view of the ship, but for Grant, Mouse and Sue, it was a known, if not welcome, sight. Grant had briefed everyone earlier on what was expected of them when they reached this point and the group settled into the cover that the creek bed provided without a word. Unsure of how long they would be there, some tried to get comfortable. Most, however, were too wound up and Grant noticed with satisfaction that several were silently checking their weapons for any problems that might have occurred on the march. Grant crept to each of the others to provide assistance if needed. To everyone, he gave encouragement.

After making sure everyone else was in place and that no problems had arisen, Grant settled down also. He kept his pack on and, taking a seated position, leaned back against it. He looked toward the Minith ship, the top of the massive vehicle still visible from this distance and angle. Like the others, he wondered how long they would have to wait.

The waiting is the hardest part, Grant thought. He recalled the last mission with his team six hundred years ago. The one from which he had never returned. There was some similarity, he decided, looking around at the figures around him. Even after six hundred years, being a soldier still required a great deal of "hurry up and wait." They had hurried to reach this site and now they waited for a sign to hurry on to their next destination, the alien ship.

## CHAPTER TWENTY-THREE

Tap. Tap. Tap.

The interruption was unexpected and undesired. Zal had remained in his quarters since the receipt of Brun's message two days before. Other than an occasional message over the ship's communication system, Zal had talked to no one, seen no one, and entertained no one. It was not unusual for a commander to remain in seclusion during a wartime situation, and Zal chose to act as though he were at war with the humans. He had food, water, everything he needed in his plush commander's quarters and had no need or desire to leave. What few commands he had for his soldiers and guards were given electronically. His concentration was focused on the eradication of humans responsible for the rebellious acts that had been committed.

Occasionally, a thought or two was given to what he would tell Brun if the situation was not taken care of before his superior's arrival but, for the most part, he still held the firm belief that he would be successful. He was not concerned for the Minith position here on Earth, but for his own. To think that a weak race of beings like these humans could pose any serious harm was unrealistic. But to think that they could ruin his career with their rebellious acts was a very serious possibility. If he did not stomp them out, and soon, he would be replaced.

Zal let the visitor wait, as was his right as commander, and wished, not for the first time, that he could take care of the human problem in a manner he considered appropriate. But, although his Minith superiors would overlook a few slave deaths for the purpose of their troops' morale, they would not permit the scale of killing that needed to be done to teach these sheep a lesson. Soon after receipt of Brun's message announcing his visit, Zal received another message regarding the eradication of the human sub-farms. The message relayed the Minith Command's order that nothing was to be done which would interfere with the human's ability to meet their supply quotas. The message was sent as 'Priority Two', which meant it could be read by anyone on the ship. And it specifically mentioned protection of the human food supply and sub-farms. The spies on board had again managed to communicate Zal's activities.

The message effectively eliminated a course of action that would have ensured his success. Zal knew the humans would do anything to protect their farms. Now that leverage had been taken away by his superiors. He had to find another way to erase the putrid disease of discontent that currently tainted his human flock.

Having made him wait outside long enough, Zal bade his visitor entry. Lieutenant Treel entered his commander's room as quietly as he had approached it five minutes earlier and bowed. Zal nodded in recognition of his subordinate. He was pleased to see the other soldier's recognition of the proper protocols and hoped he had news of the human traitors.

"Speak."

"Sir, I have information regarding the slaves we seek."

Zal stepped closer to his lieutenant, eager for the news.

"Yes?"

"Sir, as you suggested, I ordered our human informants to be questioned regarding those who attacked us."

"And did they talk?" Zal's voice rose perceptibly with the excitement he felt. "What have you learned?" His eagerness for success overcame his need to appear uncaring in the presence of his subordinate.

Treel tactfully ignored his commander's professional slip and answered eagerly. "Sir. One of the humans came forth of his own volition. He has told us a very odd tale. But one which could explain how the humans have been able to act so far out of character."

"Ah? I would like to hear this 'odd tale' but first tell me what this human wanted for his information." Zal resisted the urge to hear the details of the human's information immediately. It would be unwise to show this lieutenant another sign of his concern over the human situation.

"Sir, the human requested very little for his knowledge."

At this revelation, Zal's leathered eyelids rose. Usually, humans who informed on their own kind wanted more of everything: more food, more clothing, a larger living space, human money. Of course, they never got everything they requested, but they were given enough to keep them coming back whenever they had information that they felt their masters would want to know. To find one who wanted little in return for something of such obvious importance was a curiosity indeed.

"What did he want?"

"Sir. He said... he said he wanted to return 'Peace' to his fellow humans."

A smile crossed Treel's face as he relayed this information to his commander. The human race's desire for 'Peace' was a well-worn joke among the Minith. Minith could not understand the concept, but none of them failed to be grateful for the foreign idea either. It made their conquest of this world infinitely simple.

"I see," Zal said, nodding. The concept of Peace was new to him but he recognized its unshakable hold upon these creatures. Until recently, he would have believed these humans incapable of resisting because of this concept, but something had occurred to change that, at least in a few of them.

"Tell me what this human told you."

"Sir, I... I took the liberty of bringing this human here. The story he tells is strange. There may be questions you have, and, excuse me for my presumptuousness, but there is also the Zone." The lieutenant bowed in deference to his commander's authority in the matter, but Zal did not rebuke him for his actions.

"No, Lieutenant, you have performed admirably. If this creature's story is as odd as you describe, the Zone may be the very thing we need to determine its validity."

"Thank you, sir." Treel relaxed visibly before asking, "Shall I bring the prisoner here, sir?"

"No, no," Zal said. He had already spent enough time in seclusion. He headed for the door, relieved to have a diversion from his thoughts and a focus for his anger. "We shall speak with this human in the Zone."

Treel followed his leader out the door and along the corridor. He remained a step behind and to the left of Zal and found he had to step quickly in order to keep up. They reached the Zone within minutes.

The human male was already there when they arrived. The first thing Zal noticed was the man's ample size for a human, and he said as much to Treel.

"Yes, sir," he answered in Minith. "He is apparently a human of some standing. He has no need of additional food as do many of our informants. Perhaps that is why he asked for so little in exchange for his story."

"Perhaps." The human's fear at the arrival of the two Minith was apparent, even to Zal who had little direct contact with the species. He switched to Earth Standard language.

"Speak, human. What is your name? And what can you tell me of the attacks on your masters?"

"My... my name is Mr. Blue." The human trembled, obviously frightened. He whispered words that Zal recognized a human Peace mantra.

"Speak, human!"

The fat man flinched, but began talking.

Ten minutes later, the Minith Minister of Earth knew about Tane Rolan's experiment, the six hundred year old soldier, and the efforts of the ancient soldier to train human recruits.

He also knew why this overlarge human wanted nothing in return for his information. He had been ordered by the Human Leadership Council to tell everything they knew about the rebel humans. Apparently, they had had enough killing of their population and were ready to concede. It was also apparent that they had no means of stopping the rebels themselves, and were coming to Zal for assistance in shutting down the rogue humans.

Zal asked only one question. "Where is this training being done, human?" Blue's enormous belly jiggled as he strained to catch the whispered words.

"They... they are preparing within the confines of Violent's Prison." He shrugged weakly then began to hyperventilate. His entire frame shook with each ragged breath he took.

Zal simply stared at the creature's display, unsure of what, if anything, to say to the man. The human was a slobbering coward as well as a traitor to his race. Instead of saying anything to the pitiful heap of spineless flesh, he addressed Lieutenant Treel in Minith.

"What do you make of this, Lieutenant?" The words were barely audible even to Treel. Mr. Blue was aware only of the look that passed between the immense monster and his equally sizable subordinate.

"Sir," Treel began without hesitation. He had obviously given the matter some thought since first hearing the human's story. "I disbelieve in the existence of this 'ancient soldier' which the human mentions. It is impossible for such an accomplishment, especially for this weak race of slaves. I do, however, feel there may be a soldier among them who possesses the capability to stand up against our superiority, and who may be influential enough to recruit others to his cause. Who knows what stories this human has concocted to further his cause among his own? Perhaps the slaves will follow him more readily if they believe him to be of an earlier era. As you know, sir, these humans were once a warring people."

Zal nodded at his lieutenant's words, but in fact had not known this bit of human history. It would have been counterproductive to show his lack of knowledge to his subordinate, however.

Treel continued, "It is my belief that a lone human may be attempting to recruit, train and lead other members of his weak race against us."

"Very good, Lieutenant," Zal conceded. "Anything else?"

Treel contemplated briefly, had a thought. He cleared his throat in the Minith way, and spoke his mind.

"Sir, it is my belief that humans possessing the courage we have witnessed can only come from one place on this world. This human's assertion that the human prison is the source is likely accurate." The lieutenant stopped speaking at the sign of Zal's raised fist.

Zal pondered his soldier's words carefully. The lieutenant had more time on planet than he but the studies he had undertaken upon his assignment as commander offered a single possibility.

"Of course," Zal said, more to himself than to his lieutenant. "It has to be at the human prison, does it not?" Zal's smile returned. There was no longer any doubt that he could take care of the human problem before Brun's arrival. He turned to the lieutenant.

"Ready all three Battle Groups. That should be more than enough force to eradicate a few unruly sheep. I want them at the human prison by tomorrow morning."

"It will be done, sir," the lieutenant said. He bowed to Zal and left the room with a purpose.

"Yes," Zal spoke as he left the room, the cowering human inside now forgotten. "I will show Brun how I deal with wild sheep." He smacked one of his leathered fists into his other palm. The sudden crack of noise was pleasing.

* * *

Inside the Zone, Blue's heavy form sank to the cold floor of the empty alien chamber and shivered. His stomach growled loudly and he began to cry. He had never felt so alone. He suddenly wished he had asked the aliens for something to eat before they had left him.

He did not know why the Leadership Council had asked him, of all people, to deliver this news to these aliens.

## CHAPTER TWENTY-FOUR

"Lieutenant Treel, you are in charge of the extermination."

It was apparent to Treel that his commander viewed his soldiers' mission as nothing more than an eradication of diseased vermin. Something that had to be done to reaffirm Minith dominance and, even more importantly, rescue his position as commander of that dominance. Treel cared nothing for Zal. And he knew the humans had to be removed. But he was not sure his current orders were the correct ones.

"Take no prisoners."

"I understand, sir. It will be done." Treel bowed in deference to his commander, but he still felt uneasy. Unsure of the plan. He took a deep breath, wrestling with the need to express the concerns he felt. His words, if received poorly, could mean his removal and execution. But his loyalty to his race was strong, and he could not ignore his judgment as a skilled warrior.

"Sir, do you think it wise to send our entire battle force? Surely, one third of the group is more than enough?"

Zal, in the middle of returning Treel's bow, froze for a fraction of a second, then completed the bow. Both knew the question questioned Zal's judgment, if not his authority. Treel felt the force of his commander's stare. Smelled the scent of danger wafting off his commander's skin.

"Lieutenant, I am well aware of our capabilities. I understand that your concerns are fueled by your selfless devotion to our success. However... I will hear no more objections. Is that understood?"

Treel bowed his head. He felt shame for having openly

questioned his superior. And anger at Zal for not listening to his concerns.

"Yes, sir." He bowed again.

"Very well," Zal said, ignoring Treel's second bow. "Success to you and your soldiers, Lieutenant."

Zal turned on his heel and left the ship's launching area.

Treel watched his commander leave then turned toward the soldiers under his command and shouted orders. Within minutes, a hundred armed soldiers, nearly the entire Minith force on Earth, were loaded onto the human-built carrier vehicles.

Treel thought about the nearly empty Mothership and was again struck by the poor judgment his commander displayed in leaving their base unprotected. As soon as the thought entered his head, however, he erased it and debased himself again for his lack of respect. Zal was commander. Besides, the ship still held a small force, capable of defending against a human attack. The animals might be rebelling, but they were still lacking in skill and weaponry. If anything happened, the forces on the ship should be sufficient. And they had orders to contact Treel and the carriers if anything unusual happened. With that final thought, Treel entered the lead carrier and closed the hatch.

"Onward," he commanded the pilot. The carrier lifted from the launch area and exited the ship. Five other carriers, transporting the remainder of his force, followed close behind.

\* \* \*

Sue saw the fleet of carriers and quickly pointed them out to Grant and the others. No one made a sound, but each tried their best to sink into the ground beneath them as the vehicles passed almost directly overhead. Grant kept sight of the carriers as they passed over and sighed with relief when they made no attempt to land or circle back. Their group was undetected.

He smiled when the carriers banked in the sky and headed in the direction of Violent's Prison. He nodded to the others in the group. They waited to allow any other carriers a chance to leave the ship and, when none did, the group left their temporary sanctuary and continued their silent journey toward the ship. Grant led the procession with Sue directly behind him. Then came the others with Mouse bringing up the rear.

\* \* \*

Avery stood next to Titan while he spoke with some of the soldiers of Violent's Prison. She caught only the occasional snatch of conversation as the man issued orders. Her thoughts wandered constantly to the Minith Mothership and Grant.

How was he? Had it begun? She found it difficult to concentrate on her surroundings and Titan must have guessed as much for he had stopped giving her tasks hours before. She felt badly about her inability to concentrate on the ongoing battle preparations but she could not help herself. Not that she could do much in the daylight, but she still felt like she was shirking her responsibilities. It was just a matter of time before the monsters arrived, she knew. And they would come prepared for battle.

Of all the men and women here at the Prison, she, more than anyone else, understood how the Minith acted and thought. She had lived with them long enough to understand how they would react to the uprising of their human charges. They would not be lenient with the people inside the stone walls of the prison.

One of the prisoner-soldiers interrupted her thoughts.

"Titan! Titan," the man shouted as he raced toward the group gathered around the large man. "They are coming! Davis has spotted several carriers approaching from the South!"

"Easy, man. Get back to your post and make sure that

the watchers keep their eyes open. We don't want to mistake carriers flown by men for those that will bring the enemy." The man stopped in his tracks. He had obviously not considered the possibility of humans approaching and turned to do as he was told.

Avery watched as Titan proceeded under the assumption that the carriers held Minith troopers and issued orders accordingly. Everyone was dispatched to man his or her post. With luck, the Minith expected this to be a simple operation and Avery knew that every possible step had been taken to maintain that belief for as long as possible.

"All right!" Titan yelled to the scampering men and women around him. They rushed to their places, their nervousness causing them to appear confused and frightened.

"Let's get it together! We fight for our world today!"

\* \* \*

Grant dropped suddenly to the ground. The others, having been trained in how to respond, did the same. Grant looked around and saw no one still standing in the waist high brush. He had hand picked each of them based on how well they had performed during their initial training and, so far, had not been disappointed with their performances.

He looked up and spotted the source of his concern. What had begun as a low hum soon became a roar as the strange craft dropped from the sky, not more than a mile behind them. The ship descended rapidly but slowed noticeably as it got closer to the ground. When it reached a height of a few hundred feet, the ship tipped sideways, its nose now pointed toward the Minith ship. The maneuver complete, it regained momentum and zipped speedily over their heads. Grant watched, amazed, as the craft flashed past and entered an open port in the

Mothership's near side. The entire passage, from the ship's initial appearance to its landing in the Mother Ship, had lasted no more than a few seconds.

Definitely not human.

Which meant the Minith had just received visitors from off world.

Grant silently cursed the timing. The craft and its passengers were an unexpected card in the game and Grant hoped the card was not an ace. If it delivered a fresh batch of alien recruits his small team could be in the midst of a suicide mission.

But that did not matter now. They were committed. There would be no turning back.

The group waited several minutes before continuing toward the ship. If they were quiet before the spacecraft's arrival, they were noiseless now. There is nothing like the sudden arrival of the unexpected to slap you back into reality, Grant thought.

\* \* \*

Lieutenant Treel ordered the Minith battle force to fly once around the prison. Unlike many of his kind, he was not one for rushing into a situation blindly. The effort was wasted, however, as nothing out of the ordinary could be seen. There was some activity inside the prison's walls but that was to be expected. Treel pondered his next move and elected a direct approach. His previous encounters with humans had shown him that, as a rule, they were a cowardly bunch, unable or unwilling to defend themselves against trained soldiers. Even if the humans inside the stone walls below were willing to fight, they would be unarmed and not very well trained. It would be a slaughter, and one he looked forward to. A quick scan of the soldiers in his carrier showed that they, too, were anxious for the upcoming events.

"Forces, ready!" Treel received acknowledgement from the other carriers, then ordered his pilot into the vacant area of the Inner Square.

The plan called for them to kill all of the humans in the prison. Starting with the smallest, inner square made tactical sense. It would be a simple matter to clear the square and, once cleared of the human vermin, would provide them a defensible base from which to begin clearing the larger, outer squares. One at a time. The sheep would have nowhere to flee except to the outer squares.

"Forces, deploy!"

The carriers swept down in pairs. The Minith soldiers in the first group exited the vehicles in a tight defensive formation and set up a perimeter. Once in position, the other carriers quickly followed them and, within minutes, Lieutenant Treel and the Minith force were deployed to the inner courtyard. The walls of the Inner Square of Violent's Prison surrounded them.

"Forces, report." Treel received negative contact reports from his eight subordinate officers. Each officer led a team of ten soldiers, as did he. Each reported the same thing. No humans encountered or observed.

"Forces, forward." Treel ordered his soldiers to move out. They complied at once, heading for the four doorways that led into the stone building of the First Square.

\* \* \*

Unseen or heard by the Minith, Davis, the lookout hidden atop the building of the First Square, reported the arrival of the aliens back to Titan.

Titan, upon hearing of the size of the Minith force, smiled. If Avery's estimate was correct, then the entire alien combat force on Earth had been delivered into his hands. Just as Grant had predicted. He keyed the communication device at his side and relayed that information to Tane. He got the appropriate response and knew that Grant would soon know that the first step in his plan had worked to perfection.

## CHAPTER TWENTY-FIVE

Brun's arrival a full day ahead of his announced schedule was an unpleasant interruption. Zal chafed at being bothered now, when the human situation was not yet under control. The attack on the human prison was just getting underway. Worse than the interruption it caused, the early arrival revealed how little faith his superiors had in his abilities.

Zal struggled to restrain his anger as he rushed to the launch area. Other than the scheduled flights to ferry troops on and off Earth once every four months, the launch area was never used. The reliance on human vehicles for on world transportation left this part of the ship vacant most of the time. This was good. It meant none of the few remaining troops should be in the area. He needed to intercept Brun before he had a chance to talk with any of the crew. He did not want Brun's spies spreading false rumors or planting seeds of doubt. But mostly, he wanted to deliver the news of the humans' pending defeat personally.

He nearly collided with Brun as he turned into the final corridor leading to the launch area. Brun was accompanied by three soldiers and all were well armed. Zal took notice of this with some discomfort and wondered briefly if they were there to apprehend him. If so, he would not go willingly.

"General Brun, I am honored by your visit." Zal wanted desperately to ask his superior why he had chosen to arrive early but suppressed the urge. It would be unwise to question the actions of his commander, even though Zal considered him a bumbling fool.

"Yes, Zal, yes." Never one to avoid a subject, Brun got right to the point of why he had returned to Earth.

"How is the problem coming? Have we taken care of our unruly flock?"

Zal rankled at the 'we' part of Brun's question. The leathered bastard had done nothing to take care of the rebellious slaves and the insinuation that he could take any credit for what would certainly be accomplished chafed. He allowed none of his displeasure to show however and answered.

"Yes, Commander. The sheep are being sheared as we speak. Lieutenant Treel has been dispatched to exterminate the rebellious few."

Brun tipped his head and looked carefully at Zal. "Tell me, Zal. What is happening?"

"In summation, Commander, I learned that the humans were sowing their seeds of rebellion from inside their human prison. The prison where they send those who actually show some courage." Although still rankled by Brun's recent attempt to accept undue credit for his successes, Zal gave no second thought to taking credit for Treel's accomplishment of identifying Violent's Prison as the haven of human rebellion.

"Our combat forces departed not three hours ago to destroy the human slaves located there."

"The human prison? Surely the trouble makers cannot be located there, Zal. If these humans are good at anything, it is locking away those few who might dare to stand up against us. Are you certain of your information?"

"Positive, Commander. One of their own came forward with the information. He said he only wanted peace returned to his race." The word 'peace' passed from Zal's mouth like a piece of rotten carcass. His distaste for the foreign concept was clear.

"You idiot, how long have you been here on Earth?" Brun's voice took the tone of an angry stepmother scolding a much-hated child. Zal flinched slightly at the reproach, unsure of his mistake but sure of his need to answer his superior at once.

"Only a few months... you trained me, Commander."

"I know that, you fool! Did you learn nothing?" Brun raged at the Minith Minister of Earth and the three guards standing behind him looked at each other in confusion. None of the three was more confused than Zal, though and he said as much.

"Zal, humans are sent to the prison for life! Once inside, they remain there until they die. The only ones who ever leave there are those that we take for our slaves on this ship!"

"I still don't see--"

"Are you truly stupid?" Brun stepped close to Zal, their faces separated by inches. "How can these prisoners attack us if they are incarcerated? That could not happen unless..." Brun ceased his ranting as quickly as he had begun. "Have you questioned the human Leadership Council?"

"No, commander," Zal offered. His thoughts went to the recent raid upon their chambers. "But we have paid them a visit. They were warned against any rebellion! They could not have condoned the actions that have been taken against us."

Now it was Zal who fell back into an explanation of how their human slaves behaved. "They are sworn to uphold the concepts of 'Peace.' Never have they gone against their beliefs in this area. To do so would mean that they support the rebellion, encourage it even."

"Yes," Brun answered, thinking. "It would. Perhaps we were wrong to allow this human council a free hand. We have always stayed out of their activities as long as the quotas were met. Perhaps they have finally become tired of the slave's life."

Zal heard his commander's words and recognized them as being his own wish. He did not say that, however.

"Is this possible?"

"It is unlikely. These humans have proven themselves to be weak. Unwilling, unable even, to fight against us. You saw it yourself at the human farm when you first arrived." Zal recalled how Brun killed the human family while the father refused to act.

"But one thing is certain," Brun vowed to his subordinate. "We will not permit a successful rebellion. This planet will be destroyed first."

"Of course, Brun. But that should not be necessary. When we have destroyed the human prison, we will visit the human leaders again. They will know the price that must be paid for standing against their masters."

"You should hope so, Zal. As Minister of this planet, it will be your responsibility to accomplish its destruction. Personally."

Zal understood what would be expected of him and immediately dismissed the possibility.

\* \* \*

Treel ordered all nine teams to proceed. The darkness inside the stone building was complete and his troops advanced slowly, carefully. All ears were tuned for the slightest noise in the eerie blackness, but they heard little. An occasional thump or shuffle, but nothing that would indicate the presence of the humans for which they searched.

Treel had studied maps of the human prison and knew its layout well. All nine teams were inside the stone building of the Second Square. They had crossed through the inner, First Square building and the open area between it and the second building in under ten minutes.

So far, they had seen none of the slaves and Treel suspected the humans had been alerted to their presence and had retreated to the fifth, outermost square. He liked the thought of the humans retreating before them and felt the faint stirrings of pleasure that came to him with each battle. The humans were not fighters but their blood smelled just as sweet as any other animal's. Many Minith warriors were driven in battle by the cries of their prey; some enjoyed the fear of their opponents. But for Treel, there was no greater pleasure on any world he had ever visited – and there were many – like the smell of fresh blood.

The darkness gave way to light as Treel and the three teams he now led reached the East-facing doorway that led into the open space between the Second and Third Square buildings. The other six teams were divided into groups of two teams each, with each group assigned to take either the North-, South- or West-facing doorways. Treel ordered his soldiers to wait inside the doorway while he contacted the other three groups.

When he received news that all were in place, he considered the next move. He still felt that the slaves were cowering in the further areas of the prison but he could not ignore the possibility that he was being led into a trap. Their force was divided and the further they entered the prison, the more separated they would become. Already it would be difficult to reach any of the other groups if they were attacked.

"Treel, why are we waiting?" Lieutenant Groft, another of the team leaders expressed his impatience. Treel considered reprimanding Groft for his impertinence but realized that the other lieutenant was speaking for the group. A quick glance at the leathered faces around him showed Treel that they were all anxious for the killing to begin.

Treel took a breath and conceded that he was being overly cautious – not a good trait for a Minith leader who wanted to remain a leader. Groft would no doubt enjoy taking over should Treel show bad judgment and, as a lieutenant also, would be well within his bounds to do so. All it would take was for a majority of the soldiers to agree that the move was necessary to accomplish their mission. Treel did not plan to

allow that to happen.
> He reached for the radio.
> "Forces, forward," he ordered.

\* \* \*

Titan looked down on the Minith soldiers with mixed feelings of excitement and anger. The excitement came from knowing that, in just a few seconds, the foul beings below him would meet up with the wrong end of human vengeance.

The anger was more complex. He hated the aliens with every fiber of his being. These aliens had enslaved his world and his race. They controlled the world with threats of death, and demanded that its population labor to meet their quotas for resources and wealth. Resources that they stole and sent to another planet. But it was more than just the slavery. It was the needless killing of a race not able to defend itself that most angered Titan. They killed for sport. They killed out of boredom. They killed to send a message: do what we want or more of you will be killed. Yes, his anger was justified and so was the violence that would soon follow.

From a very young age, Titan knew he was different from those around him. Unlike most of his race, he did not abhor violence. He did not turn away from intentional slights or blatant injustices just for the purpose of Peace. When he saw a wrong, he wanted to right it. If that meant someone needed to get hurt, so be it. As a young child, there were few children his age in the sub-farm where his family worked. As a result, he often tagged along behind his brother, Stefan, and Stefan's group of six or seven friends when he could. He never played their games or joined their conversations; the five years that separated them made him a barely tolerated irritant to the older boys. But he did not need to actively participate in their activities; he was content to just be around Stefan.

He was five when one of his bother's friends, an eleven year old named Jerald, started complaining to Stefan.

"He's always hanging around Stefan. How are we going to have any fun with your baby brother hanging around?"

At first, Stefan just shook his head and ignored Jerald. But as the weeks went by, and Jerald's complaints increased, others in the group began parroting Jerald's demands. Eventually, Stefan had no choice. He gave in to the pressure from the group and told Titan to stop following them. Even at his young age, Titan understood. And he complied.

It was a week after being told to keep his distance when he came across the group of boys, playing in one of the apple orchards that were part of their sub-farm. Titan had no idea his brother's group was going to be there. He had just wanted an apple. He entered the orchard, plucked an apple from the closest tree and was turning to leave when Jerald stepped in front of him.

"I thought you weren't going to follow us any more?"

Titan looked up at Jerald, unsure of what to say. He hadn't been following them, he just wanted an apple. He looked to Stefan for assistance, but his brother stood off to one side, looking at the ground.

"Well? What are you doing here?"

"Just wanted an apple."

"Well, these are our apples and you can't have any." Jerald snatched the apple from the younger boy's hand. Wiped it on his shirt and took a bite.

Stefan's explanation to their parents that evening described the scene accurately. Jerald's bloody nose and two black eyes were a result of his younger brother standing up for himself. The circumstances, however, did not mitigate the consequences. Titan was subjected to psychological re-training for the first time. It wasn't the last.

Titan had performed well in the beat or be beaten

environment that existed within these squares of stone. Despite the rumors to the contrary, he wasn't a monster. He didn't start out looking to mete out violence. He just believed that violence was sometimes necessary and he was not averse to using it.

He viewed this situation in the same light. These alien monsters had his world in chains and he had been called upon to do away with them. The monsters thirty feet below him certainly deserved whatever punishment they received. *And they will receive a lot*, Titan thought as the aliens neared the center of the open area between the Second and Third Square buildings.

The trap had been set up exactly as planned by Grant. When the Minith landed inside the Inner Square, Titan and his soldiers had ascended to the tops of the four inner squares and remained still. The plan called for the men and women of the prison to wait quietly for the alien force to move between the Second and Third Squares and then attack. Unlike the aliens below, Titan had a clear view of all of his own forces. From the top of the Second Square, he could see the tops of the other squares as well as the people stationed on them. The attack would be concentrated between the square he occupied and the third, but reserves had been placed on the First and Fourth Squares in case some of the aliens below escaped the initial trap and tried to escape.

Grant had used the phrase 'like shooting fish in a barrel' but Titan had not understood what he had meant. Now, as the aliens made their way across the clearing, Titan understood clearly. The Minith soldiers, although well trained and heavily armed, had little hope. There was no cover for them to take once the battle began.

Titan held up a hand, the signal to get ready, to the men and women on his right and left. He looked across the open space to the top of the Third Square to make sure the soldiers stationed there saw him also. He hoped no one would jump the signal because of nerves, the alien soldiers needed to reach the center of the open space for the trap to be fully effective. Titan held his breath and waited with his hand still held high.

"Just a few more steps," he whispered to himself.

*   *   *

Treel stopped and dropped to one knee. The Minith soldiers behind him did likewise. Unsure if his ears were playing tricks on him, Treel searched the doorway of the next building for signs of human presence. His senses were heightened by the totally unexpected nature of the situation. They had searched nearly half of the human prison without any sign of humans.

"Groft," Treel muttered softly, so that only the Minith around him could hear. "Did you hear anything just now?"

Lieutenant Groft cocked his head, listening for the faintest of sounds. He thought he had heard something, but it was very brief and he could not be certain. He said as much to Treel.

Treel, wary now, searched the doorway that they had just left but saw nothing there. Almost as an afterthought, Treel looked up at the top of the building they had just left and, shocked, saw a human with his arm in the air. Treel keyed his radio as the man's arm flashed downward.

"Forces, back!" Treel shouted as the first shot rang out.

Titan fired his weapon before his arm completed its downward motion and felt satisfaction as his bullet struck one of the large, green aliens below. The elation he felt at shooting one of the Minith quickly erased the initial concern he had felt when one of them had spotted him. The aliens had not quite reached the center of the open space, but they were still vulnerable enough to the hail of fire that was rained upon them. Between shots, Titan took note of the alien soldiers dropping at an incredible rate. Now, only a few seconds after the trap had been sprung, over half the alien force was down. The rest were trying to make it back to the Second Square building while firing an occasional, wild shot at the human soldiers on the building.

The sound of the explosive rounds being fired from the tops of two buildings was a deafening shock to his system. Titan had no idea that war sounded so thunderous, but it helped to confuse the aliens below. The smoke and the smell from the rounds also hung in the air and added to the surreal sense of chaos that he observed.

It was over quickly and the shooting slowed to a trickle. Stopped completely as no further targets presented themselves.

Only three of the aliens below Titan made it to the relative safety of the Second Square building. The rest lay in the space below, dead or dying. So much carnage. The ground was covered with the purple, alien blood.

"All right," Titan yelled across the space to the men and women on the Third Square. "Keep them pinned! Don't let them come back out of that door!" He got an acknowledging wave and several whoops and shouts of triumph in return.

"The rest of you," Titan ordered to those men and women around him, "back to the other side of the square. We cannot let them reach the carriers at the Inner Square."

Titan checked with Pound and the other three group leaders on the Second Square. Pound's group and one of the others had allowed none of the aliens to escape. Only four aliens from the fourth doorway found their way back into the building. In all, of the hundred or so aliens who had entered Violent's Prison, only seven remained.

*And they cannot last inside the confines of this building forever*, Titan mused.

"Pound!" Titan called to the former leader of the Outer Square. "You are in charge, now. Do you know what to do?"

Titan knew Pound was capable of rooting out the remaining alien soldiers and eliminating them.

"What? Of course, but where are you going?"

Titan smiled and turned toward the Inner Square.. "I'm going to see if our friend Grant needs help."

"Titan!" The unexpected voice caught the giant man by surprise and he turned to face its owner.

"What are you doing here?" he asked.

"I asked Pound if I could come," Avery answered defiantly. She acted as if she expected Titan to argue. He knew her well enough to steer clear of that mistake.

"Very well," he answered. Titan knew what she wanted now and was not about to permit it. "But you are not going with me to the Minith ship."

"But, Titan, I can---"

"No," he said simply but with an authority that Avery recognized as unshakable. "You will stay here."

Her shoulders sagged but she quickly gathered herself. "Very well then. But do one thing for me."

Titan raised his eyebrows, slightly amused that she had accepted his refusal so readily.

"Certainly, what is it?"

She reached out, grabbed his hand, and squeezed tightly. "Do not allow anything to happen to Grant. Make sure he comes back to me."

Titan knew he could not make such a promise and expect to keep it. He was new to the machinations of war but not so new to its concept that he could expect to save a man like Grant Justice if the winds of fate that blew across the battlefield chose to take him. He knew it was impossible to guarantee any man's safety on a battlefield.

But he made the promise anyway.

Fifteen minutes later, he and two carriers of the prisoner's soldiers were on their way to the Minith ship. Unlike Grant and his flight, Titan wasted no time attempting to conceal their origin or destination.

## CHAPTER TWENTY-SIX

"Now what, Grant," Mouse asked.

They entered the ship through the launch bay and stood next to the Minith spacecraft they had seen entering the larger ship an hour before. The entry port had been left open, probably to permit the craft's speedy departure, or in expectation of the return of the carrier vehicles that had been sent to the prison. Whatever the reason, Grant accepted the good fortune with a disbelieving shake of the head. It seemed as though these creatures would never learn to lock all of their doors. The outer portals had been secured against another entry into the ship, but the large portal had been left wide open.

"First, we go to the Zone. Then we find the heart of the ship – the command and control room."

Grant took the map that Avery had made for them out of his pack and spread it on the polished metallic floor of the launching area. It took a few seconds for Grant to align it with their current position but Avery's blind drawings were very good and he quickly had their position identified. He referred to the drawing several times while comparing it to what he could see of the ship from where they were. Within moments, he had their path through the alien ship planned and everyone was briefed.

"Okay, follow close," Grant said as he folded the map and returned it to his pack.

"I don't know who or what we'll run into, but keep your eyes open and make as little noise as possible. We made it past the outer sensors, now we have to make it past their own ears and eyes." He checked his weapon and moved the firing selector button from the 'safe' position. The others did the same.

"Keep close and be careful. We don't want any of our folks getting killed. Just the other assholes." Grant made eye contact with every member of the party. "Any questions?"

No one had any and they began their journey deeper into the alien ship.

\* \* \*

Lieutenant Treel leaned against the wall. He placed a hand against his shoulder to stem the flow of purple blood that seeped from the hole the human weapon had created. The pressure against the wound had an immediate effect and the seeping flow slowed to a mere trickle. He looked around the dark interior of the building and made out the shapes of only two of his comrades.

The humans had led them into a trap!

*No*, he amended. *I led us into a trap.*

The flow of blood soon stopped and within minutes the wound closed entirely. Having taken care of himself, he crawled over to the doorway and peered outside. The act nearly cost him his life as one of the humans on the opposite roof put a bullet into the doorframe not ten inches from his head. He jerked back into the darkened building but not before he saw his soldiers lying in the clearing outside. Several were moving but shots were being taken and Treel knew they would not be moving for long. He confirmed this with another look from well within the protection of the doorway.

He could do nothing for those outside and turned his attention to the two Minith inside the building with him. Groft and one of the newer soldiers were lying unmoving and a quick check by Treel found Groft barely alive, though not for much longer, he guessed. The other trooper was already dead from a severe stomach wound and Treel wondered how the soldier had made it back into the building.

"Groft, can you hear me?" Treel knelt beside the other soldier and noticed the wounds that stitched the length of his left side. The body fought to stop the bleeding and close the wounds but Treel knew it would not react in time.

"Groft?" Groft opened his eyes and looked weakly at Treel.

"You... you were... right, Treel. We... should have..."

Groft had no time to finish his sentence. His body gave up its last hold on life. Treel moved away from his fallen comrades and shook his head. They had seriously underestimated these humans. They were not sheep at all. To use an old human saying, they were wolves in sheep's clothing.

Treel considered his next moves carefully. Retreat to the carriers was his only hope for returning to the ship, but that possibility seemed remote at best. If these humans were intelligent enough to plan such a trap, they would not have left an escape open. He wondered if any of the other three groups had been attacked and a quick check of the radio brought him nothing but silence.

"Damn!" Unwilling to sit still and be hunted down, he checked his weapon and began to move through the building toward the other doors. It was possible that some of the others had been spared. He hurried, certain that the humans would not permit him to live long now that they had him trapped inside.

An hour later, he neared the last of the four doorways and approached the dimly lit area with caution. Checks of the other doors had revealed only the sprawled corpses of Minith soldiers in the open area between the second and third buildings. None of those soldiers had made it back to the doorway and he began to consider what his chances for survival would have been if he had not seen the human before the firing had begun. This final doorway was his only hope to find some of his comrades alive.

As if in answer to his hopes, he saw a movement ahead

and recognized the unmistakable uniform of the Minith Earth Forces.

"Troopers!" he blurted, no longer feeling alone. He rushed forward to greet his fellow soldiers.

He was brought up short by a sound behind him and he turned to face the noise. Treel saw a brief glint of steel before a white light exploded and he crumpled to the ground.

\* \* \*

"Damn, did you have to hit him so hard?" Pound cried. "I told you I wanted him alive!"

"Uh, sorry," the man answered lamely. "I was a little nervous. I've never been this close to a live one before, you know?"

"Well, hell. No damage done, I guess. He's alive," Pound said after checking the large monster. There was a large purple stain of the alien's blood on his uniform but Pound found no indication of a wound.

"Here, help me tie him up. You," he shouted to another of the human soldiers hiding in the darkness of the building. "Go fetch Avery. We'll need her to talk to this thing."

The boy, who was probably no older than sixteen or seventeen, Pound guessed, nodded and rushed out to find her.

"This is the last of them," Pound announced to no one in particular. "All the rest are dead."

It took four men to carry the unconscious beast toward the Inner Square. They had to step over four alien bodies lying inside the doorway as they made their way out. The four had been killed by Pound and his soldiers almost an hour before, trying to make it back to the Inner Square and the carrier vehicles there.

\* \* \*

Brun and Zal were in the ship's command center. The large room doubled as the ship's bridge when in space. They waited for news of the raid on the human prison.

While they waited, Zal relayed the human traitor's tale of the six hundred year old soldier and Brun listened with much interest. He knew the humans were extremely advanced in some areas of the physical sciences but this degree of advancement was thoroughly impossible, he agreed.

"I have to agree with you, Zal. It seems impossible that the humans could have accomplished such a feat." He picked at the dry skin on his fingers while he talked. The layers of dried, green flesh came off in thin sheets that he dropped to the floor.

"Still, I would enjoy speaking with this human. It might help pass time while we wait for Lieutenant... Tril, was it?"

"Lieutenant Treel, sir," Zal corrected. "I can have the prisoner brought here if you wish. Perhaps one of your personal guards would be so kind?"

"Ah, yes. I almost forgot. All but a handful of your soldiers are at the prison." It was a mild rebuke. His way of telling Zal that leaving the ship virtually unprotected was most unwise.

Zal ignored the admonishment. He would have the last word once his forces destroyed the human resistance.

"Certainly, you may order Corporal Drant, there, to retrieve the slave."

Drant, upon hearing his summons, bowed to both Zal and Brun.

"The human is in the Zone, Drant," Zal directed the underling. The corporal bowed again and left the room.

\* \* \*

With the assistance of Avery's map, Grant went about the business of relocating the Zone. Although he had been there before, the layout of the ship would easily have had him lost without the map. It was laid out in a circular pattern, much like the square pattern of Violent's Prison. Instead of stone walls separated by open spaces, the ship consisted of rooms laid out in six concentric circles. Separating the circles of rooms were equally concentric corridors approximately ten feet wide. These circular corridors were broken up by six straight hallways that began at the ship's center and continued to the outermost circle of rooms. To Grant, the map of the ship resembled a series of six giant wheels, each smaller than the one surrounding it, connected by six large spokes.

After one false turn that was quickly corrected, Grant found the Zone. He opened the door quickly and entered it with his weapon held high. There were no Minith present but there was one human and Grant walked over to where he lay sleeping on the same table where Avery had been restrained only days before.

"Blue," Grant prodded the sleeping man with his toe. "Get up." The obese administrator opened his eyes. When he saw that it was Grant who had disturbed his rest, he sat up as quickly as his overweight body would allow.

"Well, it certainly took you long enough!" Blue reprimanded. "The beasts damn near killed me with their torture!"

Grant looked the man over carefully with trained eyes and detected no signs of torture or rough treatment.

"I'll have Rolan's job for this maltreatment," he ranted.

Grant rolled his eyes at Blue's huffy manner.

"I should have refused the Council's request. I mean, a man of my stature being degraded at the hands of these monster!

It's... it's preposterous!"

Grant had heard enough.

"It was an order from the Leadership Council, not a request, Blue. And if you don't be quiet, I'll treat you twice as rough as the Minith did."

"Well, I... I mean... how could you even think of harming me? Who do you think you are?"

Grant took Blue's arm and gave a small but firm squeeze.

"I'll tell you who I think I am, Blue. I'm the man that's going to try and save your ass! If you don't shut your mouth, I may have to reconsider."

He released Blue's arm and the man massaged it gently. He kept his mouth shut, though, and Grant nodded his approval.

"Very good, Blue. It's nice to know that a man of such stature can be intelligent as well."

Blue swallowed a reply and looked at the ground. He was not happy but Grant had no time to care.

Grant dropped his pack to the ground and took out the map once again. This time, he plotted the quickest path to the command center. The room was directly in the center of the ship and any of the spoke corridors would lead them to it.

He put the map back and told everyone, "All right. It's show time. So far we've been fortunate in not meeting any Minith soldiers but you can bet your ass there will be at least a few where we're headed now."

"We? What do you mean we?" Blue asked incredulously. "I'm no soldier. I'll wait for you here."

A quick glare shut the man up, but Grant knew the man could not keep quiet for long. It was not in his nature to do so.

"Do you want to stay here? Fine. But I'm not sure if we'll have time to pick you up on our way out."

Grant turned his back on Blue to let him soak in that thought for a while. Maybe a dose of fear would bring him to his senses.

"The rest of you get ready to move out."

"Hey, Grant." Mouse said matter of factly from the doorway. He had been keeping watch on the corridor and Grant had a sinking feeling he knew what the man was going to say.

"Yeah, Mouse? Don't tell me we have company."

"You guessed it, boss. One soldier, wearing a side arm. I think he heard us, but he doesn't seem to be concerned."

"Yeah, well good for us and bad for him," Grant said to Mouse, switching to his native Afc'n language. He did not want to tip their hand by speaking Earth Standard. Not many of the Minith knew the language but there was always that chance.

He motioned for everyone else to be silent.

"What's he doing?"

"He's heading this way. Listening to what we're saying but he doesn't understand." Mouse, speaking in his own native tongue, looked directly at Grant and smiled. "If he did, he wouldn't be acting so nonchalant."

"Probably thinks we're just a couple of the ship's slaves."

"What do we do?" Mouse raised his rifle slightly but Grant shook his head.

"No. We have to take him out quietly if we can. We don't want to alert the rest of the ship if we can help it."

Mouse nodded and quickly removed a knife from his right boot. Sue, not understanding what Grant nor Mouse was saying but certain of what the knife meant, took out her own knife and stood on the opposite side of the door. Blue, realizing what the two at the door were planning, gasped in horror. Grant saw Blue's reaction but did not act quickly enough to stop the man from alerting the Minith soldier.

"No! You can't kill him! He may be Minith, but you cannot commit violence upon him."

The shout itself would have been enough to alert the approaching soldier, but Blue yelled in Earth Standard.

"Shit, he's drawing his weapon!" Mouse yelled.

Grant dropped his pack and raced for the door. He entered the corridor and turned directly for the alien soldier who did indeed have his weapon drawn. Grant covered the ten feet between himself and the Minith in seconds but the Minith had plenty of time to fire his weapon and he did so just as Grant left his feet to deliver a kick to the monster's chest. The blast from the alien gun seared a streak along the left side of Grant's face. Grant's right foot struck the alien square in the chest and knocked him down.

If the alien had been human, he would have had a broken sternum floating around in his chest. As it was, the alien simply crumpled under the blow and lay unconscious in the middle of the corridor.

The Minith soldier had been stopped before he had a chance to hurt anyone but the damage was done, Grant knew. Though not as loud as a human weapon, the blast from the Minith's weapon had to have alerted the ship's crew.

"Everyone get ready!" Grant shouted, no longer worried about maintaining silence. The element of surprise was taken away. Now speed had to rule their movements. "We have to move. To the command center. NOW!"

\* \* \*

The human voice resounded around the command center. One of the crew had opened a communication line into the Zone when he heard the weapon discharge just moments before.

"Humans! They're inside the ship!"

"It's probably just one of our slaves, Brun!" Zal insisted illogically. He raged at the thought that a human would dare to enter a Minith ship without permission.

"Get a grip, Zal. Denial is not called for in this situation!" Brun openly chastised Zal in front of his subordinates.

"Your actions have been bordering on incompetence for weeks now. It is fortunate that I had the foresight to leave Lieutenant Treel behind as my confident. Without the lieutenant's reports, Minith Command might still be ignorant of the situation here on Earth."

"Treel! He is the spy?"

Confusion and anger at having been deceived by someone he had trusted fought for dominance within Zal and anger won out. His fury made him more certain than ever about his plans. He would not be stopped by anyone. This was his command and he meant to keep it or die trying, he no longer cared which.

Brun obviously had other ideas. There were eight crew members staffing the command center and he pointed to three of them.

"You three, head toward the Zone. Stop the intruders. Tinag, Yat, guard the doorway!"

Zal stared in disbelief at what was transpiring in front of him. Brun had just ordered three of his men, as well as two of Brun's own personal guards, to fighting positions. His command was being stolen from him!

"You, on the communications console, what is your name?"

The Minith who had brought them the voices of the humans from the Zone turned toward Brun.

"Nial, sir."

"Nial, you have acted admirably. You are hereby promoted to the rank of sergeant."

"Thank you, sir."

"Do not thank me, sergeant. The promotion was earned.

Now, get me a communication line with the Minith War Council."

"The War Council? But why, Brun? This is nothing but a slight inconvenience! I can handle this, I assure you," Zal exploded. The Minith Minister of Earth advanced a step toward the general, his fists clenched.

Sergeant Nial hesitated but a moment before carrying out Brun's order.

"Zal, you are hereby relieved of your command. I will assume responsibility for this ship and this planet. As soon as the corridors are cleared of these human rodents, you will report to your quarters and remain there until directed to do otherwise."

Brun's words were crisp and precise. He obviously wanted Zal to understand them without question and without argument. His wishes were not granted, however.

"You will not do this, Brun! This is my command! These are my soldiers. And this is my ship!"

"Not anymore," Brun cited calmly. He turned his back to Zal in dismissal and addressed Nial. "Have you received a reply yet, Sergeant?"

"Still waiting, uh, sir," the sergeant stammered. The argument between two senior commanders seemed to be taking its toll on the young soldier. "It...It normally takes a few minutes, sir!"

"Very well, then. We shall wait." Brun was turning back toward Zal when the blast took him between the shoulders.

Purple blood splattered about the command center and Brun, former General of the Minith War Council, fell to the floor. None of those in the room doubted that he was dead.

The remaining soldiers stared in horror at Zal. He appeared calm except for the hand holding the weapon. It shook uncontrollably.

The soldiers stared at Zal, unsure of what to do for

several seconds. Nial broke the silence.

"I have the War Council on the line, sir."

Zal's hand stopped shaking at once and he looked toward the communication specialist.

"Inform them that Commander Brun has arrived safely and that the human situation is under control."

"Yes, sir," Sergeant Nial whispered.

## CHAPTER TWENTY-SEVEN

Grant took Blue and six of the prisoners down one of the corridors leading to the center of the ship. Mouse led the remaining seven, including Sue, down the next corridor. They agreed that assaulting the command center from two directions made the most sense, especially if there was going to be significant resistance. Grant's group reached the innermost corridor of the ship without incident and turned right toward their destination. The corridor at this point in the alien ship was curved and they could not see further than thirty meters or so ahead. This slowed them down since Grant did not welcome the idea of running blindly into a Minith ambush.

They did not encounter an ambush, but they did run into a team of three Minith soldiers. Except for Blue, the three aliens seemed more surprised to see the humans running at them than vice versa. Blue began to wail as soon as he spotted the approaching aliens. The noise he made distracted the aliens momentarily and Grant was able to take out the lead soldier before the alien giant could fire his weapon.

They were not so fortunate with the other two, however, and both got off shots. Two of Grant's men went down with holes burned through their torsos. Grant shoved Blue, who wailed even louder at the sight of the two men dying, to the ground. Grant wondered why he bothered but, despite his dislike for Blue, he couldn't just leave him unprotected.

The rest of the group hit the ground around them and got off shots at the alien soldiers. The two former 'masters' were quickly dispatched, but not before taking out another of Grant's recruits.

Grant checked the three fallen men. Nothing could be

done for them so he, Blue and the three remaining soldiers continued on. They heard firing before they reached the command center and Grant surmised that Mouse's contingent had reached the goal first. They stopped at the final turn and Grant peered quickly around the curve of the hallway.

He spied Mouse and his group assembled on the opposite side of the command center's open doorway. He also saw two large alien bodies sprawled in front of the door and watched as several blasts were released from inside the room. The firing was very effective at keeping Mouse and his soldiers away from the doorway.

Grant motioned for two of his group to remain in the corridor as rear guards. He did not want any alien soldiers coming up behind them while they were occupied with the command center. He whispered to Blue to stay with them. The large man nodded and slumped to the floor.

Grant and the remaining prisoner, a woman who had picked things up quickly in training, moved forward to link up with Mouse.

Mouse waved and smiled as Grant approached. The reaction from the rest of Mouse's group was mixed. Some nodded, a couple seemed to be crying, and one was seated on the ground, his head in his hands. The sight reminded Grant that these individuals – some of the most violent on the planet – were not warriors. For the most part, they were products of the Peaceful world to which they had been born.

He hoped they would hold up to finish the battle just ahead.

The blasts pouring from the command center slowed. Stopped. Grant wasn't sure if the aliens were conserving their weapons or waiting for the humans to make the next move.

In a low voice, Grant asked Mouse in Afc'n if he had placed a rear guard.

Mouse shook his head, but quickly corrected the

problem. One of the crying soldiers was dispatched to the task.

"Welcome to the party," Mouse jibed, then fired a wild volley of rounds into the room. He did not aim. Just jabbed the rifle into the doorway and pulled the trigger. Grant doubted he hit anything, but it would keep the Minith away from the door.

Another hot flash sizzled through the doorway in response, struck the opposite side of the corridor. The metal wall was darkened, blistered by the heat of successive blasts.

Grant just nodded. "We ran into a small problem. It's under control, though. You ready to do this?"

Mouse smiled. "Oh yeah."

Grant switched from Afc'n to Minith and addressed the aliens trapped inside the command center.

\* \* \*

"There is no way out. We demand your surrender," the human voice shouted from the corridor.

Zal glared disbelief at the open doorway, slammed his fist into a control panel.

*It's him!* Zal thought.

The Minith underlings looked to Zal. The stares were full of questions but Zal did not know what to do. He was staggered by the revelation. He *always* knew what to do.

The humans had them trapped. He did not know how many there were, but they were well armed. Well enough, at least. One thing was certain. Surrender was not an option. He would destroy the ship and the planet before surrendering to these weak slaves.

He quickly ran through his options and came up with the only one that offered any hope of his success.

"You three," Zal pointed to the remaining guards who

had arrived with Brun. They and their weapons had been key in keeping the humans from entering the command center.

"Rush the humans at the door. Kill them quickly."

The three soldiers looked at each other. Two stole furtive glances toward the fallen Brun. The purple stain around the body was large, but had stopped spreading. Zal wondered how they would react to the order and waited. They finally looked at him and he waved the weapon he had used to kill Brun. The gun, along with Zal's obvious willingness to use it, became a threat as real as the one posed by the humans.

Two of the soldiers received a curt nod from the third.

"Sergeant Nial," Zal addressed the communication specialist, certain to use the soldier's new rank. Like Brun, he wanted the trooper's unquestioning loyalty and readily offered that small token in return. "Prepare to lead them."

The soldier nodded, drew his weapon and joined the other three.

\* \* \*

Grant heard the exchange. Marveled at the stupidity of whoever gave them. The Minith soldiers had just been ordered to commit suicide.

"They're going to try to rush us!" Grant relayed the information to Mouse in Afc'n.

Mouse looked back with disbelief. Grant merely shrugged and instructed Mouse to take his team back to the corridor. It would provide cover for the group when the aliens rushed the doorway. He turned and signaled for the soldier with him to head back to their corridor.

"Bring 'em on, then." Mouse hefted his weapon and motioned for his team to retreat.

Grant, taking a chance that the Minith would need a few moments to prepare for their assault, quickly poked his head around the frame to see what was going on inside. In the fraction of a second that his head was exposed to their fire, Grant saw several of the large alien soldiers checking or drawing their weapons.

"I do believe they're coming."

He waited until Mouse's small force retreated to their corridor and dared another quick look inside. Grant nearly lost his face to a beam of heat from a Minith weapon. The aliens were making their way slowly toward the door.

Grant backed away from the door and took two grenades from his belt. He pulled the pins and rolled the grenades carefully.

One...

As planned, they stopped a foot away from the entrance to the command center. Grant sprinted down the hall.

Two...

He grabbed the woman and pulled her around the corner of the intersecting corridor. He hoped Mouse had seen his move and had the foresight to have his team take cover.

Three...

He heard the sizzle and felt the heat of the Minith weapons being fired behind him.

Four...

The explosion lifted him into the air. He had time to think that at least one of the aliens had been caught in the blast. Then he slammed cruelly into the hard metallic floor.

He tried to push himself up. His body refused, suddenly unable to inhale. His lungs strained to draw breath, were rewarded with ragged, empty gasps.

*I'm fucking dying!*
*Wind knocked out. You'll be fine.*
*No, I'm fucking dying!*

*Not dying!*
*I'm dying!*
*Not dying!*

It seemed like hours, but was really less than six seconds. Grant finally wrestled that first, sweet breath back into his lungs.

He pulled in a second full breath.

A third.

When the fourth breath arrived the emotional part of his brain finally began agreeing with the rational.

*I'm not dying!*

Grant pushed himself to his hands and knees.

He was nominally aware that Blue was sitting a few yards away and the rest of his small group was running past him toward the command center. He was fully aware of the ringing in his ears.

He shook his head and struggled to rise. The sounds of rifles firing came to him clearly, even through the ringing in his ears. The firing stopped after a few seconds. Grant regained his feet slowly and turned toward the control center. His slow steps turned into a jog.

He expected the others to be waiting outside of the doorway, still held at bay by the Minith soldiers inside. Instead, all he saw were several dead aliens and the corridor painted purple from a lot of Minith blood.

He jumped over the alien bodies and stopped outside the door to the command center. He touched the side of his face and felt the burned skin.

He dared a quick glance inside the room.

The glance showed Mouse, Sue and the rest of the prisoners from Violent's Prison. Their weapons were all pointed at a single alien figure. Stepping over another alien body, Grant joined them.

The single Minith solider stood in a large pool of blood. At his feet, and the reason for the stain, lay yet another dead alien.

In his hands, the alien held a strange device topped with a flashing purple light.

*It would be purple*, Grant thought.

"Grant," Mouse explained, "this ugly fucker says he's holding a bomb."

"Not just a bomb."

The alien's Earth Standard was very good but spoken in quiet tones. Grant strained to catch the words. "No, this is not just a bomb."

"Speak up, asshole. Not everyone here has pancakes for ears!"

Grant had no doubt that the alien held a very powerful device, but he was not about to give up control of the situation. So the fucker had a bomb? He might kill the few of them, but that still meant that they had won. This fight was over.

"Ah! You must be the leader of these sheep. Yes?" The Minith spoke louder but Grant still had to listen carefully.

"I don't think you consider us sheep, but it does paint a nice picture: We are the sheep who have devoured the wolves."

"Devoured? Really, human, I would hardly describe killing a few of my men as devouring us. We are a strong race, much stronger than your own. Besides, the bulk of my command should be returning soon. I should think you'd want to be gone when they arrive. A few armed humans are nothing compared to a trained Minith battle force."

The Minith's mouth turned upward and Grant had the impression the alien was attempting a human-like smile. He obviously felt as though he had the upper hand in this game of cat and mouse – or sheep and wolf – but Grant knew otherwise.

"I don't think your 'battle force' will be returning from Violent's Prison anytime soon."

Grant dropped his own bomb. Watched as it exploded in surprise upon the alien's face.

"Uh... I'm sorry. I don't know your name. You ugly bastards have names, don't you?"

"How did you know about that?" the alien exclaimed.

As Grant suspected, the alien had no idea that they knew about the Minith raid on the prison.

"We know, because we wanted you to send your forces to the prison. You don't think you could have figured that out for yourself, do you?"

Grant toyed with the Minith but was constantly aware of the device in the alien's hands.

"And I'm sorry. But I still don't know your name."

"My name is Zal! I am commander of the Minith forces here on Earth." The Minith answered in a tone that Grant took to be a shout. "Now, how did you know our plans?"

Grant turned to Sue who stood near the door.

"Bring Blue."

Sue returned a minute later. She had to push the overweight administrator from behind to get him into the room. The man's pallor resembled his name. He gagged as he stepped over the Minith bodies. He wiped the sweat from his brow with a shirtsleeve and sagged against a wall.

"He's not a very good specimen of a human," Grant offered Zal apologetically. "But he did okay when the chips were down."

"You mean he lied to us about Violent's Prison? Humans are not being trained there?"

A muscle in Zal's face began twitching and Grant wondered if the movement was involuntary, and if it was, did it indicate the same stress in a Minith, as it would have in a human?

"Oh, no, Zal." Grant assured the Minith. "Everything Blue told you was the truth. We thought you'd put him through the torture of the Zone so it had to be the truth." Grant raised his right hand. "And nothing but the truth. So help me God."

"What?" Zal was confused. "But what about that nonsense of a six hundred year old human? Clearly a falsehood."

Grant just shook his head and tapped himself on the chest.

"That's me. But, to be exact, I'm six hundred and thirty-four years old."

"I don't believe it! You lie."

"Look, you can believe what you want to believe. I'm not interested in trying to convince you." Grant pointed at the device in Zal's large paws. "I just want to know how we're going to resolve this situation."

Mouse lifted his weapon.

"Let me resolve it, Grant. It will only take a second and then we can be on our way."

Grant shook his head and signaled for Mouse to lower the gun. Mouse sighed, obviously not pleased.

Zal glanced down at the bomb. Grant had the feeling that the Minith soldier had temporarily forgotten about it. Now that he remembered, he seemed to gather strength from the blinking contraption.

"Oh. Well that is simple. You and your flock are going to leave this ship at once. Then I am going to leave the planet." Zal gave the gathered humans another parody of a smile. "That is what you want is it not? For the Minith to be gone so that you can rule yourselves?"

"Something like that, Zal. Something like that," Grant acknowledged with a thoughtful nod. "But you're not leaving this planet. Either you put down that bomb and surrender to us, or you go ahead and use it to blow us up. Your choice.

"But this ship is not going back to wherever it came from. That's unacceptable."

"It seems we have a problem then, human. You see, this bomb will not only destroy this ship." The Minith shook his head rapidly.

"No. This device will destroy the entire planet! Who do you think you are trying to bargain with, you lamb? This is not our first conquest. Nor will it be our last. You cannot win!"

The alien's words had an effect on Grant's soldiers. They murmured excitedly to each other, a couple even retreated a step. They had been watchfully silently before, resigned that they might give up their own lives in return for ridding the planet of the Minith. Now, the concern shifted.

"He's lying, Grant!" Mouse interjected. "That little thing? He would have a hard time blowing up this room with that. There's no way it can blow up the entire planet!"

Grant did not waste time explaining to Mouse that the device was probably just the detonation mechanism. Instead he considered the alien's revelation in silence. He had no reason to doubt the Minith's words. What was worse was that he did not feel the alien was bluffing. He quickly concluded that the bomb was probably built into the ship and that it most likely could do exactly what the alien said. Destroy the entire Earth.

"What if I killed you outright?"

Zal had that planned also. "This ship has been programmed to depart this planet in exactly," he consulted an odd looking object on the nearest control panel that Grant took for a time piece, "thirty-four minutes and eight seconds. So you see, even if you kill me, the ship will return on its own to Minith."

"You bastard," Mouse growled. He stepped by Grant and went for Zal but Grant put out a hand to stop him.

"It's your decision, human. You can leave this ship now and trust me when I say that none of my race will return... or you can pay the ultimate price for certain liberation."

The alien indicated the bomb he held, "Which will it be?"

"How do I know you won't activate the bomb when your ship is out of danger, Zal?"

"You won't. It is a matter of trust."

"I don't trust you at all." Grant aimed his pulse weapon at the alien and tightened his finger on the weapon's trigger.

"Then you'll just have to kill me and take your chances that I don't hit this switch when I fall," Zal said, indicating a toggle switch on the bomb. His thumb hovered above it precariously. "Even if I don't fall on the switch, there's no way you can stop the ship from taking off. It's well protected against any damage you could hope to inflict upon it. It's sabotage-proof."

Grant's mind raced. The firing of their weapons and the explosions from the grenades had done little more than blacken the walls of the ship and Grant had to concede that what Zal said about the ship was true. They would not be able to prevent the ship from leaving.

"Okay, Zal. Let me see if I have this right," Grant ventured. "I can let you and the ship leave without any interference... or I can try to kill you and hope you don't blow us all to hell in the process. But if I do kill you without setting off the device, then the ship will leave anyway?"

"I think that's an accurate description of what we have here, human. Leave the ship now and I will depart Earth. Kill me and, if I do not set off the device, the ship leaves anyway. Either way, it will arrive on Minith within a few months. What is your decision?"

"We don't have any choice but to trust him, Grant," Mr. Blue whined from behind Grant. "We have to let him go." Several of the men from the prison mumbled their agreement.

Not for the first time, Grant felt like hitting the administrator.

"Now there's an intelligent male human," Zal observed wryly. "And what do you say, my little lamb?"

Grant's face was blank as his mind worked. Mouse and the others watched him nervously.

"I say screw you, you ugly bastard.'"

The blast struck the alien's skull at a point directly between the eyes and exited, with a burst of purple and yellow gore, from the back of Zal's head.

Zal fell backwards.

The blinking device tumbled, end over end, from the alien's hands. It landed in the middle of the large purple pool with a resounding smack and slid across the slick floor. It came to rest, flashing button up, next to Grant's left boot. The entire group released their breaths.

Grant reached down to retrieve the bomb.

"Okay, everyone," he said as he checked the time on the ship's control panel. "This flight leaves in exactly thirty-two minutes and thirty-one seconds. Everyone not holding a ticket to the planet Minith is asked to please depart the vessel at this time."

The men and women looked at Grant and then at each other, unsure of what to do.

"How do I...which way is out?" Blue asked in a wavering voice and Grant felt that the man was not such a fool after all. Hell, the man had even played a very important part in their mission, Grant conceded. No one spoke and Blue, giving up on them for assistance, turned for the door intent on finding his own way out.

Grant turned and caught Sue's eye.

"Can you help Blue find the exit?" Sue nodded and left the command center at a run. Grant took the radio from his belt, and handed it to the woman soldier who had been with him in the corridor.

"Get Tane. Tell him we need those carriers here NOW! Tell him to land them as close to the ship as possible and get ready to accept passengers."

The woman took the radio and ran for an exit where she could get a signal. Grant was glad their plan had included coordinating for extra carriers to be on hand. They knew they would be evacuating the humans from the ship, but they had not known it would be an emergency evacuation. He just hoped they were close enough to arrive, get loaded, and be on their way before the Minith ship lifted off. He remembered the scorched ring of earth surrounding the ship. It would be close.

"The rest of you, search the ship quickly. There are humans here. Find them and get them outside. We don't have much time!"

Understanding settled among the group and they hustled to follow out their orders. Only Grant and Mouse remained in the Minith ship's command center.

"That was a hell of a gamble just to kill one alien, man. Shit, the ship's leaving anyway. You should have let him go with it." Mouse was obviously shaken over Grant's unnecessary gamble.

"You don't understand, Mouse. This ship is leaving in thirty minutes for the planet of Minith. If I allowed Zal to go with it, he would have brought back reinforcements and we would have been back to square one." Grant inspected the bomb as he talked. He cleaned the purple stains from it, unsure of how the blood might affect its operation.

"And what do you think is going to happen when this ship returns to Minith with no one alive on board? They're going to send their soldiers here anyway!"

"That's just it, Mouse. The ship won't arrive at Minith with no one on board."

He finished cleaning the blood from the bomb and set it down next to the Minith clock. It read twenty-eight minutes and forty-two seconds until lift off.

Grant looked at the large black man straight in the eye and grinned.

"I plan to be on it."

## CHAPTER TWENTY-EIGHT

The Minith ship was a beehive of activity as the two carriers swept downward. Titan watched men and women running from the alien vessel, while others milled about outside the ship uncertainly.

"What is going on?" He spoke to no one in particular. They knew as little as he did. He did not plan to remain in the dark, though.

"Land right in the middle of that group," he pointed.

As the carrier settled to the ground, Titan had a clearer view of what was happening. He recognized several of the soldiers that Grant had taken with him. They were helping other, unarmed persons out of the ship and through the sparse growth of grass and shrubs towards several waiting carriers. They were all leaving the Minith ship as quickly as they could. Titan watched the scene as he stepped from the carrier and realized that the unarmed men and women were blind.

They were the slaves the Minith had on the ship!

"You men," he ordered to the group who arrived with him from the prison, "help get these people out of the ship and into these carriers! And quickly!"

He was not sure why they had to hurry but took his cue from the panic he saw on the faces of the soldiers who had come with Grant. He hailed one of the soldiers who was assisting a blind woman from the ship.

"What's going on here? Where's Grant?"

The young soldier's urgency was evident but he stopped what he was doing and answered.

"We beat them!" he shouted. "We kicked their leather asses! But the ship's been programmed to take off! We only have a few minutes to get these people out of here!" Like Grant, Titan had also noticed the large circle of burnt earth surrounding the alien ship and understood what had caused it. No wonder these people were hurrying to get away from the ship!

"Put them aboard these carriers!" Titan ordered the young man. The soldier looked at the vehicle as if seeing it for the first time. He nodded in understanding and yelled for the others to quickly load the carriers.

Titan turned to the pilot and gave him his instructions. He went to the second carrier and did the same.

"Get these people loaded! As many as you can. I don't know how much time we have left."

The pilot nodded and immediately began directing the prisoner-soldiers and blind civilians where to sit in the carrier to maximize its capacity. They had arrived at less than half capacity. They would be leaving at more than full capacity.

Within a minute both carriers were full.

But there were still a couple dozen people left without transportation. Titan made the tough call.

"Get these people out of here! Travel at least ten miles beyond where the earth is burned, drop them off and get your ass back as soon as possible! I don't want to cook when this thing takes off!" Titan jerked his thumb toward the huge alien ship.

The pilot gave him a thumb's up sign and closed the hatch.

Titan watched as the carriers rose and headed off to the north. He did not know how long they had until the ship took off, but hoped it was long enough for the carriers to return for them. They had to get well away from the barren area surrounding the ship in order to be safe, and that would take at least three or four minutes.

"There's no one left inside! I think we got them all," one of the prisoner-soldiers informed Titan. "Except for Mouse and

Grant. They're still inside!"

"Damn," Titan swore. "How much time?"

"Can't be more than ten or fifteen minutes left, I'd guess," he answered.

Titan was about to say it wouldn't matter anyway when he noticed a group of three carriers landing close by. He smiled when Tane Roland stepped from one of them.

"Alright," Titan ordered the soldier. "Get the rest of these folks loaded and out of here. You too."

He then trotted over to Tane.

\* \* \*

Grant and Mouse continued to argue. They were facing away from the dead aliens scattered outside the door of the command center. Not because they cared about the aliens or felt badly about the violence that caused the deaths. They faced away so they could watch the clock set into the alien control panel. The seconds ticked away quickly and Grant knew he had to make his point soon so that Mouse could be on his way.

"Why, Grant?"

"Because it has to be done, Mouse. It's the only way! I've kicked this around in my head since Tane brought me back from my... my sleep. There has never been a way of making sure they never come back. But now there is! Don't you see? They've given us a way," Grant said, indicating the dead aliens lying at their feet. He picked up the Minith bomb. Checked the alien clock to see how much time remained.

"In this hand I have a bomb that is supposed to be strong enough to destroy a planet the size of Earth. And in twelve minutes, this ship is leaving for Minith. You tell me what has to be done, Mouse?"

"Aw, man," Mouse growled.

Grant knew he was right, and he could see that Mouse

knew it also. There was only one way to defeat these monsters once and for all and they held the key to that puzzle in their hands.

"Can't we rig up something that would set it off automatically when the ship lands?"

"Yeah, maybe we could. If we had more time. But not now. What if something went wrong and the bomb didn't go off? That's a chance we can't afford to take."

Grant had considered the possibilities and options and the only one that afforded even modest success was if one of them accompanied the alien vessel back to its home planet and set off the bomb when they arrived.

"Then let me do it, Grant. I'll go."

"No, Mouse, I can't do that. It's my responsibility. I have to go."

"Why you? Why are you so quick to volunteer, huh?"

Grant thought about the question for less than a second. He did not need any longer than that.

"Because I don't belong here, Mouse. My time for living was up a long time ago."

Grant cursed the fates that had placed him in such a position and wondered if there was really a God and if there was, did He enjoy the joke he was playing?

"Hell, Mouse, these aren't even my own," Grant said, holding out his arms and slapping his legs. "Tane brought me back and gave me these for only one reason. So I could stop the Minith from killing Earth."

Grant put a hand on his friend's shoulder.

"Mouse, it's my destiny," Grant whispered hoarsely. Avery's face swam before his eyes and he hated himself for having dragged her into this. She would be hurt by what he had to do and that was his only regret. "You'd better get going. There's less than eleven minutes left."

"Okay, my friend," Mouse finally said. "I understand."

* * *

"But I don't."

Titan's fist slammed into the side of Grant's head. The blow, while not fair, felt good considering who he was hitting. It was just a small pay back for the beating Grant had dealt him inside the prison.

"What the -- ?" Mouse yelled, spinning around to face the other man.

Titan smiled in return. He had entered the control room while Grant and Mouse were turned away from the door and had heard everything. Grant never knew what hit him. He just fell limply into Mouse's arms. Titan reached out and caught the bomb deftly before it had a chance to hit the floor.

"Why did you hit him?" Mouse held Grant's still form and glared daggers of anger at Titan.

"Get him out of here," Titan said. He placed the bomb on the control panel next to the clock. "You've got ten and a half minutes to get him loaded onto a carrier and away from here. Just pray there's a carrier waiting for you when you get outside."

"I can't take him out! Someone has to go with the ship, you giant idiot!"

"I'm going, Mouse," Titan calmly explained. He chose to ignore the man's threatening tone and was surprised that he was able to do so. It was a first for him. Somehow, his release of violence upon the Minith allowed him to tolerate this threat from another human. Before, he would have been enraged at any man for speaking to him in such a manner. Now, he simply brushed his anger aside as irrelevant.

"There's nothing for me here, Mouse. I'm a man of violence on a world of Peace. Besides," he added, looking down at Grant's unconscious form. "I made a promise to Avery."

Mouse nodded, and Titan knew that he understood. Both about the promise to Avery as well as being a man of violence. He wondered briefly how Mouse and Grant were going to cope in the new world that they had just helped forge.

"Good luck."

"Thanks, Mouse. Tell Grant I'm sorry about the sneak attack. Now, you'd better hurry."

"You got it!" Mouse agreed. He tossed Grant's body over his shoulder and headed for the door. He stopped just before he reached it and turned around. "I could have taken you, Titan. I just wanted you to know that."

Titan threw back his head and laughed.

"Then you should have tried me, little one! I do not roll over so easy. But let's not discuss what might have been. You have very little time."

"I hear you, friend," Mouse said as he left the room and started to run. "I hear you."

\* \* \*

Grant came to as he was being loaded onto a carrier. His head hurt. And he was pissed.

He felt the carrier lift off the ground. Heard the whine of the engines as the pilot maxed out his speed. He opened his eyes and saw Mouse looking down at him.

"Why?" It was all he could manage for the moment. His head felt like a blacksmith's anvil after a hard day of shoeing.

"Titan clobbered you, man. He said he's sorry he had to sneak it in on you. But I got the feeling he was kind of happy to oblige. If you know what I mean."

Grant stared stupidly at Mouse, unsure of what the other

man was talking about.

"Titan? He's at the prison."

"No, Grant. Titan is on that Minith ship getting ready to take a long trip."

The whine of the carrier vehicle was suddenly eclipsed by another, louder sound. Grant knew the source of the noise right away and sat up. He turned to look out the back viewing window and saw the Minith ship on fire. No. Not on fire, just sitting on a platform of fire. A platform that began rising as the alien ship lifted off of the ground.

Grant looked down for the ring of scorched earth but he couldn't make it out. They would have to hope they were beyond the destructive path of the Mothership and he settled back, suddenly content to just let things happen. There was nothing he could do now anyway. Nothing except watch the ship as it rose higher and higher.

When it was gone, he lay down on the floor of the carrier.

He slept and dreamed of Avery.

## EPILOGUE

Grant soaked up the sunshine. Their picnic finished, he and Avery had laid out a blanket. They were snuggled together, her head nestled comfortably in the crook of his arm. The crest of this grass covered hill was a favorite spot and they visited it often. Grant marveled at the joy he had found in this new world as his wife slept.

His thoughts and the quiet that surrounded them were interrupted as a carrier rushed overhead. He opened one eye and watched the vehicle settle at the bottom of the hill.

Two figures got out.

One began the short trek to the top. The other hung back.

Grant waited a few moments before gently removing his arm from under Avery's sleeping form. He sat up and waited for Tane to reach the summit.

The scientist stopped fifteen feet from the blanket and nodded his head. Grant got the impression that Tane felt he was intruding and was unwilling to close the remaining distance. Tane's thoughtfulness was one of the things Grant loved about his best friend.

"Hello, Grant." Tane eyes met Grant's for the briefest moment before settling on a patch of ground midway between them. Having become attuned to Tane's mannerisms, Grant knew that something very important was on the scientist's mind.

"Hi, Tane. What's up?"

"I've just received word from the Leadership Council." Grant waited for his friend to continue, but had to prod him to go on.

"And? What did our gracious Council have to say that's got you so nervous, Tane?"

Tane squatted down. He pulled several blades of grass from the ground and tossed them into the air where they were caught by a slight breeze. Grant noticed that the wind was blowing from its usual direction of west to east. He also recognized that Tane was delaying what he needed to say for as long as possible. He decided to wait. Tane would speak when he was ready.

"They have received word from one of the deep space telescopes we had installed in S'merca."

That got Grant's full attention.

"And?"

"They have detected a large object headed toward our solar system."

"A large object? You mean a ship?" Grant tried to sound calm, but could not keep the sudden, tight tension from creeping into his voice.

Avery must have detected the change, because she stirred beside him. Sat up. Her secondary eyelids blinked down to cut the glare of the mid-day sun and she looked down the hill. Waved to the figure walking there.

Tane held up his hands. He was asking Grant to remain calm, at Peace.

"We do not know that. It could be an asteroid or a meteor. It is too soon to tell for sure."

"Right, Tane. It could be. But it could also be them right?" Grant didn't need Tane to answer. He already knew that the Minith's return was a possibility. Perhaps even a probability.

"That has not been ruled out."

"Well then, I guess I have work to do." Grant stood up and stretched. He looked down the hill at the second visitor, who was now running towards them.

Avery was fully awake now and having heard the last few

exchanges, knew what to expect. She packed up their blanket and the remains of the picnic without another word.

They had planned for this day. Hoped it wouldn't come, but planned for it nonetheless. If the object hurtling toward Earth was an asteroid or a meteor, great. If it was the Minith, then they were ready.

The running figure reached the top of the hill. Did not slow down. Launched himself into the air toward Grant.

"Daaadddy!"

Grant timed the jump perfectly, as he always did. Plucked the five year old cleanly out of the air and swung him around and around. His son stuck out his arms and made plane noises.

All three adults laughed. They knew the child wanted to be a jet fighter pilot when he grew up.

Just like his Uncle Mouse.

Not a boring old general like his dad.

*The End*

# Acknowledgements

I wrote the first draft of this book more than ten years ago. It languished in a drawer for all of those years simply because I didn't know what to do with it. I didn't have an agent. I didn't know anyone in the publishing world. For me, the purpose and drive behind the book was in the writing, not in the publishing. Then I bought a Kindle from Amazon and downloaded Edward C. Patterson's title, *Are You Still Submitting Your Work to a Traditional Publisher?* That short e-book gave me a roadmap for publishing my book – in a format that I enjoyed. I would encourage other authors who may have a book stashed away to grab a copy of Patterson's book and follow his roadmap. It's not easy, but it may be worth it. It was for me – the result is in your hands. I hope you enjoy it, but if you don't, it's entirely my fault and none of Patterson's.

I need to thank some great Brother's of the Leaf. Dan Lockhart (MrWolf) helped by reading the draft and offering suggestions. Jimmy Rodriguez (eljimmy) and Keith Norek (shamrocker) assisted me over a couple of technical hurdles. All were a great help en route to finishing this book. Thanks, guys!

Thanks also to Sabrina C. Kleis for use of her art, *A Dark Starry Night*, as the background for the book's cover. You can see more of her outstanding work on her website: www.7-days.net.

# About the Author

Steven L. Hawk spent six years as a Military Intelligence Specialist with the U.S. Army's 82nd Airborne Division before joining the ranks of corporate America. He has a B.S. in Business Management from Western Governor's University and is a certified Project Management Professional (PMP). He has traveled extensively across the United States and, at various times, has lived in Georgia, North Carolina, West Virginia, Massachusetts, California and Idaho.

Steve currently resides in Boise, Idaho with his wife, Juanita. Together, they have a blended family of five sons: Paul, Gordo, Aaron, Taylor and Steven Jr.

This is his first published novel. For more information, you can follow him via the following channels:

Website:   www.SteveHawk.com

Linkedin:  http://www.linkedin.com/in/stevenhawk

Twitter:   @stevenhawk

Facebook:  http://www.facebook.com/steven.hawk1